DAY AND NIGHT STORIES

DAY AND NIGHT STORIES

By
ALGERNON BLACKWOOD

CASSELL AND COMPANY, LTD
London, New York, Toronto and Melbourne

First Published 1917

TO

M. S-K.

CONTENTS

DAY AND NIGHT STORIES

I

THE TRYST

As he got out of the train at the little wayside station he remembered the conversation as if it had been yesterday, instead of fifteen years ago —and his heart went thumping against his ribs so violently that he almost heard it. The original thrill came over him again with all its infinite yearning. He felt it as he had felt it *then*— not with that tragic lessening the interval had brought to each repetition of its memory. Here, in the familiar scenery of its birth, he realised with mingled pain and wonder that the subsequent years had not destroyed, but only dimmed it. The forgotten rapture flamed back with all the fierce beauty of its genesis, desire at white heat. And the shock of the abrupt discovery shattered time. Fifteen years became a negligible moment; the crowded experiences that had intervened seemed but a dream. The farewell scene, the conversation on the steamer's deck, were clear as of the day before. He saw the hand holding her big hat that fluttered in the wind, saw the flowers on the dress where the long coat was blown open a moment, recalled the face of a hurrying steward who had jostled them; he even heard the voices—his own and hers :

"Yes," she said simply; "I promise you. You have my word. I'll wait——"

"Till I come back," he interrupted.

Steadfastly she repeated his actual words, then added : "Here; at home—that is."

"I'll come to the garden gate as usual," he told her, trying to smile. "I'll knock. You'll open the gate—as usual—and come out to me."

These words, too, she attempted to repeat, but her voice failed, her eyes filled suddenly with tears; she looked into his face and smiled. It was just then that her little hand went up to hold the hat on—he saw the very gesture still. He remembered that he was vehemently tempted to tear his ticket up there and then, to go ashore with her, to stay in England, to brave all opposition—when the siren roared its third horrible warning . . . and the ship put out to sea.

Fifteen years, thick with various incident, had passed between them since that moment. His life had risen, fallen, crashed, then risen again. He had come back at last, fortune won

by a lucky coup—at thirty-five; had come back
to find her, come back, above all, to keep his
word. Once every three months they had
exchanged the brief letter agreed upon: " I
am well; I am waiting; I am happy; I am
unmarried. Yours ——." For his youthful
wisdom had insisted that no "man" had the
right to keep "any woman" too long waiting;
and she, thinking that letter brave and splendid,
had insisted likewise that he was free—if freedom called him. They had laughed over this
last phrase in their agreement. They put five
years as the possible limit of separation. By
then he would have won success, and obstinate
parents would have nothing more to say.

But when the five years ended he was " on
his uppers " in a western mining town, and with
the end of ten in sight those uppers, though
changed, were little better, apparently, than
patched and mended. It was just then, too, that
the change which had been stealing over him
first betrayed itself. He realised it abruptly,
a sense of shame and horror in him. The discovery was made unconsciously: it disclosed
itself. He was reading her letter as a labourer
on a Californian fruit farm: " Funny she doesn't
marry—someone else!" he heard himself say.
The words were out before he knew it, and
certainly before he could suppress them. They
just slipped out, startling him into the truth;

and he knew instantly that the thought was
fathered in him by a hidden wish. . . . He was
older. He had lived. It was a memory he
loved.

Despising himself in a contradictory fashion
—both vaguely and fiercely—he yet held true
to his boyhood's promise. He did not write
and offer to release her as he knew they did in
stories; he persuaded himself that he meant
to keep his word. There was this fine, stupid,
selfish obstinacy in his character. In any case,
she would misunderstand and think he wanted
to set free—himself. "Besides—I'm still—
awfully fond of her," he asserted. And it was
true; only the love, it seemed, had gone its
way. Not that another woman took it; he kept
himself clean, held firm as steel. The love,
apparently, just faded of its own accord; her
image dimmed, her letters had ceased to thrill,
then ceased to interest him.

Subsequent reflection made him realise other
details about himself. In the interval he had
suffered hardships, had learned the uncertainty
of life that depends for its continuance on a
little food, but that food often hard to come
by, and had seen so many others go under that
he held it more cheaply than of old. The
wandering instinct, too, had caught him, slowly
killing the domestic impulse; he lost his desire
for a settled place of abóde, the desire for

children of his own, lost the desire to marry at
all. Also—he reminded himself with a smile—
he had lost other things: the expression of
youth *she* was accustomed to and held always
in her thoughts of him, two fingers of one hand,
his hair! He wore glasses, too. The gentlemen-
adventurers of life get scarred in those wild
places where he lived. He saw himself a rather
battered specimen well on the way to middle
age.

There was confusion in his mind, however,
and in his heart: a struggling complex of
emotions that made it difficult to know exactly
what he did feel. The dominant clue concealed
itself. Feelings shifted. A single, clear deter-
minant did not offer. He was an honest fellow.
" I can't quite make it out," he said. " What
is it I really feel? And why?" His motive
seemed obscured. To keep the flame alight for
ten long buffeting years was no small achieve-
ment; better men had succumbed in half the
time. Yet something in him still held fast to
the girl as with a band of steel that *would* not
let her go entirely. Occasionally there came
strong reversions, when he ached with longing,
yearning, hope; when he loved her again; remembered passionately each detail of the far-off
courtship days in the forbidden rectory garden
beyond the small, white garden gate. Or was
it merely the image and the memory he loved

" again "? He hardly knew himself. He could not tell. That "again" puzzled him. It was the wrong word surely. . . . He still wrote the promised letter, however; it was so easy; those short sentences could not betray the dead or dying fires. One day, besides, he would return and claim her. He meant to keep his word.

And he had kept it. Here he was, this calm September afternoon, within three miles of the village where he first had kissed her, where the marvel of first love had come to both; three short miles between him and the little white garden gate of which at this very moment she was intently thinking, and behind which some fifty minutes later she would be standing, waiting for him. . . .

He had purposely left the train at an earlier station; he would walk the three miles in the dusk, climb the familiar steps, knock at the white gate in the wall as of old, utter the promised words, "I have come back to find you," enter, and—keep his word. He had written from Mexico a week before he sailed; he had made careful, even accurate calculations: "In the dusk, on the sixteenth of September, I shall come and knock," he added to the usual sentences. The knowledge of his coming, therefore, had been in her possession seven days. Just before sailing, moreover, he had heard from her—though not in answer, naturally. She was well; she was happy; she was unmarried; she was waiting.

And now, as by some magical process of restoration—possible to deep hearts only, perhaps, though even to them quite inexplicable—the state of first love had blazed up again in him. In all its radiant beauty it lit his heart, burned unextinguished in his soul, set body and mind on fire. The years had merely veiled it. It burst upon him, captured, overwhelmed him with the suddenness of a dream. He stepped from the train. He met it in the face. It took him prisoner. The familiar trees and hedges, the unchanged countryside, the " field-smells known in infancy," all these, with something subtly added to them, rolled back the passion of his youth upon him in a flood. No longer was he bound upon what he deemed, perhaps, an act of honourable duty; it was love that drove him, as it drove him fifteen years before. And it drove him with the accumulated passion of desire long forcibly repressed; almost as if, out of some fancied notion of fairness to the girl, he had deliberately, yet still unconsciously, said " No " to it; that *she* had not faded, but that he had decided, " *I* must forget her." That sentence: " Why doesn't she marry—someone else?" had not betrayed change in himself. It surprised another motive: " It's not fair to—her!"

His mind worked with a curious rapidity, but worked within one circle only. The stress of sudden emotion was extraordinary. He remembered a thousand things; yet, chief among them, those occasional reversions when he had felt he "loved her again." Had he not, after all, deceived himself? Had she ever really "faded" at all? Had he not felt he ought to let her fade—release her that way? And the change in himself?—that sentence on the Californian fruit-farm—what did they mean? Which had been true, the fading or the love?

The confusion in his mind was hopeless, but, as a matter of fact, he did not think at all: he only felt. The momentum, besides, was irresistible, and before the shattering onset of the sweet revival he did not stop to analyse the strange result. He knew certain things, and cared to know no others: that his heart was leaping, his blood running with the heat of twenty, that joy recaptured him, that he must see, hear, touch her, hold her in his arms—and marry her. For the fifteen years had crumbled to a little thing, and at thirty-five he felt himself but twenty, rapturously, deliciously in love.

He went quickly, eagerly, down the little street to the inn, still feeling only, not thinking anything. The vehement uprush of the old emotion made reflection of any kind impossible. He gave no further thought to those long years "out there," when her name, her letters, the very image of her in his mind had found him, if not cold, at least without keen response. All that was forgotten as though it had not been. The steadfast thing in him, this strong holding to a promise which had never wilted, ousted the recollection of fading and decay that, whatever caused them, certainly had existed. And this steadfast thing now took command. This enduring quality in his character led him. It was only towards the end of the hurried tea he first received the singular impression—vague, indeed, but undeniably persistent—that he was *being* led.

Yet, though aware of this, he did not pause to argue or reflect. The emotional displacement in him, of course, had been more than considerable : there had been upheaval, a change whose abruptness was even dislocating, fundamental in a sense he could not estimate—shock. Yet he took no count of anything but the one mastering desire to get to her as soon as possible, knock at the small, white garden gate, hear her answering voice, see the low wooden door swing open —take her. There was joy and glory in his heart, and a yearning sweet delight. At this very moment she was expecting him. And he —had come.

Behind these positive emotions, however, there lay concealed all the time others that were

B

of a negative character. Consciously, he was
not aware of them, but they were there; they
revealed their presence in various little ways
that puzzled him. He recognised them absent-
mindedly, as it were; did not analyse or investi-
gate them. For, through the confusion upon his
faculties, rose also a certain hint of insecurity
that betrayed itself by a slight hesitancy or miscalculation in one or two unimportant actions.
There was a touch of melancholy, too, a sense
of something lost. It lay, perhaps, in that tinge
of sadness which accompanies the twilight of an
autumn day, when a gentler, mournful beauty
veils a greater beauty that is past. Some trick
of memory connected it with a scene of early
boyhood, when, meaning to see the sunrise, he
overslept, and, by a brief half-hour, was just—
too late. He noted it merely, then passed on;
he did not understand it; he hurried all the
more, this hurry the only sign that it *was*
noted. "I must be quick," flashed up across
his strongly positive emotions.

And, due to this hurry, possibly, were the
slight miscalculations that he made. They were,
very trivial. He rang for sugar, though the bowl
stood just before his eyes, yet when the girl
came in he forgot completely what he rang for
—and inquired instead about the late trains back
to London. And, when the time-table was laid
before him, he examined it without intelligence,

then looked up suddenly into the maid's face with a question about flowers. Were there flowers to be had in the village anywhere? What kind of flowers? "Oh, a bouquet or a "—he hesitated, searching for a word that tried to present itself, yet was not the word *he* wanted to make use of—" or a wreath—of some sort?" he finished. He took the very word he did not want to take. In several things he did and said, this hesitancy and miscalculation betrayed themselves—such trivial things, yet significant in an elusive way that he disliked. There was sadness, insecurity somewhere in them. And he resented them, though aware of their existence only because they qualified his joy. There was a whispered "No" floating somewhere in the dusk. Almost—he felt disquiet. He hurried, more and more eager to be off upon his journey—the final part of it.

Moreover, there were other signs of an odd miscalculation—dislocation, perhaps, properly speaking—in him. Though the inn was familiar from his boyhood days, kept by the same old couple, too, he volunteered no information about himself, nor asked a single question about the village he was bound for. He did not even inquire if the rector—her father—still were living. And when he left he entirely neglected the gilt-framed mirror above the mantelpiece of plush, dusty pampas-grass in waterless vases

on either side. It did not matter, apparently,
whether he looked well or ill, tidy or untidy.
He forgot that when his cap was off the absence
of thick, accustomed hair must alter him con-
siderably, forgot also that two fingers were
missing from one hand, the right hand, the hand
that she would presently clasp. Nor did it
occur to him that he wore glasses, which must
change his expression and add to the appearance
of the years he bore. None of these obvious and
natural things seemed to come into his thoughts
at all. He was in a hurry to be off. He did
not think. But, though his mind may not
have noted these slight betrayals with actual
sentences, his attitude, nevertheless, expressed
them. This was, it seemed, the feeling in him :
" What could such details matter to her *now* ?
Why, indeed, should he give to them a single
thought? It was himself she loved and waited
for, not separate items of his external, physical
image." As well think of the fact that she, too,
must have altered—outwardly. It never once
occurred to him. Such details were of To-day.
. . . He was only impatient to come to her
quickly, very quickly, instantly, if possible.
He hurried.

There was a flood of boyhood's joy in him.
He paid for his tea, giving a tip that was twice
the price of the meal, and set out gaily and
impetuously along the winding lane. Charged

to the brim with a sweet picture of a small,
white garden gate, the loved face close behind
it, he went forward at a headlong pace, singing
" Nancy Lee " as he used to sing it fifteen
years before.

With action, then, the negative sensations
hid themselves, obliterated by the positive ones
that took command. The former, however,
merely lay concealed; they waited. Thus, perhaps, does vital emotion, overlong restrained,
denied, indeed, of its blossoming altogether,
take revenge. Repressed elements in his psychic
life asserted themselves, selecting, as though
naturally, a dramatic form.

The dusk fell rapidly, mist rose in floating
strips along the meadows by the stream; the old,
familiar details beckoned him forwards, then
drove him from behind as he went swiftly past
them. He recognised others rising through the
thickening air beyond; they nodded, peered,
and whispered, sometimes they almost sang.
And each added to his inner happiness; each
brought its sweet and precious contribution, and
built it into the reconstructed picture of the
earlier, long-forgotten rapture. It was an
enticing and enchanted journey that he made,
something impossibly blissful in it, something,
too, that seemed curiously irresistible.

For the scenery had not altered all these
years, the details of the country were un-

changed, everything he saw was rich with dear and precious association, increasing the momentum of the tide that carried him along. Yonder was the stile over whose broken step he had helped her yesterday, and there the slippery plank across the stream where she looked above her shoulder to ask for his support; he saw the very bramble bushes where she scratched her hand, a-blackberrying, the day before . . . and, finally, the weather-stained signpost, "To the Rectory." It pointed to the path through the dangerous field where Farmer Sparrow's bull provided such a sweet excuse for holding, leading—protecting her. From the entire landscape rose a steam of recent memory, each incident alive, each little detail brimmed with its cargo of fond association.

He read the rough black lettering on the crooked arm—it was rather faded, but he knew it too well to miss a single letter—and hurried forward along the muddy track; he looked about him for a sign of Farmer Sparrow's bull; he even felt in the misty air for the little hand, that he might take and lead her into safety. The thought of her drew him on with such irresistible anticipation that it seemed as if the cumulative drive of vanished and unsated years evoked the tangible phantom almost. He actually felt it, soft and warm and clinging in his own, that was no longer incomplete and mutilated.

Yet it was not he who led and guided now, but, more and more, he who was being led. The hint had first betrayed its presence at the inn; it now openly declared itself. It had crossed the frontier into a positive sensation. Its growth, swiftly increasing all this time, had accomplished itself; he had ignored, somehow, both its genesis and quick development; the result he plainly recognised. She was expecting him, indeed, but it was more than expectation; there was calling in it—she summoned him. Her thought and longing reached him along that old, invisible track love builds so easily between true, faithful hearts. All the forces of her being, her very voice, came towards him through the deepening autumn twilight. He had not noticed the curious physical restoration in his hand, but he was vividly aware of this more magical alteration—that *she* led and guided him, drawing him ever more swiftly towards the little, white garden gate where she stood at this very moment, waiting. Her sweet strength compelled him; there was this new touch of something irresistible about the familiar journey, where formerly had been delicious yielding only, shy, tentative advance.

His footsteps hurried, faster and ever faster; so deep was the allurement in his blood, he almost ran. He reached the narrow, winding lane, and raced along it. He knew each bend,

each angle of the holly hedge, each separate
incident of ditch and stone. He could have
plunged blindfold down it at top speed. The
familiar perfumes rushed at him—dead leaves
and mossy earth and ferns and dock leaves,
bringing the bewildering currents of strong
emotion in him all together as in a rising wave.
He saw, then, the crumbling wall, the cedars
topping it with spreading branches, the chimneys
of the rectory. On his right bulked the outline
of the old, grey church; the twisted, ancient
yews, the company of gravestones, upright and
leaning, dotting the ground like listening figures.
But he looked at none of these. For, a little
beyond, he already saw the five rough steps of
stone that led from the lane towards a small,
white garden gate. That gate at last shone
before him, rising through the misty air. He
reached it.

He stopped dead a moment. His heart, it
seemed, stopped too, then took to violent
hammering in his brain. There was a roaring
in his mind, and yet a marvellous silence—just
behind it. Then the roar of emotion died away.
There was utter stillness. This stillness, silence,
was all about him. The world seemed preter-
naturally quiet.

But the pause was too brief to measure.
For the tide of emotion had receded only to
come on again with redoubled power. He

turned, leaped forward, clambered impetuously up the rough stone steps, and flung himself, breathless and exhausted, against the trivial barrier that stood between his eyes and—hers. In his wild, half violent impatience, however, he stumbled. That roaring, too, confused him. He fell forward, it seemed, for twilight had merged in darkness, and he misjudged the steps, the distances he yet knew so well. For a moment, certainly, he lay at full length upon the uneven ground against the wall; the steps had tripped him. And then he raised himself and knocked. His right hand struck upon the small, white garden gate. Upon the two lost fingers he felt the impact. "I am here," he cried, with a deep sound in his throat as though utterance was choked and difficult. "I have come back."

For a fraction of a second he waited, while the world stood still and waited with him. But there was no delay. Her answer came at once: "I am well. . . . I am happy. . . . I am waiting."

And the voice was dear and marvellous as of old. Though the words were strange, reminding him of something dreamed, forgotten, lost, it seemed, he did not take special note of them. He only wondered that she did not open instantly that he might see her. Speech could follow, but sight came surely first! There was

this lightning-flash of disappointment in him.
Ah, she was lengthening out the marvellous
moment, as often and often she had done before.
It was to tease him that she made him wait.
He knocked again; he pushed against the unyielding surface. For he noticed that it was
unyielding; and there was a depth in the tender
voice that he could not understand.

"Open!" he cried again, but louder than
before. "I have come back!" And, as he
said it, the mist struck cold against his face.

But her answer froze his blood.

"I cannot open."

And a sudden anguish of despair rose over
him; the sound of her voice was strange; in
it was faintness, distance as well as depth. It
seemed to echo. Something frantic seized him
then—the panic sense.

"Open, open! Come out to me!" he tried
to shout. His voice failed oddly; there was no
power in it. Something appalling struck him
between the eyes. "For God's sake, open.
I'm waiting here! Open, and come out to
me!"

The reply was muffled by distance that
already seemed increasing; he was conscious of
freezing cold about him—in his heart:

"I cannot. You must come in to me."

He knew not exactly then what happened,
for the cold grew dreadful and the icy mist was

in his throat. No words would come. He rose
to his knees, and from his knees to his feet. He
stooped. With all his force he knocked again;
in a blind frenzy of despair he hammered and
beat against the unyielding barrier of the small,
white garden gate. He battered it till the skin
of his knuckles was torn and bleeding—the first
two fingers of a hand already mutilated. He
remembers the torn and broken skin, for he
noticed in the gloom that stains upon the gate
bore witness to his violence; it was not till afterwards that he remembered the other fact—that
the hand had already suffered mutilation, long,
long years ago. The power of sound was feebly
in him; he called aloud; there was no answer.
He tried to scream, but the scream was muffled
in his throat before it issued properly; it was a
nightmare scream. As a last resort he flung
himself bodily upon the unyielding gate, with
such precipitate violence, moreover, that his
face struck against its surface.

From the friction, then, along the whole
length of his cheek he knew that the surface
was not smooth. Cold and rough that surface
was; but also—it was not of wood. Moreover,
there was writing on it he had not seen before.
How he deciphered it in the gloom, he never
knew. The lettering was deeply cut. Perhaps
he traced it with his fingers; his right hand
certainly lay stretched upon it. He made out

a name, a date, a broken verse from the Bible, and strange words : "*Je suis la première au rendez-vous. Je vous attends.*" The lettering was sharply cut with edges that were new. For the date was of a week ago; the broken verse ran, "When the shadows flee away . . ." and the small, white garden gate was unyielding because it was of—stone.

At the inn he found himself staring at a table from which the tea things had not been cleared away. There was a railway time-table in his hands, and his head was bent forwards over it, trying to decipher the lettering in the growing twilight. Beside him, still fingering a florin, stood the serving-girl; her other hand held a brown tray with a running dog painted upon its dented surface. It swung to and fro a little as she spoke, evidently continuing a conversation her customer had begun. For she was giving information—in the colourless, disinterested voice such persons use :

"We all went to the funeral, sir, all the country people went. The grave was her father's—the family grave. . . ." Then, seeing that her customer was too absorbed in the time-table to listen further, she said no more but began to pile the tea things on to the tray with noisy clatter.

Ten minutes later, in the road, he stood

hesitating. The signal at the station just opposite was already down. The autumn mist was rising. He looked along the winding road that melted away into the distance, then slowly turned and reached the platform just as the London train came in. He felt very old—too old to walk three miles. . . .

II

THE TOUCH OF PAN

1

An idiot, Heber understood, was a person in whom intelligence had been arrested—instinct acted, but not reason. A lunatic, on the other hand, was someone whose reason had gone awry —the mechanism of the brain was injured. The lunatic was out of relation with his environment; the idiot had merely been delayed *en route*.

Be that as it might, he knew at any rate that a lunatic was not to be listened to, whereas an idiot—well, the one he fell in love with certainly had the secret of some instinctual knowledge that was not only joy, but a kind of sheer natural joy. Probably it was that sheer natural joy of living that reason argues to be untaught, degraded. In any case—at thirty— he married her instead of the daughter of a duchess he was engaged to. They lead to-day that happy, natural, vagabond life called idiotic, unmindful of that world the majority of reasonable people live only to remember.

Though born into an artificial social clique that made it difficult, Heber had always loved the simple things. Nature, especially, meant much to him. He would rather see a woodland misty with bluebells than all the châteaux on the Loire; the thought of a mountain valley in the dawn made his feet lonely in the grandest houses. Yet in these very houses was his home established. Not that he under-estimated worldly things—their value was too obvious—but that it was another thing he wanted. Only he did not know precisely *what* he wanted until this particular idiot made it plain.

Her case was a mild one, possibly; the title bestowed by implication rather than by specific mention. Her family did not say that she was imbecile or half-witted, but that she was "not all there" they probably did say. Perhaps she saw men as trees walking, perhaps she saw through a glass darkly. . . . Heber, who had met her once or twice, though never yet to speak to, did not analyse her degree of sight, for in him, personally, she woke a secret joy and wonder that almost involved a touch of awe. The part of her that was "not all there" dwelt in an "elsewhere" that he longed to know about. He wanted to share it with her. She seemed aware of certain happy and desirable things that reason and too much thinking hid.

He just felt this instinctively without analysis. The values they set upon the prizes of life were similar. Money to her was just stamped metal, fame a loud noise of sorts, position nothing. Of people she was aware as a dog or bird might be aware—they were kind or unkind. Her parents, having collected much metal and achieved position, proceeded to make a loud noise of sorts with some success; and since she did not contribute, either by her appearance or her tastes, to their ambitions, they neglected her and made excuses. They were ashamed of her existence. Her father in particular justified Nietzsche's shrewd remark that no one with a loud voice can listen to subtle thoughts.

She was, perhaps, sixteen; for, though she did not look it, eighteen or nineteen was probably more in accord with her birth certificate. Her mother was content, however, that she should dress the lesser age, preferring to tell strangers that she was childish, rather than admit that she was backward.

"You'll never marry at all, child, much less marry as you might," she said, "if you go about with that rabbit expression on your face. That's not the way to catch a nice young man of the sort we get down to stay with us now. Many a chorus-girl with less than you've got has caught them easily enough.

Your sister's done well. Why not do the same? There's nothing to be shy or frightened about.''

"But I'm not shy or frightened, mother. I'm bored. I mean *they* bore me."

It made no difference to the girl; she was herself. The bored expression in the eyes— the rabbit, not-all-there expression—gave place sometimes to another look. Yet not often, nor with anybody. It was this other look that stirred the strange joy in the man who fell in love with her. It is not to be easily described. It was very wonderful. Whether sixteen or nineteen, she then looked—a thousand.

The house-party was of that up-to-date kind prevalent in Heber's world. Husbands and wives were not asked together. There was a cynical disregard of the decent (not the stupid) conventions that savoured of abandon, perhaps of decadence. He only went himself in the hope of seeing the backward daughter once again. Her millionaire parents afflicted him, the smart folk tired him. Their peculiar affectation of a special language, their strange belief that they were of importance, their treatment of the servants, their calculated self-indulgence, all jarred upon him more than usual. At bottom he heartily despised the whole vapid set. He felt uncomfortable and out of place. Though

c

not a prig, he abhorred the way these folk believed themselves the climax of fine living. Their open immorality disgusted him, their indiscriminate love-making was merely rather nasty; he watched the very girl he was at last to settle down with behaving as the tone of the clique expected over her final fling—and, bored by the strain of so much "modernity," he tried to get away. Tea was long over, the sunset interval invited, he felt hungry for trees and fields that were not self-conscious—and he escaped. The flaming June day was turning chill. Dusk hovered over the ancient house, veiling the pretentious new wing that had been added. And he came across the idiot girl at the bend of the drive, where the birch trees shivered in the evening wind. His heart gave a sudden leap.

She was leaning against one of the dreadful statues—it was a satyr—that sprinkled the lawn. Her back was to him; she gazed at a group of broken pine trees in the park beyond. He paused an instant, then went on quickly, while his mind scurried to recall her name. They were within easy speaking range.

"Miss Elizabeth!" he cried, yet not too loudly, lest she might vanish as suddenly as she had appeared. She turned at once. Her eyes and lips were smiling welcome at him without pretence. She showed no surprise.

"You're the first one of the lot who's said it properly," she exclaimed, as he came up. "Everybody calls me Elizabeth instead of Elspeth. It's idiotic. They don't even take the trouble to get a name right."

"It is," he agreed, "quite idiotic." He did not correct her. Possibly he had said Elspeth after all—the names were similar. Her perfectly natural voice was grateful to his ear, and soothing. He looked at her all over with an open admiration that she noticed and, without concealment, liked. She was very untidy, the grey stockings on her slim, vigorous legs were torn, her short skirt was spattered with mud. Her nut-brown hair, glossy and plentiful, flew loose about neck and shoulders. In place of the usual belt she had tied a coloured handkerchief round her waist. She wore no hat. What she had been doing to get in such a state, while her parents entertained a "distinguished" party, he did not know, but it was not difficult to guess. Climbing trees or riding bareback and astride was probably the truth. Yet her dishevelled state became her well, and the welcome in her face delighted him. She remembered him, she was glad. He, too, was glad, and a sense both happy and reckless stirred in his heart. "Like a wild animal," he said, "you come out in the dusk——"

"To play with my kind," she answered in

a flash, throwing him a glance of invitation that made his blood go dancing.

He leaned against the statue a moment, asking himself why this young Cinderella of a parvenu family delighted him when all the London beauties left him cold. There was a lift through his whole being as he watched her, slim and supple, grace shining through the untidy modern garb—almost as though she wore no clothes. He thought of a panther standing upright. Her poise was so alert—one arm upon the marble ledge, one leg bent across the other, the hip-line showing like a bird's curved wing. Wild animal or bird, flashed across his mind : something untamed and natural. Another second and she might leap away—or spring into his arms.

It was a deep, delicious sensation in him that produced the mental picture. "Pure and natural," a voice whispered with it in his heart, "as surely as *they* are just the other thing !" And the thrill struck with unerring aim at the very root of that unrest he had always known in the state of life to which he was called. She made the natural clean and pure. This girl and himself were somehow kin. The primitive thing broke loose in him.

In two seconds, while he stood with her beside the vulgar statue, these thoughts passed through his mind. But he did not at first give

utterance to any of them. He spoke more
formally, although laughter, due to his happiness, lay close behind :

"They haven't asked you to the party,
then? Or you don't care about it? Which is
it?"

"Both," she said, looking fearlessly into his
face. "But I've been waiting here ten minutes
already. Why were you so long?"

This outspoken honesty was hardly what he
expected, yet in another sense he was not surprised. Her eyes were very penetrating, very
innocent, very frank. He felt her as clean and
sweet as some young fawn that asks plainly to
be stroked and fondled. He told the truth:
"I couldn't get away before. I had to play
about and——" when she interrupted with
impatience :

"*They* don't want you," she exclaimed
scornfully. "I do."

And, before he could choose one out of the
several answers that rushed into his mind, she
nudged him with her foot, holding it out a
little so that he saw the shoelace was unfastened.
She nodded her head towards it, and pulled
her skirt up half an inch as he at once stooped
down.

"And, anyhow," she went on as he fumbled
with the lace, touching her ankle with his hand,
"you're going to marry one of them. I read

it in the paper. You'll be miserable. It's idiotic."

The blood rushed to his head, but whether owing to his stooping or to something else, he could not say.

"I only came—I only accepted," he said quickly, "because I wanted to see you again."

"Of course. I made mother ask you."

He did an impulsive thing. Kneeling as he was, he bent his head a little lower and suddenly kissed the soft grey stocking—then stood up and looked her in the face. She was laughing happily, no sign of embarrassment in her anywhere, no trace of outraged modesty. She only looked very pleased.

"I've tied a knot that won't come undone in a hurry——" he began, then stopped dead. For as he said it, gazing into her smiling face, another expression looked forth at him from the two big eyes of hazel. Something rushed from his heart to meet it. It may have been that playful kiss, it may have been the way she took it; but, at any rate, there was a strength in the new emotion that made him unsure of who he was and of whom he looked at. He forgot the place, the time, his own identity and hers. . . . The lawn swept from beneath his feet the English sunset with it. He forgot his host and hostess, his fellow guests, even his father's name and his own into the bargain. He was carried away upon a great tide, the girl always beside him. He left the shore-line in the distance, already half forgotten, the shore-line of his education, learning, manners, social point of view—everything to which his father had most carefully brought him up as the scion of an old-established English family. This girl had torn up the anchor. Only the anchor had previously been loosened a little, perhaps, by his own unconscious and restless efforts. . . .

Where was she taking him to? Upon what island would they land . . . ?

"I'm younger than you—a good deal," she broke in upon his rushing mood. "But that doesn't matter a bit, does it? We're about the same age really."

With the happy sound of her voice the extraordinary sensation passed—or, rather, it became normal. But that it lasted an appreciable time was proved by the fact that they had left the statue on the lawn, the house was no longer visible behind them, and they were now walking side by side between the massive rhododendron clumps. They brought up against a five-barred gate into the park. They leaned upon the topmost bar, and he felt her shoulder touching his—edging into it—as they looked across to the grove of pines.

"I feel absurdly young," he said without a

sign of affectation, "and yet I've been looking
for you a thousand years and more."

The afterglow lit up her face; it fell on her
loose hair and tumbled blouse, turning them
amber red. She looked not only soft and
comely, but extraordinarily beautiful. The
strange expression haunted the deep eyes again,
the lips were a little parted, the young breast
heaving slightly, joy and excitement in her
whole presentment. And as he watched her he
knew that all he had just felt was due to her
close presence, her atmosphere, her perfume,
her physical warmth and vigour. It had
emanated directly from her being.

"Of course," she said, and laughed so that
he felt her breath upon his face. He bent
lower to bring his own on a level, gazing straight
into her eyes that were still fixed upon the
field beyond. They were clear and luminous as
pools of water, and in their centre, sharp as a
photograph, he saw the reflection of the pine
grove, perhaps a hundred yards away. With
detailed accuracy he saw it, empty and motionless in the glimmering June dusk.

Then something caught his eye. He
examined the picture more closely. He drew
slightly nearer. He almost touched her face
with his own, forgetting for a moment whose
were the eyes that served him for a mirror.
For, looking intently thus, it seemed to him

that there was movement, a passing to and fro, a stirring as of figures among the trees. . . . Then suddenly the entire picture was obliterated. She had dropped her lids. He heard her speaking—the warm breath was again upon his face:

"*In the heart of that wood dwell I.*"

His heart gave another leap—more violent than the first—for the sentence caught him like a spell. There was a lilt and rhythm in the words, a wonder and a beauty, that made it poetry. She laid emphasis upon the pronoun and the nouns. It seemed the last line of some delicious runic verse:

" In the *heart* of that *wood*—dwell *I*. . . ."

And it flashed across him: That living, moving, inhabited pine wood was her thought. It was thus she thought it, saw it. Her nature flung back to a life she understood, a life that needed, claimed her. The ostentatious and artificial values that surrounded her she denied, even as the distinguished house-party of her ambitious, masquerading family neglected her. Of course she was unnoticed by them—just as a swallow or a wild-rose were unnoticed.

He knew her secret then, for she had told it to him. It was his own secret too. They were akin, as the birds and animals were akin. They belonged together in some free and open life, natural, wild, untamed. That unhampered life was flowing about them now, rising, beating with delicious tumult in her veins and his, yet innocent as the sunlight and the wind—because it was as freely recognised.

"Elspeth!" he cried, "come, take me with you! We'll go at once. Come—hurry—before we forget to be happy, or remember to be wise again——!"

His words stopped half-way towards completion, for a perfume floated past him, born of the summer dusk, perhaps, yet sweet with a penetrating magic that made his senses reel with some remembered joy. No flower, no scented garden-bush delivered it. It was the perfume of young, spendthrift life, sweet with the purity that reason had not yet stained. The girl moved closer. Gathering her loose hair between her fingers, she brushed his cheeks and eyes with it, her slim, warm body pressing against him as she leaned over laughingly.

"*In the darkness*," she whispered in his ear; "*when the moon puts the house upon the statue!*"

And he understood. Her world lay behind the vulgar, staring day. He turned. He heard the flutter of skirts—just caught the grey stockings, swift and light, as they flew behind the rhododendron masses. And she was gone.

He stood a long time, leaning upon that five-barred gate. . . . It was the dressing-gong

that recalled him at length to what seemed the
present. By the conservatory door, as he went
slowly in, he met his distinguished cousin—who
was helping the girl he himself was to marry
to enjoy her "final fling." He looked at his
cousin. He realised suddenly that he was
merely vicious. There was no sun and wind,
no flowers—there was depravity only, lust
instead of laughter, excitement in place of
happiness. It was calculated, not spontaneous.
His mind was in it. Without joy it was. He
was not natural.

"Not a girl in the whole lot fit to look at,"
his cousin exclaimed with peevish boredom, ex-
cusing himself stupidly for his illicit conduct.
"I'm off in the morning." He shrugged his
blue-blooded shoulders. "These millionaires!
Their shooting's all right, but their mixum-
gatherum week-ends—bah!" His gesture
completed all he had to say about this one in
particular. He glanced sharply, nastily, at his
companion. "_You_ look as if you'd found something!" he added, with a suggestive grin. "Or
have you seen the ghost that was paid for with
the house?" And he guffawed and let his eye-
glass drop. "Lady Hermione will be asking
for an explanation—eh?"

"Idiot!" replied Heber, and ran upstairs
to dress for dinner.

But the word was wrong, he remembered,

as he closed his door. It was lunatic he had
meant to say, yet something more as well. He
saw the smart, modern philanderer somehow as
a beast.

2

It was nearly midnight when he went up to
bed, after an evening of intolerable amusement.
The abandoned moral attitude, the common
rudeness, the contempt of all others but themselves, the ugly jests, the horseplay of tasteless
minds that passed for gaiety, above all the
shamelessness of the women that behind the
cover of fine breeding aped emancipation,
afflicted him to a boredom that touched
desperation.

He understood now with a clarity unknown
before. As with his cousin, so with these.
They took life, he saw, with a brazen effrontery
they thought was freedom, while yet it was
life that they denied. He felt vampired and
degraded; spontaneity went out of him. The
fact that the geography of bedrooms was
studied openly seemed an affirmation of vice
that sickened him. Their ways were nauseous
merely. He escaped—unnoticed.

He locked his door, went to the open
window, and looked out into the night—then
started. For silver dressed the lawn and park,
the shadow of the building lay dark across the

elaborate garden, and the moon, he noticed, was just high enough to put the house upon the statue. The chimney-stacks edged the pedestal precisely.

"Odd!" he exclaimed. "Odd that I should come at the very moment——!" then smiled as he realised how his proposed adventure would be misinterpreted, its natural innocence and spirit ruined—if he were seen. "And someone would be sure to see me on a night like this. There are couples still hanging about in the garden." And he glanced at the shrubberies and secret paths that seemed to float upon the warm June air like islands.

He stood for a moment framed in the glare of the electric light, then turned back into the room; and at that instant a low sound like a bird-call rose from the lawn below. It was soft and flutey, as though someone played two notes upon a reed, a piping sound. He had been seen, and she was waiting for him. Before he knew it, he had made an answering call, of oddly similar kind, then switched the light out.

Three minutes later, dressed in simpler clothes, with a cap pulled over his eyes, he reached the back lawn by means of the conservatory and billiard-room. He paused a moment to look about him. There was no one, although the lights were still ablaze. "I am an idiot," he

chuckled to himself. " I'm acting on instinct ! "
He ran.

The sweet night air bathed him from head
to foot; there was strength and cleansing in it.
The lawn shone wet with dew. He could almost
smell the perfume of the stars. The fumes of
wine, cigars, and artificial scent were left behind,
the atmosphere exhaled by civilisation, by heavy
thoughts, by bodies overdressed, unwisely stimulated—all, all forgotten. He passed into a
world of magical enchantment. The hush of
the open sky came down. In black and white
the garden lay, brimmed full with beauty, shot
by the ancient silver of the moon, spangled with
the stars' old-gold. And the night wind rustled
in the rhododendron masses as he flew between
them.

In a moment he was beside the statue,
engulfed now by the shadow of the building,
and the girl detached herself silently from the
blur of darkness. Two arms were flung about
his neck, a shower of soft hair fell on his cheek
with a heady scent of earth and leaves and grass,
and the same instant they were away together
at full speed—towards the pine wood. Their
feet were soundless on the soaking grass. They
went so swiftly that they made a whir of
following wind that blew her hair across his
eyes.

And the sudden contrast caused a shock that

put a blank, perhaps, upon his mind, so that he lost the standard of remembered things. For it was no longer merely a particular adventure; it seemed a habit and a natural joy resumed.

It was not new. He realised the momentum of an accustomed happiness, mislaid, it may be, but certainly familiar. They sped across the gravel paths that intersected the well-groomed lawn, they leaped the flower-beds, so laboriously shaped in mockery, they clambered over the ornamental iron railings, scorning the easier five-barred gate into the park. The longer grass then shook the dew in soaking showers against his knees. He stooped, as though in some foolish effort to turn up something, then realised that his legs, of course, were bare. *Her* garment was already high and free, for she, too, was barelegged like himself. He saw her little ankles, wet and shining in the moonlight, and flinging himself down, he kissed them happily, plunging his face into the dripping, perfumed grass. Her ringing laughter mingled with his own, as she stooped beside him the same instant; her hair hung in a silver cloud; her eyes gleamed through its curtain into his; then, suddenly, she soaked her hands in the heavy dew and passed them over his face with a softness that was like the touch of some scented southern wind.

"Now you are anointed with the Night," she cried. "No one will know you. You are forgotten of the world. Kiss me!"

"We'll play for ever and ever," he cried, "the eternal game that was old when still the world was young," and lifting her in his arms he kissed her eyes and lips. There was some natural bliss of song and dance and laughter in his heart, an elemental bliss that caught them together as wind and sunlight catch the branches of a tree. She leaped from the ground to meet his swinging arms, and in an instant was upon his shoulders. He ran with her, then tossed her off and caught her neatly as she fell. Evading a second capture, she danced ahead, holding out one shining arm that he might follow. Hand in hand they raced on together through the clean summer moonlight. Yet there remained a smooth softness as of fur against his neck and shoulders, and he saw then that she wore skins of tawny colour that clung to her body closely, that he wore them too, and that her skin, like his own, was of a sweet dusky brown.

Then, pulling her towards him, he stared into her face. She suffered the close gaze a second, but no longer, for with a burst of sparkling laughter again she leaped into his arms, and before he shook her free she had pulled and tweaked the two small horns that hid in the thick curly hair behind, and just above, the ears.

And that wilful tweaking turned him wild and reckless. That touch ran down him deep into the mothering earth. He leaped and ran and sang with a great laughing sound. The wine of eternal youth flushed all his veins with joy, and the old, old world was young again with every impulse of natural happiness intensified with the Earth's own foaming tide of life.

From head to foot he tingled with the delight of Spring, prodigal with creative power. Of course he could fly the bushes and fling wild across the open! Of course the wind and moonlight fitted close and soft about him like a skin! Of course he had youth and beauty for playmates, with dancing, laughter, singing, and a thousand kisses! For he and she were natural once again. They were free together of those long-forgotten days when "Pan leaped through the roses in the month of June . . .!"

With the girl swaying this way and that upon his shoulders, tweaking his horns with mischief and desire, hanging her flying hair before his eyes, then bending swiftly over again to lift it, he danced to join the rest of their companions in the little moonlit grove of pines beyond. . . .

D

3

THEY rose somewhat pointed, perhaps, against
the moonlight, those English pines—more with
the shape of cypresses, some might have
thought. A stream gushed down between their
roots, there were mossy ferns, and rough grey
boulders with lichen on them. But there was
no dimness, for the silver of the moon sprinkled
freely through the branches like the faint sunlight that it really was, and the air ran out to
meet them with a heady fragrance that was
wiser far than wine.

The girl, in an instant, was whirled from her
perch on his shoulders and caught by a dozen
arms that bore her into the heart of the merry,
careless throng. Whisht! Whew! Whir!
She was gone, but another, fairer still, was in
her place, with skins as soft and knees that
clung as tightly. Her eyes were liquid amber,
grapes hung between her little breasts, her arms
entwined about him, smoother than marble, and
as cool. She had a crystal laugh.

But he flung her off, so that she fell plump
among a group of bigger figures lolling against
a twisted root and roaring with a jollity that
boomed like wind through the chorus of a
song. They seized her, kissed her, then sent
her flying. They were happier, after all,
with their glad singing. They held stone

goblets, red and foaming in their broad-palmed hands.

"The mountains lie behind us!" cried someone dancing past. "We are come at last into our valley of delight. Grapes, breasts, and rich red lips! Ho! Ho! It is time to press them that the juice of life may run!" The figure waved a cluster of ferns across the air and vanished amid a cloud of song and laughter.

"It is ours. Use it!" answered a deep, ringing voice. "The valleys are our own. No climbing now!" And a wind of echoing cries gave answer from all sides. "Life! Life! Life! Abundant, flowing over—use it, use it!"

A troop of nymphs rushed forth, escaped from clustering arms and lips they yet openly desired. He chased them in and out among the waving branches, while she who had brought him ever followed, and sped past him and away again. He caught three gleaming soft brown bodies, then fell beneath them, smothered, bubbling with joyous laughter—next freed himself and, while they sought to drag him captive again, escaped and raced with a leap upon a slimmer, sweeter outline that swung up—only just in time—upon a lower bough, whence she leaned down above him with hanging net of hair and merry eyes. A few feet beyond his reach, she laughed and teased him—the one who had brought him in, the one he ever sought, and who for ever sought him too. . . . .

It became a riotous glory of wild children who romped and played with an impassioned glee beneath the moon. For the world was young and they, her happy offspring, glowed with the life she poured so freely into them. All intermingled, the laughing voices rose into a foam of song that broke against the stars. The difficult mountains had been climbed and were forgotten. Good! Then, enjoy the luxuriant, fruitful valley and be glad! And glad they were, brimful with spontaneous energy, natural as birds and animals that obeyed the big, deep rhythm of a simpler age —natural as wind and innocent as sunshine.

Yet, for all the untamed riot, there was a lift of beauty pulsing underneath. Even when the wildest abandon approached the heat of orgy, when the recklessness appeared excess— there hid that marvellous touch of loveliness which makes the natural sacred. There was coherence, purpose, the fulfilling of an exquisite law: and—there was worship. The form it took, haply, was strange as well as riotous, yet in its strangeness dreamed innocence and purity, and in its very riot flamed that spirit which is divine.

For he found himself at length beside her once again; breathless and panting, her sweet brown limbs aglow from the excitement of escape denied; eyes shining like a blaze of stars, and pulses beating with tumultuous life —helpless and yielding against the strength that pinned her down between the roots. His eyes put mastery on her own. She looked up into his face, obedient, happy, soft with love, surrendering with the same delicious abandon that had swept her for a moment into other arms. "You caught me in the end," she sighed. "I only played awhile."

"I hold you for ever," he replied, half wondering at the rough power in his voice.

It was here the hush of worship stole upon her little face, into her obedient eyes, about her parted lips. She ceased her wilful struggling.

"Listen!" she whispered. "I hear a step upon the glades beyond. The iris and the lily open; the earth is ready, waiting; we must be ready too! *He* is coming!"

He released her and sprang up; the entire company rose too. All stood, all bowed the head. There was an instant's subtle panic, but it was the panic of reverent awe that preludes a descent of deity. For a wind passed through the branches with a sound that is the oldest in the world and so the youngest. Above it there rose the shrill, faint piping of a little reed. . . .

Only the first, true sounds were audible— wind and water : the tinkling of the dewdrops as

they fell, the murmur of the trees against the
air. This was the piping that they heard. And
in the hush the stars bent down to hear, the
riot paused, the orgy passed and died. The
figures waited, kneeling then with one accord.
They listened with—the Earth.

"He comes. . . . He comes . . ." the
valley breathed about them.

A footfall from far away came treading
across a world unruined and unstained. It
fell with the wind and water, sweetening the
valley into life as it approached. Across the
rivers and forests it came gently, tenderly, but
swiftly and with a power that knew majesty.

"He comes. . . . He comes . . .!" rose
with the murmur of the wind and water from
the host of lowered heads.

The footfall came nearer, treading a world
grown soft with worship. It reached the grove.
It entered. There was a sense of intolerable
loveliness, of brimming life, of rapture. The
thousand faces lifted like a cloud. They heard
the piping close. . . . And so He came.

But He came with blessing. With the
stupendous Presence there was joy, the joy of
abundant, natural life, pure as the sunlight and
the wind. He passed among them. There was
great movement—as of a forest shaking, as of
deep water falling, as of a cornfield swaying to
the wind, yet gentle as of a harebell shedding

its burden of dew that it has held too long because of love. He passed among them, touching every head. The great hand swept with tenderness each face, lingered a moment on each beating heart. There was sweetness, peace, and loveliness; but above all, there was —life. He sanctioned every natural joy in them and blessed each passion with his power of creation. . . . Yet each one saw him differently : some as a wife or maiden desired with fire, some as a youth or stalwart husband, others as a figure veiled with stars or cloaked in luminous mist, hardly attainable; others, again—the fewest these, not more than two or three—as that mysterious wonder which tempts the heart away from known familiar sweetness into a wilderness of undecipherable magic without flesh and blood. . . .

To two, in particular, He came so near that they could feel his breath of hills and fields upon their eyes. He touched them with both mighty hands. He stroked the marble breasts, He felt the little hidden horns . . . and, as they bent lower so that their lips met together for an instant, He took her arms and twined them about the curved, brown neck that she might hold him closer still. . . .

Again a footfall sounded far away upon an unruined world . . . and He was gone—back into the wind and water whence He came.

The thousand faces lifted; all stood up; the
hush of worship still among them. There was
a quiet as of the dawn. The piping floated
over woods and fields, fading into silence. All
looked at one another. . . . And then once
more the laughter and the play broke loose.

4

"We'll go," she cried, "and peep upon that
other world where life hangs like a prison on
their eyes!"

And, in a moment, they were across the
soaking grass, the lawn and flower-beds, and
close to the walls of the heavy mansion. He
peered in through a window, lifting her up
to peer in with him. He recognised the
world to which he outwardly belonged; he
understood; a little gasp escaped him; and
a slight shiver ran down the girl's body into
his own. She turned her eyes away. "See,"
she murmured in his ear, "it's ugly, it's not
natural. They feel guilty and ashamed. There
is no innocence!" She saw the men; it was
the women that he saw chiefly.

Lolling ungracefully, with a kind of bold-
ness that asserted independence, the women
smoked their cigarettes with an air of invitation
they sought to conceal and yet showed plainly.
He saw his familiar world in nakedness. Their

backs were bare, for all the elaborate clothes they wore; they hung their breasts uncleanly; in their eyes shone light that had never known the open sun. Hoping they were alluring and desirable, they feigned a guilty ignorance of that hope. They all pretended. Instead of wind and dew upon their hair, he saw flowers grown artificially to ape wild beauty, tresses without lustre borrowed from the slums of city factories. He watched them manœuvring with the men; heard dark sentences; caught gestures half delivered whose meaning should just convey that glimpse of guilt they deemed to increase pleasure. The women were calculating, but nowhere glad; the men experienced, but nowhere joyous. Pretended innocence lay cloaked with a veil of something that whispered secretly, clandestine, ashamed, yet with a brazen air that laid mockery instead of sunshine in their smiles. Vice masqueraded in the ugly shape of pleasure; beauty was degraded into calculated tricks. They were not natural. They knew not joy.

" The forward ones, the civilised!" she laughed in his ear, tweaking his horns with energy. " *We* are the backward!"

" Unclean," he muttered, recalling a catchword of the world he gazed upon.

They were the civilised! They were refined and educated—advanced. Generations of careful breeding, mate cautiously selecting mate,

laid the polish of caste upon their hands and
faces where gleamed ridiculous, untaught jewels
—rings, bracelets, necklaces hanging absurdly
from every possible angle.

"But—they are dressed up—for fun," he
exclaimed, more to himself than to the girl in
skins who clung to his shoulders with her naked
arms.

"*Un*dressed!" she answered, putting her
brown hand in play across his eyes. "Only
they have forgotten even that!" And another
shiver passed through her into him. He turned
and hid his face against the soft skins that
touched his cheek. He kissed her body. Seizing his horns, she pressed him to her, laughing
happily.

"Look!" she whispered, raising her head
again; "they're coming out." And he saw
that two of them, a man and a girl, with an
interchange of secret glances, had stolen from
the room and were already by the door of the
conservatory that led into the garden. It
was his wife to be—and his distinguished
cousin.

"Oh, Pan!" she cried in mischief. The
girl sprang from his arms and pointed. "We
will follow them. We will put natural life into
their little veins!"

"Or panic terror," he answered, catching
the yellow panther skin and following her

swiftly round the building. He kept in the
shadow, though she ran full into the blaze of
moonlight. "But they can't see us," she
called, looking over her shoulder a moment.
"They can only feel our presence, perhaps."
And, as she danced across the lawn, it seemed
a moonbeam slipped from a sapling birch tree
that the wind curved earthwards, then tossed
back against the sky.

Keeping just ahead, they led the pair, by
methods known instinctively to elemental blood
yet not translatable—led them towards the little
grove of waiting pines. The night wind
murmured in the branches; a bird woke into a
sudden burst of song. These sounds were
plainly audible. But four little pointed ears
caught other, wilder, notes behind the wind and
music of the bird—the cries and ringing laughter, the leaping footsteps and the happy singing
of their merry kin within the wood.

And the throng paused then amid the revels
to watch the "civilised" draw near. They
presently reached the trees, halted, looked
about them, hesitated a moment—then, with
a hurried movement as of shame and fear lest
they be caught, entered the zone of shadow.

"Let's go in here," said the man, without
music in his voice. "It's dry on the pine
needles, and we can't be seen." He led the
way; she picked up her skirts and followed over

the strip of long wet grass. "Here's a log all ready for us," he added, sat down, and drew her into his arms with a sigh of satisfaction. "Sit on my knee; it's warmer for your pretty figure." He chuckled; evidently they were on familiar terms, for though she hesitated there was no real resistance in her, and she allowed the ungraceful roughness. "But are we *quite* safe? Are you sure?" she asked between his kisses.

"What does it matter, even if we're not?" he replied, establishing her more securely on his knees. "But, as a matter of fact, we're safer here than in my own house." He kissed her hungrily. "By Jove, Hermione, but you're divine," he cried passionately, "divinely beautiful. I love you with every atom of my being—with my very soul."

"Yes, dear, I know—I mean, I know you do, but——"

"But what?" he asked impatiently.

"Those horrid detectives——"

He laughed. Yet it seemed to annoy him. "My wife *is* a beast, isn't she?—to have me watched like that," he said quickly.

"They're everywhere," she replied, a sudden hush in her tone. She looked at the encircling trees a moment, then added bitterly : "I hate her, simply *hate* her for it."

"I love you," he cried, crushing her to him,

"that's all that matters now. Don't let's waste time talking about the rest." She contrived to shudder, and hid her face against his coat, while he showered kisses on her neck and hair.

And the solemn pine trees watched them, the silvery moonlight fell on their faces, the scent of new-mown hay went floating past.

" I love you with my very soul," he repeated with intense conviction. " I'd do anything, give up anything, bear anything—just to give you a moment's happiness. I swear it—before God!"

There was a faint sound among the trees behind them, and the girl sat up, alert. She would have scrambled to her feet, but that he held her tight.

" What the devil's the matter with you to-night?" he asked in a different tone, his vexation plainly audible. " You're as nervy as if *you* were being watched, instead of me."

She paused before she answered, her finger on her lip. Then she spoke slowly, hushing her voice a little:

" Watched!" she repeated. " That's exactly what I did feel. I've felt it ever since we came into the wood."

" Nonsense, Hermione. It's too many cigarettes." He drew her back into his arms, forcing her head up so that he could kiss her better.

"I suppose it is nonsense," she said, smiling. "It's gone now, anyhow."

He began admiring her hair, her dress, her shoes, her pretty ankles, while she resisted in a way that proved her practice. "It's not *me* you love," she pouted, yet drinking in his praise. She listened to his repeated assurances that he loved her with his "soul" and was prepared for any sacrifice.

"I feel so safe with you," she murmured, knowing the moves in the game as well as he did. She looked up guiltily into his face, while he looked down with a passion that he thought perhaps was joy.

"You'll be married before the summer's out," he said, "and all the thrill and excitement will be over. Poor Hermione!" She lay back in his arms, drawing his face down with both hands, and kissing him on the lips. "You'll have more of him than you can do with—eh? As much as you care about, anyhow."

"I shall be much more free," she whispered. "Things will be easier. And I've got to marry someone——"

She broke off with another start. There was a sound again behind them. The man heard nothing. The blood in his temples pulsed too loudly, doubtless.

"Well, what is it this time?" he asked sharply.

She was peering into the wood, where the patches of dark shadow and moonlit spaces made odd, irregular patterns in the air. A low branch near them waved slightly in the wind.

"Did you hear?" she asked nervously.

"Wind," he replied, annoyed that her change of mood disturbed his pleasure.

"But something moved——"

"Only a branch. We're quite alone, quite safe, I tell you," and there was a rasping sound in his voice as he said it. "Don't be so imaginative. I can take care of you."

She sprang up. The moonlight caught her figure, revealing its exquisite young curves beneath the smother of the costly clothing. Her hair had dropped a little in the struggle. The man eyed her eagerly, making a quick, impatient gesture towards her, then stopped abruptly. He saw the terror in her eyes.

"Oh, hark! What's that?" she whispered in a startled voice. She put her finger up. "Oh, let's go back. I don't like this wood. I'm frightened."

"Rubbish," he said, and tried to catch her by the waist.

"It's safer in the house—my room—or yours——" She broke off again. "There it is—don't you hear? It's a footstep!" Her face was whiter than the moon.

"I tell you it's the wind in the branches,"

he repeated gruffly. "Oh, come on, *do*. We were just getting jolly together. There's nothing to be afraid of. Can't you believe me?" He tried to pull her down upon his knee again with force. His face wore an unpleasant expression that was half leer, half grin.

But the girl stood away from him. She continued to peer nervously about her. She listened intently.

"You give me the creeps," he exclaimed crossly, clawing at her waist again with passionate eagerness that now betrayed exasperation. His disappointment turned him coarse.

The girl made a quick movement of escape, turning so as to look in every direction. She gave a little scream.

"That *was* a step. Oh, oh, it's close beside us. I heard it. We're being watched!" she cried in terror. She darted towards him, then shrank back. He did not try to touch her this time.

"Moonshine!" he growled. "You've spoilt my—spoilt our chance with your silly nerves."

But she did not hear him apparently. She stood there shivering as with sudden cold.

"There! I saw it again. I'm sure of it. Something went past me through the air."

And the man, still thinking only of his own pleasure frustrated, got up heavily, something like anger in his eyes. "All right," he said testily; "if you're going to make a fuss, we'd better go. The house *is* safer, possibly, as you say. You know my room. Come along!" Even that risk he would not take. He loved her with his "soul."

They crept stealthily out of the wood, the girl slightly in front of him, casting frightened backward glances. Afraid, guilty, ashamed, with an air as though they had been detected, they stole back towards the garden and the house, and disappeared from view.

And a wind rose suddenly with a rushing sound, poured through the wood as though to cleanse it, swept out the artificial scent and trace of shame, and brought back again the song, the laughter, and the happy revels. It roared across the park, it shook the windows of the house, then sank away as quickly as it came. The trees stood motionless again, guarding their secret in the clean, sweet moonlight that held the world in dream until the dawn stole up, and sunshine took the earth again with joy.

III

THE WINGS OF HORUS

BINOVITCH had the bird in him somewhere : in his features, certainly, with his piercing eye and hawk-like nose; in his movements, with his quick way of flitting, hopping, darting; in the way he perched on the edge of a chair; in the manner he pecked at his food; in his twittering, high-pitched voice as well; and, above all, in his airy, flashing mind. He skimmed all subjects and picked their heart out neatly, as a bird skims lawn or air to snatch its prey. He had the bird's-eye view of everything. He loved birds and understood them instinctively; could imitate their whistling notes with astonishing accuracy. Their one quality he had not was poise and balance. He was a nervous little man; he was neurasthenic. And he was in Egypt by doctor's orders.

Such imaginative, unnecessary ideas he had! Such uncommon beliefs!

"The old Egyptians," he said laughingly, yet with a touch of solemn conviction in his manner, "were a great people. Their consciousness was different from ours. The bird idea, for instance, conveyed a sense of deity to them—of bird deity, that is : they had sacred birds—hawks, ibis, and so forth—and worshipped them." And he put his tongue out as though to say with challenge, "Ha, ha!"

"They also worshipped cats and crocodiles and cows," grinned Palazov. Binovitch seemed to dart across the table at his adversary. His eyes flashed; his nose pecked the air. Almost one could imagine the beating of his angry wings.

"Because everything alive," he half screamed, "was a symbol of some spiritual power to them. Your mind is as literal as a dictionary and as incoherent. Pages of ink without connected meaning! Verb always in the infinitive! If you were an old Egyptian, you—you "—he flashed and spluttered, his tongue shot out again, his keen eyes blazed— "you would take all those words and spin them into a great interpretation of life, a cosmic romance, as they did. Instead, you get the bitter, dead taste of ink in your mouth, and spit it over us—like that "—he made a quick movement of his whole body as a bird that shakes itself—"in empty phrases."

Khilkoff ordered another bottle of champagne, while Vera, his sister, said half nervously, "Let's go for a drive; it's moonlight." There was enthusiasm at once. Another of the party called the head waiter and told him to pack food and drink in baskets. It was only eleven o'clock. They would drive out into the desert, have a meal at two in the morning, tell stories, sing, and see the dawn.

It was in one of those cosmopolitan hotels in Egypt which attract the ordinary tourists as well as those who are doing a " cure," and all these Russians were ill with one thing or another. All were ordered out for their health, and all were the despair of their doctors. They were as unmanageable as a bazaar and as in-coherent. Excess and bed were their routine. They lived, but none of them got better. Equally, none of them got angry. They talked in this strange personal way without a shred of malice or offence. The English, French, and Germans in the hotel watched them with remote amazement, referring to them as " that Russian lot." Their energy was elemental. They never stopped. They merely disappeared when the pace became too fast, then reappeared after a day or two, and resumed their " living " as before. Binovitch, despite his neurasthenia, was the life of the party. He was also a special patient of Dr. Plitzinger, the famous psychi-atrist, who took a peculiar interest in his case. It was not surprising. Binovitch was a man of unusual ability and of genuine, deep culture.

But there was something more about him that stimulated curiosity. There was this striking originality. He said and did surprising things.

"I could fly if I wanted to," he said once when the airmen came to astonish the natives with their biplanes over the desert, "but without all that machinery and noise. It's only a question of believing and understanding——"

"Show us!" they cried. "Let's see you fly!"

"He's got it! He's off again! One of his impossible, delightful moments!"

These occasions when Binovitch let himself go always proved wildly entertaining. He said monstrously incredible things as though he really believed them. They loved his madness, for it gave them new sensations.

"It's only levitation, after all, this flying," he exclaimed, shooting out his tongue between the words, as his habit was when excited; "and what is levitation but a power of the air? None of you can hang an orange in space for a second, with all your scientific knowledge; but the moon is always levitated perfectly. And the stars. D'you think they swing on wires? What raised the enormous stones of ancient Egypt? D'you really believe it was heaped-up sand and ropes and clumsy leverage and all our weary and laborious mechanical contrivances? Bah! It was levitation. It was the powers of the air.

Believe in those powers, and gravity becomes a mere nursery trick—true where it is, but true nowhere else. To know the fourth dimension is to step out of a locked room and appear instantly on the roof or in another country altogether. To know the powers of the air, similarly, is to annihilate what you call weight—and fly."

"Show us, show us!" they cried, roaring with delighted laughter.

"It's a question of belief," he repeated, his tongue appearing and disappearing like a pointed shadow. "It's in the heart; the power of the air gets into your whole being. Why should I show you? Why should I ask my deity to persuade your scoffing little minds by any miracle? For it is deity, I tell you, and nothing else. I know it. Follow *one* idea like that, as I follow my bird-idea—follow it with the impetus and undeviating concentration of a projectile—and you arrive at power. You know deity—the bird-idea of deity, that is. *They* knew that. The old Egyptians knew it."

"Oh, show us, show us!" they shouted impatiently, wearied of his nonsense-talk. "Get up and fly! Levitate yourself, as they did! Become a star!"

Binovitch turned suddenly very pale, and an odd light shone in his keen brown eyes. He rose slowly from the edge of the chair where he was perched. Something about him changed. There was silence instantly.

"I *will* show you," he said calmly, to their intense amazement; "not to convince your disbelief, but to prove it to myself. For the powers of the air are with me here. I believe. And Horus, great falcon-headed symbol, is my patron god."

The suppressed energy in his voice and manner was indescribable. There was a sense of lifting, upheaving power about him. He raised his arms; his face turned upward; he inflated his lungs with a deep, long breath, and his voice broke into a kind of singing cry, half prayer, half chant:

"O Horus,
  Bright-eyed deity of wind,
 [1] Feather my soul
  Though earth's thick air,
  To know thy awful swiftness——"

He broke off suddenly. He climbed lightly and swiftly upon the nearest table—it was in a deserted card-room, after a game in which he had lost more pounds than there are days in the year—and leaped into the air. He hovered a second, spread his arms and legs in space, appeared to float a moment—then buckled, rushed down and forward, and dropped in a

[1] The original is untranslatable. The phrase means, "Give my life wings."

heap upon the floor, while everyone roared with laughter.

But the laughter died out quickly, for there was something in his wild performance that was peculiar and unusual. It was uncanny, not quite natural. His body had seemed, as with Mordkin and Nijinski, literally to hang upon the air a moment. For a second he gave the distressing impression of overcoming gravity. There was a touch in it of that faint horror which appals by its very vagueness. He picked himself up unhurt, and his face was as grave as a portrait in the Academy, but with a new expression in it that everybody noticed with this strange, half-shocked amazement. And it was this expression that extinguished the claps of laughter as wind takes away the sound of bells. Like many ugly men, he was an inimitable actor, and his facial repertory was endless and incredible. But this was neither acting nor clever manipulation of expressive features. There was something in his curious Russian physiognomy that made the heart beat slower. And that was why the laughter died away so suddenly.

"You ought to have flown farther," cried someone. It expressed what all had felt.

"Icarus didn't drink champagne," another replied, with a laugh; but nobody laughed with him.

"You went too near to Vera," said Palazov, "and passion melted the wax." But his face twitched oddly as he said it. There was something he did not understand, and so heartily disliked.

The strange expression on the features deepened. It was arresting in a disagreeable, almost in a horrible way. The talk stopped dead; all stared; there was a feeling of dismay in everybody's heart, yet unexplained. Some lowered their eyes, or else looked stupidly elsewhere; but the women of the party felt a kind of fascination. Vera, in particular, could not move her sight away. The joking reference to his passionate admiration for her passed unnoticed. There was a general and individual sense of shock. And a chorus of whispers rose instantly:

"Look at Binovitch! What's happened to his face?"

"He's changed—he's changing!"

"God! Why he looks like a—bird!"

But no one laughed. Instead, they chose the names of birds—hawk, eagle, even owl. The figure of a man leaning against the edge of the door, watching them closely, they did not notice. He had been passing down the corridor, had looked in unobserved, and then had paused. He had seen the whole performance. He watched Binovitch narrowly now with calm, discerning eyes. It was Dr. Plitzinger, the great psychiatrist.

For Binovitch had picked himself up from the floor in a way that was oddly self-possessed, and precluded the least possibility of the ludicrous. He looked neither foolish nor abashed. He looked surprised, but also he looked half angry and half frightened. As someone had said, he "ought to have flown farther." That was the incredible impression his acrobatics had produced—incredible, yet somehow actual. This uncanny idea prevailed, as at a séance where nothing genuine is expected to happen, and something genuine, after all, does happen. There was no pretence in this: Binovitch had flown.

And now he stood there, white in the face —with terror and with anger white. He looked extraordinary, this little, neurasthenic Russian, but he looked at the same time half terrific. Another thing, not commonly experienced by men, was in him, breaking out of him, affecting *directly* the minds of his companions. His mouth opened; blood and fury shone in his blazing eyes; his tongue shot out like an ant-eater's, though even in this the comic had no place. His arms were spread like flapping wings, and his voice rose poignantly:

"He failed me, he failed me!" he tried to shout. "Horus, my falcon-headed deity, my power of the air, deserted me! Hell take him! Hell burn his wings and blast his piercing sight! Hell scorch him into dust for his false prophecies! I curse him—I curse Horus!''

The voice that should have roared across the silent room emitted, instead, this high-pitched, bird-like scream. The added touch of sound, the reality it lent, was ghastly. Yet it was marvellously done and acted. The entire thing was a bit of instantaneous inspiration—his voice, his words, his gestures, his whole wild appearance. Only—here was the reality that caused the sense of shock—the expression on his altered features was genuine. *That* was not assumed. There was something new and alien in him, something cold and difficult to human life, something alert and swift and cruel, of another element than earth. A strange, rapacious grandeur had leaped upon the struggling features. The face looked hawk-like.

And he came forward suddenly and sharply toward Vera, whose fixed, staring eyes had never once ceased to watch him with a kind of anxious yet eager fascination. She was both drawn and beaten back. Binovitch advanced on tiptoe. No doubt he still was acting, still pretending this mad nonsense that he worshipped Horus, the falcon-headed deity of forgotten days, and that Horus had failed him in his hour of need; but somehow there was just

a hint of too much reality in the way he moved
and looked.   The girl, a little creature, with
fluffy golden hair, opened her lips; her cigarette
fell to the floor; she shrank back; she looked
for a moment like some smaller, coloured bird
trying to escape from a great pursuing hawk;
she screamed.   Binovitch, his arms wide, his
bird-like face thrust forward, had swooped upon
her.   He leaped.   Almost he caught her.

No one could say exactly what happened.
Play, become suddenly and unexpectedly too
real, confuses the emotions.   The change of key
was swift.   From fun to terror is a dislocating
jolt upon the mind.   Someone—it was Khilkoff,
the brother—upset a chair; everybody spoke at
once; everybody stood up.   An unaccountable
feeling of disaster was in the air, as with those
drinkers' quarrels that blaze out from nothing,
and end in a pistol-shot and death, no one able
to explain clearly how it came about.   It was
the silent, watching figure in the doorway who
saved the situation.   Before anyone had noticed
his approach, there he was among the group,
laughing, talking, applauding—between Binovitch and Vera.   He was vigorously patting his
patient on the back, and his voice rose easily
above the general clamour.   He was a strong,
quiet personality; even in his laughter there was
authority.   And his laughter now was the only
sound in the room, as though by his mere

presence peace and harmony were restored.
Confidence came with him. The noise subsided;
Vera was in her chair again. Khilkoff poured
out a glass of wine for the great man.

"The Czar!" said Plitzinger, sipping his
champagne, while all stood up, delighted with
his compliment and tact. "And to your opening night with the Russian ballet," he added
quickly a second toast, "or to your first performance at the Moscow Théâtre des Arts!"
Smiling significantly, he glanced at Binovitch;
he clinked glasses with him. Their arms were
already linked, but it was Palazov who noticed
that the doctor's fingers seemed rather tight
upon the creased black coat. All drank, looking
with laughter, yet with a touch of respect,
toward Binovitch, who stood there dwarfed
beside the stalwart Austrian, and suddenly as
meek and subdued as any mole. Apparently
the abrupt change of key had taken his mind
successfully off something else.

"Of course—'The Fire-Bird,'" exclaimed
the little man, mentioning the famous Russian
ballet. "The very thing!" he exclaimed.
"For *us*," he added, looking with devouring
eyes at Vera. He was greatly pleased. He
began talking vociferously about dancing and
the rationale of dancing. They told him he was
an undiscovered master. He was delighted.
He winked at Vera and touched her glass again

with his. "We'll make our début together,"
he cried. "We'll begin at Covent Garden, in
London. I'll design the dresses and the posters
'The Hawk and the Dove!' *Magnifique!* I in
dark grey, and you in blue and gold! Ah,
dancing, you know, is sacred. The little self
is lost, absorbed. It is ecstasy, it is divine.
And dancing in air—the passion of the birds
and stars—ah! they are the movements of the
gods. You know deity that way—by living it."

He went on and on. His entire being had
shifted with a leap upon this new subject. The
idea of realising divinity by dancing it absorbed
him. The party discussed it with him as though
nothing else existed in the world, all sitting now
and talking eagerly together. Vera took the
cigarette he offered her, lighting it from his
own; their fingers touched; he was as harmless
and normal as a retired diplomat in a drawing-
room. But it was Plitzinger whose subtle
manœuvring had accomplished the change so
cleverly, and it was Plitzinger who presently
suggested a game of billiards, and led him off,
full now of a fresh enthusiasm for cannons,
balls, and pockets, into another room. They
departed arm in arm, laughing and talking
together.

Their departure, it seemed, made no great
difference at first. Vera's eyes watched him out
of sight, then turned to listen to Baron Minski,

who was describing with gusto how he caught wolves alive for coursing purposes. The speed and power of the wolf, he said, was impossible to realise; the force of their awful leap, the strength of their teeth, which could bite through metal stirrup-fastenings. He showed a scar on his arm and another on his lip. He was telling truth, and everybody listened with deep interest. The narrative lasted perhaps ten minutes or more, when Minski abruptly stopped. He had come to an end; he looked about him; he saw his glass, and emptied it. There was a general pause. Another subject did not at once present itself. Sighs were heard; several fidgeted; fresh cigarettes were lighted. But there was no sign of boredom, for where one or two Russians are gathered together there is always life. They produce gaiety and enthusiasm as wind produces waves. Like great children, they plunge whole-heartedly into whatever interest presents itself at the moment. There is a kind of uncouth gambolling in their way of taking life. It seems as if they are always fighting that deep, under-lying, national sadness which creeps into their very blood.

"Midnight!" then exclaimed Palazov, abruptly, looking at his watch; and the others fell instantly to talking about that watch, admiring it and asking questions. For the moment that very ordinary timepiece became the centre of

observation. Palazov mentioned the price. "It
never stops," he said proudly, "not even under
water." He looked up at everybody, challeng-
ing admiration. And he told how, at a country
house, he made a bet that he would swim to a
certain island in the lake, and won the bet. He
and a girl were the winners, but as it was a horse
they had bet, he got nothing out of it for himself, giving the horse to her. It was a genuine
grievance in him. One felt he could have cried
as he spoke of it. "But the watch went all the
time," he said delightedly, holding the gun-
metal object in his hand to show, "and I was
twelve minutes in the water with my clothes
on."

Yet this fragmentary talk was nothing but
pretence. The sound of clicking billiard-balls
was audible from the room at the end of the
corridor. There was another pause. The pause,
however, was intentional. It was not vacuity
of mind or absence of ideas that caused it.
There was another subject, an unfinished subject,
that each member of the group was still con-
sidering. Only no one cared to begin about it,
till at last, unable to resist the strain any longer,
Palazov turned to Khilkoff, who was saying he
would take a "whisky-soda," as the champagne
was too sweet, and whispered something beneath his breath; whereupon Khilkoff, forgetting his drink, glanced at his sister, shrugged

his shoulders, and made a curious grimace.
"He's all right now"—his reply was just
audible—"he's with Plitzinger." He cocked
his head sidewise to indicate that the clicking of
the billiard-balls still was going on.

The subject was out: all turned their heads;
voices hummed and buzzed; questions were
asked and answered or half answered; eyebrows
were raised, shoulders shrugged, hands spread
out expressively. There came into the atmosphere a feeling of presentiment, of mystery,
of things half understood; primitive, buried
instinct stirred a little, the kind of racial dread
of vague emotions that might gain the upper
hand if encouraged. They shrank from looking
something in the face, while yet this unwelcome
influence drew closer round them all. They
discussed Binovitch and his astonishing performance. Pretty little Vera listened with large and
troubled eyes, though saying nothing. The
Arab waiter had put out the lights in the corridor, and only a solitary cluster burned now
above their heads, leaving their faces in shadow.
In the distance the clicking of the billiard-balls
still continued.

"It was not play; it was real," exclaimed
Minski vehemently. "I can catch wolves,"
he blurted; "but birds—ugh!—and human
birds!" He was half inarticulate. He had
witnessed something he could not understand,

F

and it had touched instinctive terror in him. "It was the way he leaped that put the wolf first into my mind, only it was not a wolf at all." The others agreed and disagreed. "It was play at first, but it was reality at the end," another whispered; "and it was no animal he mimicked, but a bird, and a bird of prey at that!"

Vera thrilled. In the Russian woman hides that touch of savagery which loves to be caught, mastered, swept helplessly away, captured utterly and deliciously by the one strong enough to do it thoroughly. She left her chair and sat down beside an older woman in the party, who took her arm quietly at once. Her little face wore a perplexed expression, mournful, yet somehow wild. It was clear that Binovitch was not indifferent to her.

"It's become an *idée fixe* with him," this older woman said. "The bird-idea lives in his mind. He lives it in his imagination. Ever since that time at Edfu, when he pretended to worship the great stone falcons outside the temple—the Horus figures—he's been full of it." She stopped. The way Binovitch had behaved at Edfu was better left unmentioned at the moment, perhaps. A slight shiver ran round the listening group, each one waiting for someone else to focus their emotion, and so explain it by saying the convincing thing. Only no one ventured. Then Vera abruptly gave a little jump.

"Hark!" she exclaimed, in a staccato whisper, speaking for the first time. She sat bolt upright. She was listening. "Hark!" she repeated. "There it is again, but nearer than before. It's coming closer. I hear it." She trembled. Her voice, her manner, above all her great staring eyes, startled everybody. No one spoke for several seconds; all listened. The halls and corridors lay in darkness, and gloom was over the big hotel. Everybody was in bed. But the clicking of the billiard-balls had ceased.

"Hear what?" asked the older woman soothingly, yet with a perceptible quaver in her voice, too. She was aware that the girl's hand tightened upon her arm.

"Do you not hear it, too?" the girl whispered.

All listened without speaking. All watched her paling face. Something wonderful, yet half incomprehensible, seemed in the air about them. There was a dull murmur, audible, faint, remote, its direction hard to tell. It had come suddenly from nowhere. They shivered. That strange racial thrill again passed into the group, unwelcome, unexplained. It was aboriginal; it belonged to the unconscious primitive mind, half childish, half terrifying.

" *What* do you hear?" her brother asked angrily—the irritable anger of nervous fear.

" When he came at me," she answered very low, " I heard it first. I hear it now again. Listen ! He's coming."

And at that minute, out of the dark mouth of the corridor, emerged two human figures, Plitzinger and Binovitch. Their game was over ; they were going up to bed. They passed the open door of the card-room. But Binovitch was being half dragged, half restrained, for he was apparently attempting to run down the passage with flying, dancing leaps. He bounded. It was like a huge bird trying to rise for flight, while his companion kept him down by force upon the earth. As they entered the strip of light, Plitzinger changed his own position, placing himself swiftly between his companion and the group in the dark corner of the room. He hurried Binovitch along as though he sheltered him from view. They passed into the shadows down the passage. They disappeared. And everyone looked significantly, questioningly, at his neighbour, though at first saying no word. It seemed that a curious disturbance of the air had followed them audibly.

Vera was the first to open her lips. " You heard it *then*," she said breathlessly, her face whiter than the ceiling.

"Damn!" exclaimed her brother furiously.
"It was wind against the outside walls—wind
in the desert. The sand is driving."

Vera looked at him. She shrank closer
against the side of the older woman, whose arm
was tight about her.

"It was *not* wind," she whispered simply.

She paused. All waited uneasily for the
completion of her sentence. They stared into
her face like peasants who expected a miracle.

"Wings," she whispered. "It was the
sound of wings."

And at four o'clock in the morning, when
they all returned exhausted from their excursion
into the desert, little Binovitch was sleeping
soundly and peacefully in his bed. They passed
his door on tiptoe. But he did not hear them.
He was dreaming. His spirit was at Edfu,
experiencing with that ancient deity who was
master of all flying life those strange enjoy-
ments upon which his own troubled human
heart was passionately set. Safe with that
mighty falcon whose powers his lips had scorned
a few hours before, his soul, released in vivid
dream, went sweetly flying. It was amazing,
it was gorgeous. He skimmed the Nile at
lightning speed. Dashing down headlong from
the height of the great Pyramid, he chased with
faultless accuracy a little dove that sought vainly

to hide from his terrific pursuit beneath the palm trees. For what he loved must worship where he worshipped, and the majesty of those tremendous effigies had fired his imagination to the creative point where expression was imperative.

Then suddenly, at the very moment of delicious capture, the dream turned horrible, becoming awful with the nightmare touch. The sky lost all its blue and sunshine. Far, far below him the little dove enticed him into nameless depths, so that he flew faster and faster, yet never fast enough to overtake it. Behind him came a great thing down the air, black, hovering, with gigantic wings outstretched. It had terrific eyes, and the beating of its feathers stole his wind away. It followed him, crowding space. He was aware of a colossal beak, curved like a scimitar and pointed wickedly like a tooth of steel. He dropped. He faltered. He tried to scream.

Through empty space he fell, caught by the neck. The huge spectral falcon was upon him. The talons were in his heart. And in sleep he remembered then that he had cursed. He recalled his reckless language. The curse of the ignorant is meaningless; that of the worshipper is real. This attack was on his soul. He had invoked it. He realised next, with a shock of ghastly horror, that the dove he chased was,

after all, the bait that had lured him purposely
to destruction . . . and awoke with a suffocating
terror upon him, and his entire body bathed in
icy perspiration. Outside the open window he
heard a sound of wings retreating with powerful
strokes into the surrounding darkness of the
sky.

The nightmare made its impression upon
Binovitch's impressionable and dramatic temperament. It aggravated his tendencies. He
related it next day to Mme. de Drühn, the
friend of Vera, telling it with that somewhat
boisterous laughter some minds use to disguise
less kind emotions. But he received no encour-
agement. The mood of the previous night was
not recoverable; it was already ancient history.
Russians never make the banal mistake of
repeating a sensation till it is exhausted; they
hurry on to novelties. Life flashes and rushes
with them, never standing still for exposure
before the cameras of their minds. Mme. de
Drühn, however, took the trouble to mention
the matter to Plitzinger, for Plitzinger, like
Freud of Vienna, held that dreams revealed
subconscious tendencies which sooner or later
must betray themselves in action.

"Thank you for telling me," he smiled
politely; "but I have already heard it from
him." He watched her eyes a moment, really
examining her soul. "Binovitch, you see," he

continued, apparently satisfied with what he saw, "I regard as that rare phenomenon—a genius without an outlet. His spirit, intensely creative, finds no adequate expression. His power of production is enormous and prolific; yet he accomplishes nothing." He paused an instant. "Binovitch, therefore, is in danger of poisoning—himself." He looked steadily into her face, as a man who weighs how much he may confide. "Now," he continued, "*if* we can find an outlet for him, a field wherein his bursting imaginative genius can produce results —above all, *visible* results"—he shrugged his shoulders—"the man is saved. Otherwise"— he looked extraordinarily impressive—"there is bound to be sooner or later——"

"Madness?" she asked very quietly.

"An explosion, let us say," he replied gravely. "For instance, take this Horus obsession of his, quite wrong archæologically though it is. *Au fond* it is megalomania of a most unusual kind. His passionate interest, his love, his worship of birds, wholesome enough in themselves, find no satisfying outlet. A man who really loves birds neither keeps them in cages, nor shoots, nor stuffs them. What, then, can he do? The commonplace bird-lover observes them through glasses, studies their habits, then writes a book about them. But a man like Binovitch, overflowing with this intense creative power of mind and imagination, is not content with that. He wants to know them from within. He wants to feel what they feel, to live their life. He wants to *become* them. . . . You follow me? Not quite. Well, he seeks to be identified with the object of his sacred, passionate adoration. All genius seeks to know the thing-itself from its own point of view. It desires union. That tendency, unrecognised by himself, perhaps, and therefore subconscious, hides in his very soul." He paused a moment. " And the sudden sight of those majestic figures at Edfu—that crystallisation of his *idée fixe* in granite—took hold of this excess in him, so to speak—and is now focusing it toward some definite act. Binovitch sometimes—feels himself a bird! You noticed what occurred last night?"

She nodded; a slight shiver passed over her.

" A most curious performance," she murmured; " an exhibition I never want to see again."

" The most curious part," replied the doctor coolly, " was its truth."

" Its truth!" she exclaimed beneath her breath. She was frightened by something in his voice and by the uncommon gravity in his eyes. It seemed to arrest her intelligence. She felt upon the edge of things beyond her. " You mean that Binovitch did for a moment—hang—

in the air?" The other verb, the right one, she could not bring herself to use.

The great man's face was enigmatical. He talked to her sympathy, perhaps, rather than to her mind.

"Real genius," he said smilingly, "is as rare as talent, even great talent, is common. It means that the personality, if only for one second, becomes everything; becomes the universe; becomes the soul of the world. It gets the flash. It is identified with the universal life. Being everything and everywhere, all is possible to it—in that second of vivid realisation. It can brood with the crystal, grow with the plant, leap with the animal and fly with the bird : genius unifies all three. That is the meaning of 'creative.' It is faith. Knowing it, you can pass through fire and not be burned, walk on water and not sink, move a mountain, fly. Because you *are* fire, water, earth, air. Genius, you see, is madness in the magnificent sense of being superhuman. Binovitch has it."

He broke off abruptly, seeing he was not understood. Some great enthusiasm in him he deliberately suppressed.

"The point is," he resumed, speaking more carefully, "that we must try to lead this passionately constructive genius of the man into some human channel that will absorb it, and therefore render it harmless."

"He loves Vera," the woman said, bewildered, yet seizing this point correctly.

"But would he marry her?" asked Plitzinger at once.

"He is already married."

The doctor looked steadily at her a moment, hesitating whether he should utter all his thought.

"In that case," he said slowly after a pause, "it is better he or she should leave."

His tone and manner were exceedingly impressive.

"You mean there's danger?" she asked.

"I mean, rather," he replied earnestly, "that this great creative flood in him, so curiously focused now upon his Horus-falcon-bird idea, may result in some act of violence——"

"Which would be madness," she said, looking hard at him.

"Which would be disastrous," he corrected her. And then he added slowly: "Because in the mental moment of creation he might overlook material laws."

The costume ball two nights later was a great success. Palazov was a Bedouin, and Khilkoff an Apache; Mme. de Drühn wore a national headdress; Minski looked almost natural as Don Quixote; and the entire Russian "set" was cleverly, if somewhat extravagantly, dressed. But Binovitch and Vera were the most successful of all the two hundred dancers who took part. Another figure, a big man dressed as a Pierrot, also claimed exceptional attention, for though the costume was commonplace enough, there was something of dignity in his appearance that drew the eyes of all upon him. But he wore a mask, and his identity was not discoverable.

It was Binovitch and Vera, however, who must have won the prize, if prize there had been, for they not only looked their parts, but acted them as well. The former in his dark grey feather tunic, and his falcon mask, complete even to the brown hooked beak and tufted talons, looked fierce and splendid. The disguise was so admirable, yet so entirely natural, that it was uncommonly seductive. Vera, in blue and gold, a charming head-dress of a dove upon her loosened hair, and a pair of little dove-pale wings fluttering from her shoulders, her tiny twinkling feet and slender ankles well visible, too, was equally successful and admired. Her large and timid eyes, her flitting movements, her light and dainty way of dancing—all added touches that made the picture perfect.

How Binovitch contrived his dress remained a mystery, for the layers of wings upon his back were real; the large black kites that haunt the

Nile, soaring in their hundreds over Cairo and
the bleak Mokattam Hills, had furnished them.
He had procured them none knew how. They
measured five feet across from tip to tip; they
swished and rustled as he swept along; they
were true falcons' wings. He danced with
nautch girls and Egyptian princesses and
Rumanian gipsies; he danced well, with
beauty, grace, and lightness. But with Vera
he did not dance at all; with her he simply
flew. A kind of passionate abandon was in him
as he skimmed the floor with her in a way that
made everybody turn to watch them. They
seemed to leave the ground together. It was
delightful, an amazing sight; but it was peculiar.
The strangeness of it was on many lips. Somehow its queer extravagance communicated itself
to the entire ball-room. They became the centre
of observation. There were whispers.

"There's that extraordinary bird-man!
Look! He goes by like a hawk. And he's
always after that dove-girl. How marvellously
he does it! It's rather awful. Who is he? I
don't envy *her*."

People stood aside when he rushed past.
They got out of his way. He seemed for ever
pursuing Vera, even when dancing with another
partner. Word passed from mouth to mouth.
A kind of telepathic interest was established
everywhere. It was a shade too real sometimes,

something unduly earnest in the chasing wildness, something unpleasant. There was even
alarm.

"It's rowdy; I'd rather not see it; it's
quite disgraceful," was heard. "*I* think it's
horrible; you can see she's terrified."

And once there was a little scene, trivial
enough, yet betraying this reality that many
noticed and disliked. Binovitch came up to
claim a dance, programme clutched in his great
tufted claws, and at the same moment the big
Pierrot appeared abruptly round the corner
with a similar claim. Those who saw it assert
he had been waiting, and came on purpose,
and that there was something protective and
authoritative in his bearing. The misunderstanding was ordinary enough—both men had
written her name against the dance—but "No.
13, Tango" also included the supper interval,
and neither Hawk nor Pierrot would give way.
They were very obstinate. Both men wanted
her. It was awkward.

"The Dove shall decide between us,"
smiled the Hawk politely, yet his taloned
fingers working nervously. Pierrot, however,
more experienced in the ways of dealing with
women, or more bold, said suavely:

"I am ready to abide by her decision "—his
voice poorly cloaked this aggravating authority,
as though he had the right to her—"only I

engaged this dance before His Majesty Horus
appeared upon the scene at all, and therefore it
is clear that Pierrot has the right of way."

At once, with a masterful air, he took her
off. There was no withstanding him. He
meant to have her and he got her. Both yielding and resisting, she was swept away. They
vanished among the maze of coloured dancers,
leaving the Hawk, disconsolate and vanquished,
amid the titters of the onlookers. His swiftness, as against this steady power, was of no
avail.

It was then that the singular phenomenon
was witnessed first. Those who saw it affirm
that he changed absolutely into the part he
played. It was dreadful; it was not possible. A
frightened whisper ran about the rooms and
corridors :

"An extraordinary thing is in the air!"

Some shrank away, while others flocked to
see. There were those who swore that a
curious, rushing sound was audible, the atmosphere visibly disturbed and shaken; that a
shadow fell upon the spot the couple had
vacated; that a cry was heard, a high, wild,
searching cry : "Horus! bright deity of wind,"
it began, then died away. One man was positive
that the windows had been opened and that
something had flown in. It was the obvious
explanation. The thing spread rapidly. As in

a fire panic, there was consternation and excitement. Confusion caught the feet of all the dancers. The music fumbled and lost time. The leading pair of tango dancers halted and looked round. It seemed that everybody pressed back, hiding, shuffling, eager to see, yet more eager not to be seen, as though something unusual, dangerous, terrible, had broken loose. In rows against the wall they stood. For a great space had made itself in the middle of the ball-room, and into this empty space reappeared suddenly the Pierrot and the Dove.

It was like a challenge. A sound of applause, half voices, half clapping of gloved hands, was heard. The couple danced exquisitely into the arena. All stared. There was an impression that a set piece had been prepared, and that this was its beginning. The music again took heart. Pierrot was strong and dignified, no whit nonplussed by this abrupt publicity. The Dove, though faltering, seemed deliciously obedient. They danced together like a single outline. She was captured utterly. And to the man who needed her the sight was naturally agonising—the protective way the Pierrot held her, the right and strength of it, the mastery, the complete possession.

" He's still got her ! " someone breathed too loud, uttering the thought of all. " Good thing it's not the Hawk ! "

And, to the absolute amazement of the throng, this sight was then apparent. A figure dropped through space. That high, shrill cry again was heard:

"Feather my soul . . . to know thy awful swiftness!"

Its singing loveliness touched the heart, its appealing, passionate sweetness was marvellous, as from an upper gallery this figure of a man, dressed as a strong, dark bird, shot down with splendid grace and ease. The feathers swept; the wings spread out as sails that take the wind. Like a hawk that darts with unerring power and aim upon its prey, this thing of mighty wings rushed down into the empty space where the couple danced. Observed by all, he entered, swooping beautifully, stretching his wings like any eagle. He dropped. He fixed his point of landing with consummate skill close beside the astonished dancers. He landed.

It happened with such swiftness that it brought the dazzle and blindness as when lightning strikes. People in different parts of the room saw different details; a few saw nothing at all after the first startling shock, closing their eyes, or holding their arms before their faces as in self-protection. The touch of panic fear caught the entire room. The nameless thing that all the evening had been vaguely felt was come. It had suddenly materialised.

G

For this incredible thing occurred in the full blaze of light upon the open floor. Binovitch, grown in some sense formidable, opened his dark, big wings about the girl. He drew her to him. The long grey feathers moved, causing powerful draughts of wind that made a rushing sound. An aspect of the terrible was about him, like an emanation. The great beaked head was poised to strike, the tufted claws were raised like fingers that shut and opened, and the whole presentiment of his amazing figure focused in an attitude of attack that was magnificent and terrible. No one who saw it doubted. Yet there were those who swore that it was not Binovitch at all, but that another outline, monstrous and shadowy, towered above him, draping his lesser proportions with two colossal wings of darkness. That some touch of strange divinity lay in it may be claimed, however confused the wild descriptions afterward. For many lowered their heads and bowed their shoulders. There was terror. There was also awe. The onlookers swayed as though some power passed over them across the air.

A sound of wings was certainly in the room.

Then someone screamed; a shriek broke high and clear; and emotion, ordinary, human emotion, unaccustomed to terrific things, swept loose. The Hawk and Vera flew—the girl with willing happiness, the man with power. Beaten

back against the wall as by a stroke of whirlwind,
the Pierrot staggered. He watched them go.
Out of the lighted room they flew, out of the
crowded human atmosphere, out of the heat
and artificial light, the walled-in, airless halls
that were a cage. All this they left behind.
They seemed things of wind and air, made free
happily of another element. Earth held them
not. Toward the open night they raced with
this extraordinary lightness as of birds, down
the long corridor and on to the southern terrace,
where great coloured curtains were hung suspended from the columns. A moment they
were visible. Then the fringe of one huge
curtain, lifted by the wind, showed their dark
outline for a second against the starry sky.
There was a cry, a leap. The curtain flapped
again and closed. They vanished. And into
the ball-room swept the cold draught of night
air from the desert.

But three figures instantly were close upon
their heels. The throng of half dazed, half
stupefied onlookers, it seemed, projected them
as though by some explosive force. The general
mass held back, but, like projectiles, these three
flung themselves after the fugitives down the
corridor at high speed — the Apache, Don
Quixote, and, last of them, the Pierrot. For
Khilkoff, the brother, and Baron Minski, the
man who caught wolves alive, had been for

some time keenly on the watch, while Dr. Plitzinger, reading the symptoms clearly, never far away, had been faithfully observant of every movement. His mask tossed aside, the great psychiatrist was now recognised by all. They reached the parapet just as the curtain flapped back heavily into place; the next second all three were out of sight behind it. Khilkoff was first, however, urged forward at frantic speed by the warning words the doctor had whispered as they ran. Some thirty yards beyond the terrace was the brink of the crumbling cliff on which the great hotel was built, and there was a drop of sixty feet to the desert floor below. Only a low stone wall marked the edge.

Accounts varied. Khilkoff, it seems, arrived in time—in the nick of time—to seize his sister, virtually hovering on the brink. He heard the loose stones strike the sand below. There was a moment's violent struggle. She resisted the interference passionately and with all her strength at first. In a sense she was beside—outside—herself. And he did a characteristic thing; he not only brought her back into the ball-room, but he *danced* her back. It was admirable. Nothing could have calmed the general excitement better. The pair of them danced in together as though nothing was amiss. Accustomed to the strenuous practice of his Cossack regiment, this young cavalry officer's muscles were equal to the semi-dead weight in his arms. At most the onlookers thought her tired, perhaps. Confidence was restored—such is the psychology of a crowd—and in the middle of a thrilling Viennese waltz he easily smuggled her out of the room, administered brandy, and got her up to bed. . . . The absence of the Hawk, meanwhile, was hardly noticed; comments were made and then forgotten; it was Vera in whom the strange, anxious sympathy had centred. And, with her obvious safety, the moment of primitive, childish panic passed away. Don Quixote, too, was presently seen dancing gaily as though nothing untoward had happened; supper intervened; the incident was over; it had melted into the general wildness of the evening's irresponsibility. The fact that Pierrot did not appear again was noticed by no single person.

But Dr. Plitzinger was otherwise engaged, his heart and mind and soul all deeply exercised. A death-certificate is not always made out quite so simply as the public thinks. That Binovitch had died of suffocation in his swift descent through merely sixty feet of air was not conceivable; yet that his body lay so neatly placed upon the desert after such a fall was stranger still. It was not crumpled, it was not torn; no single bone was broken, no muscle wrenched; there was no bruise. There was no indenture in the sand. The figure lay sidewise as though in sleep, no sign of violence visible anywhere, the dark wings folded as a great bird folds them when it creeps away to die in loneliness. Beneath the Horus mask the face was smiling. It seemed he had floated into death upon the element he loved. And only Vera had seen the enormous wings that, hovering invitingly above the dark abyss, bore him so softly into another world. Plitzinger, that is, saw them, too, but he said firmly that they belonged to the big black falcons that haunt the Mokattam Hills and roost upon these ridges, close beside the hotel, at night. Both he and Vera, however, agreed on one thing : the high, sharp cry in the air above them, wild and plaintive, was certainly the black kite's cry—the note of the falcon that passionately seeks its mate. It was the pause of a second, when she stood to listen, that made her rescue possible. A moment later and she, too, would have flown to death with Binovitch.

IV

A BIT OF WOOD

HE found himself in Meran with some cousins who had various slight ailments, but, being rich and imaginative, had gone to a Sanatorium to be cured. But for the Sanatoria, Meran might be a cheerful place; their ubiquity reminds a healthy man too often that the air is really good. Being well enough himself, except for a few mental worries, he went to a Gasthaus in the neighbourhood. In the Sanatorium his cousins complained bitterly of the food, the ignorant "sisters," the inattentive doctors, and the idiotic regulations generally—which proves that people should not go to a Sanatorium unless they are really ill. However, they paid heavily for being there, so felt that something was being accomplished, and were annoyed when he called each day for tea, and told them cheerfully how much better they looked—which proved, again, that their ailments were slight and quite curable by the local doctor at home. With one of the ailing cousins, a rich and pretty girl, he believed himself half in love.

It was a three weeks' business, and he spent
his mornings walking in the surrounding hills, his
mind reflective, analytical, and ambitious, as with
a man half in love. He thought of thousands
of things. He mooned. Once, for instance, he
paused beside a rivulet to watch the buttercups
dip, and asked himself, " Will she be like this
when we're married—so anxious to be well that
she thinks fearfully all the time of getting ill? "
For, if so, he felt he would be bored. He knew
himself accurately enough to realise that he
never could stand *that*. Yet money was a
wonderful thing to have, and he, already thirty-
five, had little enough! " Am I influenced by
her money, then? " he asked himself . . . and
so went on to ask and wonder about many things
besides, for he was of a reflective temperament
and his father had been a minor poet. And
Doubt crept in. He felt a chill. He was not
much of a man, perhaps, thin-blooded and un-
successful, rather a dreamer, too, into the bargain. He had £100 a year of his own and a
position in a Philanthropic Institution (due to
influence) with a nominal salary attached. He
meant to keep the latter after marriage. He
would work just the same. Nobody should ever
say *that* of him——!

And as he sat on the fallen tree beside the
rivulet, idly knocking stones into the rushing
water with his stick, he reflected upon those

banal truisms that epitomise two-thirds of life.
The way little unimportant things can change
a person's whole existence was the one his
thought just now had fastened on. His cousin's
chill and headache, for instance, caught at a
gloomy picnic on the Campagna three weeks
before, had led to her going into a Sanatorium
and being advised that her heart was weak, that
she had a tendency to asthma, that gout was in
her system, and that a treatment of X-rays,
radium, sun-baths and light baths, violet rays,
no meat, complete rest, with big daily fees to
experts with European reputations, were imperative. "From that chill, sitting a moment
too long in the shadow of a forgotten Patri-
cian's tomb," he reflected, "has come all this"
—"all this" including his doubt as to whether
it was herself or her money that he loved,
whether he could stand living with her always,
whether he need *really* keep his work on after
marriage, in a word, his entire life and future,
and her own as well—"all from that tiny chill
three weeks ago!" And he knocked with his
stick a little piece of sawn-off board that lay
beside the rushing water.

Upon that bit of wood his mind, his mood,
then fastened itself. It was triangular, a piece
of sawn-off wood, brown with age and ragged.
Once it had been part of a triumphant, hopeful
sapling on the mountains; then, when thirty

years of age, the men had cut it down; the rest
of it stood somewhere now, at this very moment,
in the walls of the house. This extra bit was cast
away as useless; it served no purpose anywhere;
it was slowly rotting in the sun. But each tap
of the stick, he noticed, turned it sideways without sending it over the edge into the rushing
water. It was obstinate. "It doesn't want to
go in," he laughed, his father's little talent
cropping out in him, "but, by Jove, it shall!"
And he pushed it with his foot. But again it
stopped, stuck end-ways against a stone. He
then stooped, picked it up, and threw it in. It
plopped and splashed, and went scurrying away
downhill with the bubbling water. "Even that
scrap of useless wood," he reflected, rising to
continue his aimless walk, and still idly dreaming, "even that bit of rubbish may have a purpose, and may change the life of someone—
somewhere!"—and then went strolling through
the fragrant pine woods, crossing a dozen similar
streams, and hitting scores of stones and scraps
and fir cones as he went—till he finally reached
his Gasthaus an hour later, and found a note
from *her*: "We shall expect you about three
o'clock. We thought of going for a drive. The
others feel so much better."

It was a revealing touch—the way she put it
on "the others." He made his mind up then
and there—thus tiny things decide the course

of life—that he could never be happy with such an " affected creature." He went for that drive, sat next to her consuming beauty, proposed to her passionately on the way back, was accepted before he could change his mind, and is now the father of several healthy children—and just as much afraid of getting ill, or of *their* getting ill, as she was fifteen years before. The female, of course, matures long, long before the male, he reflected, thinking the matter over in his study once. . . .

And that scrap of wood he idly set in motion out of impulse also went its destined way upon the hurrying water that never dared to stop. Proud of its new-found motion, it bobbed down merrily, spinning and turning for a mile or so, dancing gaily over sunny meadows, brushing the dipping buttercups as it passed, through vineyards, woods, and under dusty roads in neat, cool gutters, and tumbling headlong over little waterfalls, until it neared the plain. And so, finally, it came to a wooden trough that led off some of the precious water to a sawmill where bare-armed men did practical and necessary things. At the parting of the ways its angles delayed it for a moment, undecided which way to take. It wobbled. And upon that moment's wobbling hung tragic issues—issues of life and death.

Unknowing (yet assuredly not unknown) it

chose the trough. It swung lightheartedly into
the tearing sluice. It whirled with the gush
of water towards the wheel, banged, spun,
trembled, caught fast in the side where the cogs
just chanced to be—and abruptly stopped the
wheel. At any other spot the pressure of the
water must have smashed it into pulp, and the
wheel have continued as before; but it was
caught in the *one* place where the various
tensions held it fast immovably. It stopped
the wheel, and so the machinery of the entire
mill.

It jammed like iron. The particular angle
at which the double-handed saw, held by two
weary and perspiring men, had cut it off a year
before just enabled it to fit and wedge itself with
irresistible exactitude. The pressure of the
tearing water combined with the weight of the
massive wheel to fix it tight and rigid. And in
due course a workman—it was the foreman of
the mill—came from his post inside to make in-
vestigations. He discovered the irritating item
that caused the trouble. He put his weight in
a certain way; he strained his hefty muscles; he
swore—and the scrap of wood was easily dislodged. He fished the morsel out, and tossed it
on the bank, and spat on it. The great wheel
started with a mighty groan. But it started
a fraction of a second before he expected it
would start. He overbalanced, clutching the

revolving framework with a frantic effort,
shouted, swore, leaped at nothing, and fell into
the pouring flood. In an instant he was turned
upside down, sucked under, drowned. He was
engaged to be married, and had put by a thousand *kronen* in the *Tiroler Sparbank*. He was
a sober and hard-working man. . . .

There was a paragraph in the local paper two
days later. The Englishman, asking the porter
of his Gasthaus for something to wrap up a
present he was taking to his cousin in the Sanatorium, used that very issue. As he folded its
crumpled and recalcitrant sheets with senti-
mental care about the precious object his eye
fell carelessly upon the paragraph. Being of an
idle and reflective temperament he stopped to
read it—it was headed " Unglücksfall," and his
poetic eye, inherited from his foolish, rhyming
father, caught the pretty expression " fliessendes
Wasser."

He read the first few lines. Some fellow,
with a picturesque Tyrolese name, had been
drowned beneath a mill-wheel; he was popular
in the neighbourhood, it seemed; he had saved
some money, and was just going to be married.
It was very sad. " Our readers' sympathy "
was with him. . . . And, being of a reflective temperament, the Englishman thought for
a moment, while he went on wrapping up the
parcel. He wondered if the man had really

loved the girl, whether she, too, had money, and whether they would have had lots of children and been happy ever afterwards.   And then he hurried out towards the Sanatorium.   "I shall be late," he reflected.   "Such little, unimportant things delay one . . . . !"

V

INITIATION

A few years ago, on a Black Sea steamer heading for the Caucasus, I fell into conversation with an American. He mentioned that he was on his way to the Baku oil-fields, and I replied that I was going up into the mountains. He looked at me questioningly a moment. "Your first trip?" he asked with interest. I said it was. A conversation followed; it was continued the next day, and renewed the following day, until we parted company at Batoum. I don't know why he talked so freely to me in particular. Normally, he was a taciturn, silent man. We had been fellow travellers from Marseilles, but after Constantinople we had the boat pretty much to ourselves. What struck me about him was his vehement, almost passionate, love of natural beauty—in seas and woods and sky, but above all in mountains. It was like a religion in him. His taciturn manner hid deep poetic feeling.

And he told me it had not always been so with him. A kind of friendship sprang up

between us. He was a New York business man
—buying and selling exchange between banks—
but was English born. He had gone out forty
years before, and become naturalised. His
talk was exceedingly "American," slangy, and
almost Western. He said he had roughed it in
the West for several years first. But what he
chiefly talked about was mountains. He said it
was in the mountains an unusual experience had
come to him that had opened his eyes to many
things, but principally to the beauty that was
now everything to him, and to the—insignificance of death.

He knew the Caucasus well where I was
going. I think that was why he was interested
in me and my journey. "Up there," he said,
"you'll feel things—and maybe find out things
you never knew before."

"What kind of things?" I asked.

"Why, for one," he replied with emotion
and enthusiasm in his voice, "that living
and dying ain't either of them of much
account. That if you know Beauty, I mean,
and Beauty is in your life, you live on in
it and with it for others—even when you're
dead."

The conversation that followed is too long
to give here, but it led to his telling me the
experience in his own life that had opened his
eyes to the truth of what he said. "Beauty is

imperishable," he declared, "and if you live with it, why, you're imperishable too!"

The story, as he told it verbally in his curious language, remains vividly in my memory. But he had written it down, too, he said. And he gave me the written account, with the remark that I was free to hand it on to others if I "felt that way." He called it "Initiation." It runs as follows:

1

In my own family this happened, for Arthur was my nephew. And a remote Alpine valley was the place. It didn't seem to me in the least suitable for such occurrences, except that it was Catholic, and the "Church," I understand—at least, scholars who ought to know have told me so—has subtle Pagan origins incorporated unwittingly in its observations of certain Saints' Days, as well as in certain ceremonials. All this kind of thing is Dutch to me, a form of poetry or superstition, for I am interested chiefly in the buying and selling of exchange, with an office in New York City, just off Wall Street, and only come to Europe now occasionally for a holiday. I like to see the dear old musty cities, and go to the Opera, and take a motor run through Shakespeare's country or round the Lakes, get in touch again with London and Paris at the Ritz Hotels—and then

H

back again to the greatest city on earth, where for years now I've been making a good thing out of it. Repton and Cambridge, long since forgotten, had their uses. They were all right enough at the time. But I'm now "on the make," with a good fat partnership, and have left all that truck behind me.

My half-brother, however—he was my senior and got the cream of the family wholesale chemical works—has stuck to the trade in the Old Country, and is making probably as much as I am. He approved my taking the chance that offered, and is only sore now because his son, Arthur, is on the stupid side. He agreed that finance suited my temperament far better than drugs and chemicals, though he warned me that all American finance was speculative and therefore dangerous. "Arthur is getting on," he said in his last letter, "and will some day take the director's place you would be in now had you cared to stay. But he's a plodder, rather." That meant, I knew, that Arthur was a fool. Business, at any rate, was not suited to his temperament. Some years ago, when I came home with a month's holiday to be used in working up connections in English banking circles, I saw the boy. He was fifteen years of age at the time, a delicate youth, with an artist's dreams in his big blue eyes, if my memory goes for anything, but with a tangle of

yellow hair and features of classical beauty that
would have made half the young girls of my
New York set in love with him, and a choice
of heiresses at his disposal when he wanted
them.

I have a clear recollection of my nephew
then. He struck me as having grit and
character, but as being wrongly placed. He
had his grandfather's tastes. He ought to
have been, like him, a great scholar, a poet, an
editor of marvellous old writings in new editions.
I couldn't get much out of the boy, except that
he "liked the chemical business fairly," and
meant to please his father by "knowing it
thoroughly" so as to qualify later for his direc-
torship. But I have never forgotten the evening
when I caught him in the hall, staring up at his
grandfather's picture, with a kind of light about
his face, and the big blue eyes all rapt and tender
(moist, too, as if from tears), and replying, when
I asked him what was up : "*That* was worth
living for. He brought Beauty back into the
world! "

" Yes," I said, " I guess that's right enough.
He did. But there was no money in it to speak
of."

The boy looked at me and smiled. He
twigged somehow or other that deep down in
me, somewhere below the money-making instinct, a poet, but a dumb poet, lay in hiding.

" You know what I mean," he said. " It's in
you too."

The picture was a copy—my father had it
made—of the presentation portrait given to
Balliol, and " the grandfather " was celebrated
in his day for the translations he made of Ana-
creon and Sappho, of Homer, too, if I remember
rightly, as well as for a number of classical studies
and essays that he wrote. A lot of stuff like that
he did, and made a name at it too. His " Lives
of the Gods " went into six editions. They
said—the big critics of his day—that he was " a
poet who wrote no poetry, yet lived it passionately in the spirit of old-world, classical Beauty,"
and I know he was a wonderful fellow in his way
and made the dons and schoolmasters all sit up.
We're proud of him all right. After thirty
years of successful " exchange " in New York
City, I confess I am unable to appreciate all
that, feeling more in touch with the commercial
and financial spirit of the age, progress, development and the rest. But, still, I'm not ashamed
of the classical old boy, who seems to have been
a good deal of a Pagan, judging by the records
we have kept. However, Arthur peering up at
that picture in the dusk, his eyes half moist with
emotion, and his voice gone positively shaky,
is a thing I never have forgotten. He stimulated my curiosity uncommonly. It stirred
something deep down in me that I hardly cared

to acknowledge on Wall Street—something burning.

And the next time I saw him was in the summer of 1910, when I came to Europe for a two months' look around—my wife at Newport with the children—and hearing that he was in Switzerland, learning a bit of French to help him in the business, I made a point of dropping in upon him just to see how he was shaping generally and what new kinks his mind had taken on. There was something in Arthur I never could quite forget. Whenever his face came into my mind I began to think. A kind of longing came over me—a desire for Beauty, I guess, it was. It made me dream.

I found him at an English tutor's—a lively old dog, with a fondness for the cheap native wines and a financial interest in the tourist development of the village. The boys learnt French in the mornings, possibly, but for the rest of the day were free to amuse themselves exactly as they pleased and without a trace of supervision—provided the parents footed the bills without demur.

This suited everybody all round; and as long as the boys came home with an accent and a vocabulary, all was well. For myself, having learned in New York to attend strictly to my own business — exchange between different countries with a profit—I did not deem it necessary to exchange letters and opinions with my brother—with no chance of profit anywhere. But I got to know Arthur, and had a queer experience of my own into the bargain. Oh, there was profit in it for me. I'm drawing big dividends to this day on the investment.

I put up at the best hotel in the village, a one-horse show, differing from the other inns only in the prices charged for a lot of cheap decoration in the dining-room, and went up to surprise my nephew with a call the first thing after dinner. The tutor's house stood some way back from the narrow street, among fields where there were more flowers than grass, and backed by a forest of fine old timber that stretched up several thousand feet to the snow. The snow at least was visible, peeping out far overhead just where the dark line of forest stopped; but in reality, I suppose, that was an effect of fore-shortening, and big slopes and pastures inter-vened between the trees and the snow-fields. The sunset, long since out of the valley, still shone on those white ridges, where the peaks stuck up like the teeth of a gigantic saw. I guess it meant five or six hours' good climbing to get up to them—and nothing to do when you got there. Switzerland, anyway, seemed a poor country, with its little bit of watch-making, sour wines, and every square yard hanging up-stairs at an angle of 60 degrees used for hay.

Picture post cards, chocolate and cheap tourists kept it going apparently, but I dare say it was all right enough to learn French in—and cheap as Hoboken to live in.

Arthur was out; I just left a card and wrote on it that I would be very pleased if he cared to step down to take luncheon with me at my hotel next day. Having nothing better to do, I strolled homewards by way of the forest.

Now what came over me in that bit of dark pine forest is more than I can quite explain, but I think it must have been due to the height—the village was 4,000 feet above sea-level—and the effect of the rarefied air upon my circulation. The nearest thing to it in my experience is rye whisky, the queer touch of wildness, of self-confidence, a kind of whooping rapture and the reckless sensation of being a tin god of sorts that comes from a lot of alcohol—a memory, please understand, of years before, when I thought it a grand thing to own the earth and paint the old town red. I seemed to walk on air, and there was a smell about those trees that made me suddenly—well, that took my mind clean out of its accustomed rut. It was just too lovely and wonderful for me to describe it. I had got well into the forest and lost my way a bit. The smell of an old-world garden wasn't in it. It smelt to me as if someone had just that minute turned out the earth all fresh and new. There

was moss and tannin, a hint of burning, something between smoke and incense, say, and a
fine clean odour of pitch-pine bark when the sun
gets on it after rain—and a flavour of the sea
thrown in for luck. That was the first I noticed,
for I had never smelt anything half so good since
my camping days on the coast of Maine. And
I stood still to enjoy it. I threw away my cigar
for fear of mixing things and spoiling it. "If
that could be bottled," I said to myself, "it'd
sell for two dollars a pint in every city in the
Union!"

And it was just then, while standing and
breathing it in, that I got the queer feeling
of someone watching me. I kept quite still.
Someone was moving near me. The sweat went
trickling down my back. A kind of childhood
thrill got hold of me.

It was very dark. I was not afraid exactly,
but I was a stranger in these parts and knew
nothing about the habits of the mountain
peasants. There might be tough customers
lurking around after dark on the chance of
striking some guy of a tourist with money in his
pockets. Yet, somehow, that wasn't the kind
of feeling that came to me at all, for, though I
had a pocket Browning at my hip, the notion
of getting at it did not even occur to me. The
sensation was new—a kind of lifting, exciting
sensation that made my heart swell out with

exhilaration. There was happiness in it. A cloud that *weighed* seemed to roll off my mind, same as that light-hearted mood when the office door is locked and I'm off on a two months' holiday—with gaiety and irresponsibility at the back of it. It was invigorating. I felt youth sweep over me.

I stood there, wondering what on earth was coming on me, and half expecting that any moment someone would come out of the darkness and show himself; and as I held my breath and made no movement at all the queer sensation grew stronger. I believe I even resisted a temptation to kick up my heels and dance, to let out a flying shout as a man with liquor in him does. Instead of this, however, I just kept dead still. The wood was black as ink all round me, too black to see the tree-trunks separately, except far below where the village lights came up twinkling between them, and the only way I kept the path was by the soft feel of the pine-needles that were thicker than a Brussels carpet. But nothing happened, and no one stirred. The idea that I was being watched remained, only there was no sound anywhere except the roar of falling water that filled the entire valley. Yet someone was very close to me in the darkness.

I can't say how long I might have stood there, but I guess it was the best part of ten minutes, and I remember it struck me that I had run up against a pocket of extra-rarefied air that had a lot of oxygen in it—oxygen or something similar—and that was the cause of my elation. The idea was nonsense, I have no doubt; but for the moment it half explained the thing to me. I realised it was all *natural* enough, at any rate—and so moved on. It took a longish time to reach the edge of the wood, and a footpath led me—oh, it was quite a walk, I tell you —into the village street again. I was both glad and sorry to get there. I kept myself busy thinking the whole thing over again. What caught me all of a heap was that million-dollar sense of beauty, youth, and happiness. Never in my born days had I felt anything to touch it. And it hadn't cost a cent!

Well, I was sitting there enjoying my smoke and trying to puzzle it all out, and the hall was pretty full of people smoking and talking and reading papers, and so forth, when all of a sudden I looked up and caught my breath with such a jerk that I actually bit my tongue. There was grandfather in front of my chair! I looked into his eyes. I saw him as clear and solid as the porter standing behind his desk across the lounge, and it gave me a touch of cold all down the back that I needn't forget unless I want to. He was looking into my face, and he had a cap in his hand, and he was speaking to me. It was my **grandfather's** picture come to life, only much

thinner and younger and a kind of light in his
eyes like fire.

"I beg your pardon, but you *are*—Uncle
Jim, aren't you?"

And then, with another jump of my nerves,
I understood.

"You, Arthur! Well, I'm jiggered. So
it is. Take a chair, boy. I'm right glad you
found me. Shake! Sit down." And I took
his hand and pushed a chair up for him. I was
never so surprised in my life. The last time I
set eyes on him he was a boy. Now he was a
young man, and the very image of his ancestor.

He sat down, fingering his cap. He wouldn't
have a drink and he wouldn't smoke. "All
right," I said, "let's talk then. I've lots to
tell you and I've lots to hear. How are you,
boy?"

He didn't answer at first. He eyed me up
and down. He hesitated. He was as handsome
as a young Greek god.

"I say, Uncle Jim," he began presently,
"it *was* you—just now—in the wood—wasn't
it?" It made me start, that question put so
quietly.

"I *have* just come through that wood up
there," I answered, pointing in the direction as
well as I could remember, "if that's what you
mean. But why? *You* weren't there, were
you?" It gave me a queer sort of feeling to

hear him say it. What in the name of heaven did he mean?

He sat back in his chair with a sigh of relief.

"Oh, that's all right then," he said, "if it *was* you. Did you see," he asked suddenly, "did you see—anything?"

"Not a thing," I told him honestly. "It was far too dark." I laughed. I fancied I twigged his meaning. But I was not the sort of uncle to come prying on him. Life must be dull enough, I remembered, in this mountain village.

But he didn't understand my laugh. He didn't mean what I meant.

And there came a pause between us. I discovered that we were talking different lingoes. I leaned over towards him.

"Look here, Arthur," I said in a lower voice, "what is it, and what do you mean? I'm all right, you know, and you needn't be afraid of telling me. What d'you mean by—did I see anything?"

We looked at each other squarely in the eye. He saw he could trust me, and I saw—well, a whole lot of things, perhaps, but I felt chiefly that he liked me and would tell me things later, all in his own good time. I liked him all the better for that too.

"I only meant," he answered slowly, "whether you really *saw*—anything?"

" No," I said straight, " I didn't see a thing, but, by the gods, I *felt* something."

He started. I started too. An astonishing big look came swimming over his fair, handsome face. His eyes seemed all lit up. He looked as if he'd just made a cool million in wheat or cotton.

" I knew—you were that sort," he whispered. " Though I hardly remembered what you looked like."

" Then what on earth was it? " I asked.

His reply staggered me a bit. " It was just that," he said—" the Earth ! "

And then, just when things were getting interesting and promising a dividend, he shut up like a clam. He wouldn't say another word. He asked after my family and business, my health, what kind of crossing I'd had, and all the rest of the common stock. It fairly bowled me over. And I couldn't change him either.

I suppose in America we get pretty free and easy, and don't quite understand reserve. But this young man of half my age kept me in my place as easily as I might have kept a nervous customer quiet in my own office. He just refused to take me on. He was polite and cool and distant as you please, and when I got pressing sometimes he simply pretended he didn't understand. I could no more get him back again to the subject of the wood than a customer could

have gotten me to tell him about the prospects
of exchange being cheap or dear—when I didn't
know myself but wouldn't let him see I didn't
know.   He was charming, he was delightful,
enthusiastic and even affectionate; downright
glad to see me, too, and to chin with me—but I
couldn't draw him worth a cent.   And in the
end I gave up trying.

And the moment I gave up trying he let
down a little—but only a very little.

"You'll stay here some time, Uncle Jim,
won't you?"

"That's my idea," I said, "if I can see
you, and you can show me round some."

He laughed with pleasure.   "Oh, rather.
I've got lots of time.   After three in the afternoon I'm free till—any time you like.   There's
a lot to see," he added.

"Come along to-morrow then," I said.
"If you can't take lunch, perhaps you can come
just afterwards.   You'll find me waiting for you
—right here."

"I'll come at three," he replied, and we
said good night.

2

HE turned up sharp on time, and I liked his
punctuality.   I saw him come swinging down
the dusty road; tall, deep-chested, his broad
shoulders a trifle high, and his head set proudly.

He looked like a young chap in training, a thoroughbred, every inch of him. At the same time there was a touch of something a little too refined and delicate for a man, I thought. That was the poetic, scholarly vein in him, I guess —grandfather cropping out. This time he wore no cap. His thick light hair, not brushed back like the London shop-boys, but parted on the side, yet untidy for all that, suited him exactly and gave him a touch of wildness.

"Well," he asked, "what would you like to do, Uncle Jim? I'm at your service, and I've got the whole afternoon till supper at seven-thirty." I told him I'd like to go through that wood. "All right," he said, "come along. I'll show you." He gave me one quick glance, but said no more. "I'd like to see if I feel anything this time," I explained. "We'll locate the very spot, maybe." He nodded. "You know where I mean, don't you?" I asked, "because you saw me there?" He just said yes, and then we started.

It was hot, and air was scarce. I remember that we went uphill, and that I realised there was considerable difference in our ages. We crossed some fields first—smothered in flowers so thick that I wondered how much grass the cows got out of it!—and then came to a sprinkling of fine young larches that looked as soft as velvet. There was no path, just a wild moun-

tain side. I had very little breath on the steep
zigzags, but Arthur talked easily—and talked
mighty well, too: the light and shade, the
colouring, and the effect of all this wilderness
of lonely beauty on the mind. He kept all this
suppressed at home in business. It was safety
valves. I twigged *that*. It was the artist in
him talking. He seemed to think there was
nothing in the world but Beauty—with a big
B all the time. And the odd thing was he took
for granted that I felt the same. It was cute
of him to flatter me that way. "Daulis and
the lone Cephissian vale," I heard; and a few
moments later—with a sort of reverence in his
voice like worship—he called out a great singing name: "*Astarte!*"

> "Day is her face, and midnight is her hair,
>   And morning hours are but the golden stair
>   By which she climbs to Night."

"Steady on, boy! I've forgotten all my
classics ages ago," I cried.

He turned and gazed down on me, his big
eyes glowing, and not a sign of perspiration on
his skin.

"That's nothing," he exclaimed in his
musical, deep voice. "You know it, or you'd
never have felt things in this wood last night;
and you wouldn't have wanted to come out
with me now!"

" How? " I gasped. " How's that? "

" You've come," he continued quietly, " to the only valley in this artificial country that has atmosphere. This valley is *alive*—especially this end of it. There's superstition here, thank God! Even the peasants know things."

It was here first that a queer change began to grow upon me too.

I stared at him. " See here, Arthur," I objected. " I'm not a Cath. And I don't know a thing—at least it's all dead in me and forgotten—about poetry or classics or your gods and pan—pantheism—in spite of grandfather——"

His face turned like a dream face.

" Hush! " he said quickly. " Don't mention *him*. There's a bit of him in you as well as in me, and it was here, you know, he wrote——"

I didn't hear the rest of what he said. A creep came over me. I remembered that this ancestor of ours lived for years in the isolation of some mountain forest where he claimed—he used that setting for his writing—to have found the exiled gods, their ghosts, their beauty, their eternal essences—or something astonishing of that sort. I had clean forgotten it till this moment. It all rushed back upon me, a memory of my boyhood.

And, as I say, a creep came over me—something as near to awe as ever could be. The

I

sunshine on the field of yellow daisies and blue
forget-me-nots turned paler. The warm valley
wind had a touch of snow in it. And, ashamed
and frightened of my baby mood, I looked at
Arthur, meaning to choke him off with all this
rubbish—and then saw something in his eyes
that fairly scared me stiff.

I admit it. What's the use? There was an
expression on his face that made my blood go
curdled.   I got cold feet right there.   It
mastered me. In him, behind him, near him
—blest if I know which, *through* him probably
—came an enormous thing that turned me in-
significant. It downed me utterly.

It was over in a second, the flash of a wing.
I recovered instantly. No mere boy should come
these muzzy tricks on me, scholar or no scholar.
For the change in me was on the increase, and
I shrank.

"See here, Arthur," I said plainly once
again, "I don't know what your game is, but
—there's something queer up here I don't quite
get at. I'm only a business man, with classics
and poetry all gone dry in me twenty years ago
and more——"

He looked at me so strangely that I stopped,
confused.

"But, Uncle Jim," he said as quietly as
though we talked tobacco brands, "you needn't
be alarmed. It's natural you should feel the

place. You and I belong to it. We've both got *him* in us. You're just as proud of him as I am, only in a different way." And then he added, with a touch of disappointment: "I thought you'd like it. You weren't afraid last night. You felt the beauty *then*."

Flattery is a darned subtle thing at any time. To see him standing over me in that superior way and talking down at my poor business mind —well, it just came over me that I was laying my cards on the table a bit too early. After so many years of city life——!

Anyway, I pulled myself together. "I was only kidding you, boy," I laughed. "I feel this beauty just as much as you do. Only, I guess, you're more accustomed to it than I am. Come on now," I added with energy, getting upon my feet, " let's push on and see the wood. I want to find that place again."

He pulled me with a hand of iron, laughing as he did so. Gee! I wished I had his teeth, as well as the muscles in his arm. Yet I, too, felt younger, somehow—youth flowed more and more into my veins. I had forgotten how sweet the winds and woods and flowers could be. Something melted in me. For it was Spring, and the whole world was singing like a dream. Beauty was creeping over me. I don't know. I began to feel all big and tender and open to a thousand wonderful sensations. The

thought of streets and houses seemed like
death. . . .

We went on again, not talking much; my
breath got shorter and shorter, and he kept looking about him as though he expected something. But we passed no living soul, not even
a peasant; there were no châlets, no cattle, no
cattle-shelters even. And then I realised that
the valley lay at our feet in haze and that we
had been climbing at least a couple of hours.
" Why, last night I got home in twenty minutes
at the outside," I said. He shook his head,
smiling. " It seemed like that," he replied,
" but you really took much longer. It was long
after ten when I found you in the hall." I
reflected a moment. " Now I come to think
of it, you're right, Arthur. Seems curious,
though, somehow." He looked closely at me.
" I followed you all the way," he said.

" You followed me ! "

" And you went at a good pace too. It was
your feelings that made it seem so short—you
were singing to yourself and happy as a dancing
faun. We kept close behind you for a long
way."

I think it was " we " he said, but for some
reason or other I didn't care to ask.

" Maybe," I answered shortly, trying uncomfortably to recall what particular capers I
had cut. " I guess that's right." And then I

added something about the loneliness, and how
deserted all this slope of mountain was. And
he explained that the peasants were afraid of it
and called it No Man's Land. From one year's
end to another no human foot went up or down
it; the hay was never cut; no cattle grazed along
the splendid pastures; no châlet had even been
built within a mile of the wood we slowly made
for. "They're superstitious," he told me.
"It was just the same a hundred years ago when
he discovered it—there was a little natural cave
on the edge of the forest where he used to sleep
sometimes—I'll show it to you presently—but
for generations this entire mountain-side has
been undisturbed. You'll never meet a living
soul in any part of it." He stopped and pointed
above us to where the pine wood hung in mid-
air, like a dim blue carpet. "It's just the place
for Them, you see."

And a thrill of power went smashing through
me. I can't describe it. It drenched me like
a waterfall. I thought of Greece—Mount Ida
and a thousand songs! Something in me—it
was like the click of a shutter—announced that
the "change" was suddenly complete. I was
another man; or rather a deeper part of me had
come on top. My very language showed it.

The calm of halcyon weather lay over all.
Overhead the peaks rose clear as crystal; below
us the village lay in a bluish smudge of smoke

and haze, as though a great finger had rubbed them softly into the earth. Absolute loneliness fell upon me like a clap. From the world of human beings we seemed quite shut off. And there began to steal over me again the strange elation of the night before. . . . We found ourselves almost at once against the edge of the wood.

It rose in front of us, a big wall of splendid trees, motionless as if cut out of dark green metal, the branches hanging stiff, and the crowd of trunks lost in the blue dimness underneath. I shaded my eyes with one hand, trying to peer into the solemn gloom. The contrast between the brilliant sunshine on the pastures and this region of heavy shadows blurred my sight.

"It's like the entrance to another world," I whispered.

"It is," said Arthur, watching me. "We will go in. You shall pluck asphodel. . . ."

And, before I knew it, he had me by the hand. We were advancing. We left the light behind us. The cool air dropped upon me like a sheet. There was a temple silence. The sun ran down behind the sky, leaving a marvellous blue radiance everywhere. Nothing stirred. But through the stillness there rose power, power that has no name, power that hides at the foundations somewhere—foundations that are changeless, invisible, everlasting.

What do I mean? My mind grew to the dimensions of a planet. We were among the roots of life—whence issues that *one thing* in infinite guise that seeks so many temporary names from the protean minds of men.

"You shall pluck asphodel in the meadows this side of Erebus," Arthur was chanting. "Hermes himself, the Psychopomp, shall lead, and Malahide shall welcome us."

Malahide . . . !

To hear him use that name, the name of our scholar-ancestor, now dead and buried close upon a century—the way he half chanted it—gave me the goose-flesh. I stopped against a tree-stem, thinking of escape. No words came to me at the moment, for I didn't know what to say; but, on turning to find the bright green slopes just left behind, I saw only a crowd of trees and shadows hanging thick as a curtain—as though we had walked a mile. And it was a shock. The way out was lost. The trees closed up behind us like a tide.

"It's all right," said Arthur; "just keep an open mind and a heart alive with love. It has a shattering effect at first, but that will pass." He saw I was afraid, for I shrank visibly enough. He stood beside me in his grey flannel suit, with his brilliant eyes and his great shock of hair, looking more like a column of light than a human being. "It's all quite right and

natural," he repeated; "we have passed the
gateway, and Hecate, who presides over gateways, will let us out again. Do not make dis-
cord by feeling fear. This is a pine wood, and
pines are the oldest, simplest trees; they are
true primitives. They are an open channel; and
in a pine wood where no human life has ever
been you shall often find gateways where Hecate
is kind to such as us."

He took my hand—he must have felt mine
trembling, but his own was cool and strong and
felt like silver—and led me forward into the
depths of a wood that seemed to me quite endless. It felt endless, that is to say. I don't
know what came over me. Fear slipped away,
and elation took its place. . . . As we advanced
over ground that seemed level, or slightly undu-
lating, I saw bright pools of sunshine here and
there upon the forest floor. Great shafts of
light dropped in slantingly between the trunks.
There was movement everywhere, though I
never could see what moved. A delicious,
scented air stirred through the lower branches.
Running water sang not very far away. Figures
I did not actually see; yet there were limbs and
flowing draperies and flying hair from time to
time, ever just beyond the pools of sunlight.
Surprise went from me too. I was on air.
The atmosphere of dream came round me, but
a dream of something just hovering outside the

world I knew—a dream wrought in gold and
silver, with shining eyes, with graceful beckoning hands, and with voices that rang like bells
of music. . . . And the pools of light grew
larger, merging one into another, until a delicate soft light shone equably throughout the
entire forest. Into this zone of light we passed
together. Then something fell abruptly at our
feet, as though thrown down . . . two marvellous, shining sprays of blossom such as I had
never seen in all my days before!

"Asphodel!" cried my companion, stooping to pick them up and handing one to me. I
took it from him with a delight I could not
understand. "Keep it," he murmured; "it is
the sign that we are welcome. For Malahide
has dropped these on our path."

And at the use of that ancestral name it
seemed that a spirit passed before my face and
the hair of my head stood up. There was a
sense of violent, unhappy contrast. A com-
posite picture presented itself, then rushed
away. What was it? My youth in England,
music and poetry at Cambridge and my passionate love of Greek that lasted two terms at
most, when Malahide's great books formed part
of the curriculum. Over against this, then, the
drag and smother of solid worldly business, the
sordid weight of modern ugliness, the bitterness of an ambitious, over-striving life. And

abruptly—beyond both pictures—a shining, marvellous Beauty that scattered stars beneath my feet and scarved the universe with gold.

All this flashed before me with the utterance of that old family name. An alternative sprang up. There seemed some radical, elemental choice presented to me—to what I used to call my soul. My soul could take it or leave it as it pleased. . . .

I looked at Arthur moving beside me like a shaft of light. What had come over me? How had our walk and talk and mood, our quite recent everyday and ordinary view, our normal relationship with the things of the world—how had it all slipped into this? So insensibly, so easily, so naturally!

" Was it worth while? "

The question—*I* didn't ask it—jumped up in me of its own accord. Was " what " worth while? Why, my present life of commonplace and grubbing toil, of course; my city existence, with its meagre, unremunerative ambitions. Ah, it was this new Beauty calling me, this shining dream that lay beyond the two pictures I have mentioned. . . . I did not argue it, even to myself. But I understood. There was a radical change in me. The buried poet, too long hidden, rushed into the air like some great singing bird.

I glanced again at Arthur moving along

lightly by my side, half dancing almost in his
brimming happiness. "Wait till you see
Them," I heard him singing. "Wait till you
hear the call of Artemis and the footsteps of her
flying nymphs. Wait till Orion thunders overhead and Selene, crowned with the crescent
moon, drives up the zenith in her white-horsed
chariot. The choice will be beyond all question
then . . . ! "

A great silent bird, with soft brown plumage,
whirred across our path, pausing an instant as
though to peep, then disappearing with a muted
sound into an eddy of the wind it made. The
big trees hid it. It was an owl. The same
moment I heard a rush of liquid song come pouring through the forest with a gush of almost
human notes, and another pair of glossy wings
flashed past us, swerving upwards to find the
open sky—blue-black, pointed wings.

"His favourites! " exclaimed my companion
with clear joy in his voice. "They all are here!
Athene's bird, Procne and Philomela too! The
owl—the swallow—and the nightingale! Tereus
and Itys are not far away." And the entire
forest, as he said it, stirred with movement, as
though that great bird's quiet wings had waked
the sea of ancient shadows. There were voices
too—ringing, laughing voices, as though his
words woke echoes that had been listening for
it. For I heard sweet singing in the distance.

The names he had used perplexed me. Yet even I, stranger as I was to such refined delights, could not mistake the passion of the nightingale and the dart of the eager swallow. That wild burst of music, that curve of swift escape, were unmistakable.

And I struck a stalwart tree-stem with my open hand, feeling the need of hearing, touching, sensing it. My link with known, remembered things was breaking. I craved the satisfaction of the commonplace. I got that satisfaction; but I got something more as well. For the trunk was round and smooth and comely. It was no dead thing I struck. Somehow it brushed me into intercourse with inanimate Nature. And next the desire came to hear my voice—my own familiar, high-pitched voice with the twang and accent the New World climate brings, so-called American :

" Exchange Place, Noo York City. I'm in that business, buying and selling of exchange between the banks of two civilised countries, one of them stoopid and old-fashioned, the other leading all creation . . . ! "

It was an effort, but I made it firmly. Only it sounded odd, remote, unreal.

" Sunlit woods and a wind among the branches," followed close and sweet upon my words. But who, in the name of Wall Street, said it?

"England's buying gold," I tried again.
"We've had a private wire. Cut in quick.
First National is selling!"

Great-faced Hephæstus, how ridiculous! It
was like saying, " I'll take your scalp unless you
give me meat." It was barbaric, savage, centuries ago. Again there came another voice that
caught up my own and turned it into common
syntax. Some heady beauty of the Earth rose
about me like a cloud.

"Hark! Night comes, with the dusk upon
her eyelids. She brings those dreams that every
dew-drop holds at dawn. Daughter of Thanatos
and Hypnos . . .!"

But again—who said the words? It surely
was not Arthur, my nephew Arthur, of To-day,
learning French in a Swiss mountain village!
I felt—well, what did I feel? In the name of
the Stock Exchange and Wall Street, what was
the cash surrender of my amazing feelings?

3

AND, turning to look at him, I made a discovery. I don't know how to tell it quite; such
shadowy marvels have never been my line of
goods. He looked several things at once—taller,
slighter, sweeter, but chiefly—it sounds so crazy
when I write it down—grander is the word, I
think. And radiating with some power that

flowed like Spring when it pours upon a landscape.   Eternally young and glorious—young,
I mean, in the sense that a field of flowers in the
Spring looks young; and glorious in the sense
the sky looks glorious at dawn or sunset.   Something big shone through him like a storm, something that would go on for ever just as the Earth
goes on, always renewing itself; something
of gigantic life that in the human sense could
never age at all—something the old gods had.
But the figure, so far as there was any figure at
all, was that old family picture come to life.   Our
great ancestor and Arthur were one being, and
that one being was vaster than a million people.
Yet it was Malahide I saw. . . .

" They laid me in the earth I loved," he said
in a low, penetrating voice like running wind
and water, " and I found eternal life.   I live now
for ever in Their divine existence.   I share the
life that changes yet can never pass away."

I felt myself rising like a cloud as he said it.
A rising beauty captured me completely.   If
I could tell it in honest newspaper language—
the common language used in flats and offices
—why, I guess I could patent a new meaning
in ordinary words, a new power of expression,
the thing that all the churches and poets and
thinkers have been trying to say since the world
began.   I caught on to a fact so fine and simple
that it knocked me silly to think I'd never

realised it before. I had read about it, yes; but now I *knew* it. The Earth, the whole bustling universe, was nothing after all but a visible production of eternal, living Powers—spiritual powers, mind you—that just happened to include the particular little type of strutting creature we called mankind. And these Powers, as seen in Nature, were the gods. It was our refusal of their grand appeal, so wild and sweet and beautiful, that caused "evil." It was this barrier between ourselves and the rest of . . .

My thoughts and feelings swept away upon the rising flood as the "figure" came upon me like a shaft of moonlight, melting the last remnant of opposition that was in me. I took my brain, my reason, chucking them aside for the futile little mechanism I suddenly saw them to be. In place of them came—oh, God, I hate to say it, for only nursery talk can get within a mile of it, and yet what I need is something simpler even than the words that children use. Under one arm I carried a whole forest breathing in the wind, and beneath the other a hundred meadows full of singing streams with golden marigolds and blue forget-me-nots along their banks. Upon my back and shoulders lay the clouded hills with dew and moonlight in their brimmed, capacious hollows. Thick in my hair hung the unaging powers that are stars and sunlight; though the sun was far away, it sweetened the currents of my blood with liquid gold. Breast and throat and face, as I advanced, met all the rivers of the world and all the winds of heaven, their strength and swiftness melting into me as light melts into everything it touches. And into my eyes passed all the radiant colours that weave the cloth of Nature as she takes the sun. I mean that the beauty of the world which never dies was one with the beauty in my soul —imperishable.

And this " figure," pouring upon me like a burst of moonlight, spoke :

" They all are in you—air, and fire, and water. . . ."

" And I—my feet stand—on the *Earth*," my own voice interrupted, power lifting through the sound of it.

" The Earth ! " He laughed gigantically. He spread. He seemed everywhere about me. He seemed a race of men. My life swam forth in waves of some immense sensation that issued from the mountain and the forest, then returned to them again. I reeled. I became afraid. I clutched at something in me that was slipping beyond control, slipping down a bank towards a deep, dark river flowing at my feet. A shadowy boat appeared, a still more shadowy outline at the helm. I was in the act of stepping into it. For the tree I caught at to save myself was only air. I couldn't stop. I tried to scream.

"You have plucked asphodel," sang the voice beside me, "and you shall pluck more. . . ."

I slipped and slipped, the speed increasing horribly. Then something caught, as though a cog held fast and stopped me—I remembered my business in New York City.

"Arthur!" I yelled. "Arthur!" I shouted again as hard as I could shout. There was frantic terror in me. I felt as though I should never get back to myself again. Death!

The answer came in his normal voice: "Keep close to me. I know the way. . . ."

The scenery dwindled suddenly; the trees came back. I was walking in the forest beside my nephew, and the moonlight lay in patches and little shafts of silver. The crests of the pines just murmured in a wind that scarcely stirred, and through an opening on our right I saw the deep valley clasped about the twinkling village lights. Towering in splendour the spectral snowfields hung upon the sky, huge summits guarding them. And Arthur took my arm—oh, solidly enough this time. Thank heaven, he asked no questions of me.

"There's a smell of myrrh," he whispered, "and we are very near the undying, ancient things."

J

I said something about the resin from the trees, but he took no notice.

"It enclosed its body in an egg of myrrh," he went on, smiling down at me; "then, setting it on fire, rose from the ashes with its life renewed. Once every five hundred years, you see——"

"What did?" I cried, feeling that loss of self stealing over me again. And his answer came like a blow between the eyes:

"The Phœnix. They called it a bird, though, of course, the true . . ."

"But my life's insured in that," I cried, for he had named the company that took large yearly premiums from me; "and I pay . . ."

"Your life's insured in *this*," he said quietly, waving his arms to indicate the Earth. "Your love of Nature and your sympathy with it make you safe." He gazed at me. There was a marvellous expression in his eyes. I understood why poets talked of stars and flowers in a human face. But behind the face crept back another look as well. There grew about his figure an indeterminate extension. The outline of Malahide again stirred through his own. A pale, delicate hand reached out to take my own. And something broke in me.

I was conscious of two things—a burst of joy that meant losing myself entirely, and a rush of terror that meant staying as I was, a small, painful, struggling item of individual life. Another spray of that awful asphodel fell fluttering through the air in front of my face. It rested on the earth against my feet. And Arthur—this weirdly changing Arthur—stooped to pick it up for me. I kicked it with my foot beyond his reach . . . then turned and ran as though the Furies of that ancient world were after me. I ran for what I called my "very life." How I escaped from that thick wood without banging my body to bits against the trees I can't explain. I ran from something I desired yet feared. I leaped along in a succession of flying bounds. Each tree I passed turned of its own accord and flung after me until the entire forest followed. But I got out. I reached the open. Upon the sloping field in the full, clear light of the moon I collapsed in a panting heap. The Earth drew back with a great shuddering sigh behind me. There was this strange, tumultuous sound upon the night. I lay beneath the open heavens that were full of moonlight. I was myself—but there were tears in me. Beauty too high for understanding had slipped between my fingers. I had lost Malahide. I had lost the gods of Earth. . . . Yet I had seen . . . and felt. I had not lost all. Something remained that I could never lose again. . . .

I don't know how it happened exactly, but

presently I heard Arthur saying : " You'll catch your death of cold if you lie on that soaking grass," and felt his hand seize mine to pull me to my feet.

"I feel safer on earth," I believed I answered. And then he said : " Yes, but it's such a stupid way to die—a chill ! "

4

I GOT up then, and we went downhill together towards the village lights. I danced—oh, I admit it—I sang as well. There was a flood of joy and power about me that beat anything I'd ever felt before. I didn't think or hesitate; there was no self-consciousness; I just let it rip for all there was, and if there had been ten thousand people there in front of me, I could have made them feel it too. That was the kind of feeling—power and confidence and a sort of raging happiness. I think I know what it was too. I say this soberly, with reverence . . . all wool and no fading. There was a bit of God in me, God's power that drives the Earth and pours through Nature—the imperishable Beauty expressed in those old-world nature-deities !

And the fear I'd felt was nothing but the little tickling pain of losing my ordinary two-cent self, the dread of letting go, the shrinking before the plunge—what a fellow feels when he's falling in love, and hesitates, and tries to think it out and hold back, and is afraid to let the enormous tide flow in and drown him.

Oh, yes, I began to think it over a bit as we raced down the mountain-side that glorious night. I've read some in my day; my brain's all right; I've heard of dual personality and subliminal uprush and conversion—no new line of goods, all that. But somehow these stunts of the psychologists and philosophers didn't cut any ice with me just then, because I'd *experienced* what they merely *explained*. And explanation was just a bargain sale. The best things can't be explained at all. There's no real value in a bargain sale.

Arthur had trouble to keep up with me. We were running due east, and the Earth was turning, therefore, with us. We all three ran together at her own pace—terrific! The moon-light danced along the summits, and the snow-fields flew like spreading robes, and the forests everywhere, far and near, hung watching us and booming like a thousand organs. There were uncaged winds about; you could hear them whistling among the precipices. But the one great thing I knew was—Beauty, a beauty of the common old familiar Earth, and a beauty that's stayed with me ever since, and given me joy and strength and a source of power and delight I'd never guessed existed before.

As we dropped lower into the thicker air of the valley I sobered down. Gradually the ecstasy passed from me. We slowed up a bit. The lights and the houses and the sight of the hotel where people were dancing in a stuffy ballroom, all this put blotting-paper on something that had been flowing.

Now you'll think this an odd thing too—but when we reached the village street, I just took Arthur's hand and shook it and said good-night and went up to bed and slept like a two-year-old till morning. And from that day to this I've never set eyes on the boy again.

Perhaps it's difficult to explain, and perhaps it isn't. I can explain it to myself in two lines —I was afraid to see him. I was afraid he might explain. I was afraid he might explain away. I just left a note—he never replied to it— and went off by a morning train. Can you understand that? Because if you can't you haven't understood this account I've tried to give of the experience Arthur gave me. Well—anyway—I'll just let it go at that.

Arthur's a director now in his father's wholesale chemical business, and I—well, I'm doing better than ever in the buying and selling of exchange between banks in New York City as before.

But when I said I was still drawing dividends on my Swiss investment, I meant it. And it's

not " scenery." Everybody gets a thrill from
" scenery." It's a darned sight more than that.
It's those little wayward patches of blue on a
cloudy day; those blue pools in the sky just
above Trinity Church steeple when I pass out of
Wall Street into Lower Broadway; it's the
rustle of the sea-wind among the Battery trees;
the wash of the waves when the Ferry's starting
for Staten Island, and the glint of the sun far
down the Bay, or dropping a bit of pearl into the
old East River. And sometimes it's the strip
of cloud in the west above the Jersey shore of the
Hudson, the first star, the sickle of the new
moon behind the masts and shipping. But
usually it's something nearer, bigger, simpler
than all or any of these. It's just the certainty
that, when I hurry along the hard stone pavements from bank to bank, I'm walking on the
—Earth. It's just that—*the Earth!*

VI

A DESERT EPISODE

1

" BETTER put wraps on now. The sun's getting low," a girl said.

It was the end of a day's expedition in the Arabian Desert, and they were having tea. A few yards away the donkeys munched their *barsim;* beside them in the sand the boys lay finishing bread and jam. Immense, with gliding tread, the sun's rays slid from crest to crest of the limestone ridges that broke the huge expanse towards the Red Sea. By the time the tea-things were packed the sun hovered, a giant ball of red, above the Pyramids. It stood in the western sky a moment, looking out of its majestic hood across the sand. With a movement almost visible it leaped, paused, then leaped again. It seemed to bound towards the horizon; then, suddenly, was gone.

" It *is* cold, yes," said the painter, Rivers. And all who heard looked up at him because of the way he said it. A hurried movement ran through the merry party, and the girls were on

their donkeys quickly, not wishing to be left to
bring up the rear. They clattered off. The
boys cried; the thud of sticks was heard; hoofs
shuffled through the sand and stones. In single
file the picnickers headed for Helouan, some five
miles distant. And the desert closed up behind
them as they went, following in a shadowy wave
that never broke, noiseless, foamless, unstreaked,
driven by no wind, and of a volume undiscover-
able. Against the orange sunset the Pyramids
turned deep purple. The strip of silvery Nile
among its palm trees looked like rising mist.
In the incredible Egyptian afterglow the enormous horizons burned a little longer, then went
out. The ball of the earth—a huge round globe
that bulged—curved visibly as at sea. It was
no longer a flat expanse; it turned. Its splendid curves were realised.

"Better put wraps on; it's cold and the sun
is low"—and then the curious hurry to get back
among the houses and the haunts of men. No
more was said, perhaps, than this, yet, the time
and place being what they were, the mind became suddenly aware of that quality which ever
brings a certain shrinking with it—vastness;
and more than vastness: that which is endless
because it is also beginningless—eternity. A
colossal splendour stole upon the heart; and the
senses, unaccustomed to the unusual stretch,
reeled a little, as though the wonder was more

than could be faced with comfort. Not all, doubtless, realised it, though to two, at least, it came with a staggering impact there was no withstanding. For, while the luminous greys and purples crept round them from the sandy wastes, the hearts of these two became aware of certain common things whose simple majesty is usually dulled by mere familiarity. Neither the man nor the girl knew for certain that the other felt it, as they brought up the rear together; yet the fact that each *did* feel it set them side by side in the same strange circle—and made them silent. They realised the immensity of a moment : the dizzy stretch of time that led up to the casual-pinning of a veil, to the tightening of a stirrup strap, to the little speech with a companion, to the roar of the vanished centuries that have ground mountains into sand and spread them over the floor of Africa; above all, to the little truth that they themselves existed amid the whirl of stupendous systems all deli-'cately balanced as a spider's web—that they were *alive*.

For a moment this vast scale of reality revealed itself, then hid swiftly again behind the debris of the obvious. The universe, containing their two tiny yet important selves, stood still for an instant before their eyes. They looked at it—realised that they belonged to it. Everything moved and had its being, *lived*—here in this

silent, empty desert even more actively than in
a city of crowded houses. The quiet Nile, sighing with age, passed down towards the sea;
there loomed the menacing Pyramids across the
twilight; beneath them, in monstrous dignity,
crouched that Shadow from whose eyes of battered stone proceeds the nameless thing that
contracts the heart, then opens it again to
terror; and everywhere, from towering mono-
liths as from secret tombs, rose that strange,
long whisper which, defying time and distance,
laughs at death. The spell of Egypt, which is
the spell of immortality, touched their hearts.

Already, as the group of picnickers rode
homewards now, the first stars twinkled overhead, and the peerless Egyptian night was on
the way. There was hurry in the passing of the
dusk. And the cold sensibly increased.

"So you did no painting after all," said
Rivers to the girl who rode a little in front of
him, "for I never saw you touch your sketch-
book once."

They were some distance now behind the
others; the line straggled; and when no answer
came he quickened his pace, drew up alongside
and saw that her eyes, in the reflection of the
sunset, shone with moisture. But she turned
her head a little, smiling into his face, so that
the human and the non-human beauty came over
him with an onset that was almost shock.

Neither one nor other, he knew, were long for him, and the realisation fell upon him with a pang of actual physical pain. The acuteness, the hopelessness of the realisation, for a moment, were more than he could bear, stern of temper though he was, and he tried to pass in front of her, urging his donkey with resounding strokes. Her own animal, however, following the lead, at once came up with him.

"You felt it, perhaps, as I did," he said some moments later, his voice quite steady again. "The stupendous, everlasting thing—the —*life* behind it all." He hesitated a little in his speech, unable to find the substantive that could compass even a fragment of his thought. She paused, too, similarly inarticulate before the surge of incomprehensible feelings.

"It's—awful," she said, half laughing, yet the tone hushed and a little quaver in it somewhere. And her voice to him was like the first sound he had ever heard in the world, for the first sound a full-grown man heard in the world would be beyond all telling—magical. "I shall not try again," she continued, leaving out the laughter this time; "my sketch-book is a farce. For, to tell the truth"—and the next three words she said below her breath—"I dare not."

He turned and looked at her for a second. It seemed to him that the following wave had caught them up, and was about to break above her too. But the big-brimmed hat and the streaming veil shrouded her features. He saw, instead, the Universe. He felt as though he and she had always, always been together, and always, always would be. Separation was inconceivable.

"It came so close," she whispered. "It—shook me!"

They were cut off from their companions, whose voices sounded far ahead. Her words might have been spoken by the darkness, or by someone who peered at them from within that following wave. Yet the fanciful phrase was better than any he could find. From the immeasurable space of time and distance men's hearts vainly seek to plumb, it drew into closer perspective a certain meaning that words may hardly compass, a formidable truth that belongs to that deep place where hope and doubt fight their incessant battle. The awe she spoke of was the awe of immortality, of belonging to something that is endless and beginningless.

And he understood that the tears and laughter were one—caused by that spell which takes a little human life and shakes it, as an animal shakes its prey that later shall feed its blood and increase its power of growth. His other thoughts—really but a single thought—he had not the right to utter. Pain this time easily routed hope as the wave came nearer.

For it was the wave of death that would shortly break, he knew, over him, but not over her. Him it would sweep with its huge withdrawal into the desert whence it came : her it would leave high upon the shores of life—alone. And yet the separation would somehow not be real. They were together in eternity even now. They were endless as this desert, beginningless as this sky . . . immortal. The realisation overwhelmed. . . .

The lights of Helouan seemed to come no nearer as they rode on in silence for the rest of the way. Against the dark background of the Mokattam Hills these fairy lights twinkled brightly, hanging in mid-air, but after an hour they were no closer than before. It was like riding towards the stars. It would take centuries to reach them. There were centuries in which to do so. Hurry has no place in the desert; it is born in streets. The desert stands still; to go fast in it is to go backwards.

Now, in particular, its enormous, uncanny leisure was everywhere—in keeping with that mighty scale the sunset had made visible. His thoughts, like the steps of the weary animal that bore him, had no progress in them. The serpent of eternity, holding its tail in its own mouth, rose from the sand, enclosing himself, the stars—and her. Behind him, in the hollows of that shadowy wave, the procession of dynasties and conquests, the great series of gorgeous civilisations the mind calls Past, stood still, crowded with shining eyes and beckoning faces, still waiting to arrive. There is no death in Egypt. His own death stood so close that he could touch it by stretching out his hand, yet it seemed as much behind him as in front. What man called a beginning was a trick. There was no such thing. He was with this girl—*now*, when Death waited so close for him—yet he had never really begun. Their lives ran always parallel. The hand he stretched to clasp approaching death caught instead in this girl's shadowy hair, drawing her in with him to the centre where he breathed the eternity of the desert. Yet expression of any sort was as futile as it was unnecessary. To paint, to speak, to sing, even the slightest gesture of the soul, became a crude and foolish thing. Silence was here the truth. And they rode in silence towards the fairy lights.

Then suddenly the rocky ground rose up close before them; boulders stood out vividly with black shadows and shining heads; a flat-roofed house slid by; three palm trees rattled in the evening wind; beyond, a mosque and minaret sailed upwards, like the spars and rigging of some phantom craft; and the colonnades of the great modern hotel, standing upon its dome of limestone ridge, loomed over them. Helouan was about them before they knew it. The desert lay behind with its huge, arrested billow. Slowly, owing to its prodigious volume, yet with a speed that merged it instantly with the far horizon behind the night, this wave now withdrew a little. There was no hurry. It came, for the moment, no farther. Rivers knew. For he was in it to the throat. Only his head was above the surface. He still could breathe—and speak—and see. Deepening with every hour into an incalculable splendour, it waited.

2

In the street the foremost riders drew rein, and, two and two abreast, the long line clattered past the shops and cafés, the railway station and hotels, stared at by the natives from the busy pavements. The donkeys stumbled, blinded by the electric light. Girls in white dresses flitted here and there, arabîyehs rattled past with people hurrying home to dress for dinner, and the evening train, just in from Cairo, disgorged its stream of passengers. There were dances in several of the hotels that night. Voices rose on all sides. Questions and answers, engagements and appointments were made, little plans and plots and intrigues for seizing happiness on the wing—before the wave rolled in and caught the lot. They chattered gaily :

" You *are* going, aren't you? You promised——"

" Of course I am."

" Then I'll drive you over. May I call for you? "

" All right. Come at ten."

" We shan't have finished our bridge by then. Say ten-thirty."

And eyes exchanged their meaning signals. The group dismounted and dispersed. Arabs standing under the lebbekh trees, or squatting on the pavements before their dim-lit booths, watched them with faces of gleaming bronze. Rivers gave his bridle to a donkey-boy, and moved across stiffly after the long ride to help the girl dismount. " You feel tired? " he asked gently. " It's been a long day." For her face was white as chalk, though the eyes shone brilliantly.

" Tired, perhaps," she answered, " but exhilarated too. I should like to be there now. I should like to go back this minute—if someone would take me." And, though she said it lightly, there was a meaning in her voice he apparently chose to disregard. It was as if she knew his secret. " Will you take me—some day soon? "

The direct question, spoken by those deter-

K

mined little lips, was impossible to ignore. He looked close into her face as he helped her from the saddle with a spring that brought her a moment half into his arms. "Some day—soon, I will," he said with emphasis; "when you are —ready." The pallor in her face, and a certain expression in it he had not known before, startled him. "I think you have been over-doing it," he added, with a tone in which authority and love were oddly mingled, neither of them disguised.

"Like yourself," she smiled, shaking her skirts out and looking down at her dusty shoes. "I've only a few days more—before I sail. We're both in such a hurry, but you are the worst of the two.

"Because my time is even shorter," ran his horrified thought—for he said no word.

She raised her eyes suddenly to his, with an expression that for an instant almost convinced him she had guessed—and the soul in him stood rigidly at attention, urging back the rising fires. The hair dropped loosely round the sun-burned neck. Her face was level with his shoulder. Even the glare of the street lights could not make her undesirable. But behind the gaze of the deep brown eyes another thing looked forth imperatively into his own. And he recog-nised it with a rush of terror, yet of singular exultation.

" It followed us all the way," she whispered. "It came after us from the desert—where it *lives*."

" At the houses," he said equally low, " it stopped." He gladly adopted her syncopated speech, for it helped him in his struggle to subdue those rising fires.

For a second she hesitated. " You mean, if we had not left so soon—when it turned cold. If we had not hurried—if we had remained a little longer——"

He caught at her hand, unable to control himself, but dropped it again the same second, while she made as though she had not noticed, forgiving him with her eyes. " Or a great deal longer," she added slowly—" for ever? "

And then he was certain that she *had* guessed—not that he loved her above all else in the world, for that was so obvious that a child might know it, but that his silence was due to his other, lesser secret : that the great Executioner stood waiting to drop the hood about his eyes. He was already pinioned. Something in her gaze and in her manner persuaded him suddenly that she understood.

His exhilaration increased extraordinarily. " I mean," he said very quietly, " that the spell weakens here among the houses and among the —so-called living." There was masterfulness, triumph, in his voice. Very wonderfully he saw her smile change; she drew slightly closer to his side, as though unable to resist. "Mingled with lesser things we should not understand completely," he added softly.

"And that might be a mistake, you mean?" she asked quickly, her face grave again.

It was his turn to hesitate a moment. The breeze stirred the hair about her neck, bringing its faint perfume—perfume of young life—to his nostrils. He drew his breath in deeply, smothering back the torrent of rising words he knew were unpermissible. "Misunderstanding," he said briefly. "If the eye be single ——" He broke off, shaken by a paroxysm of coughing. "You know my meaning," he continued, as soon as the attack had passed; "you feel the difference *here*," pointing round him to the hotels, the shops, the busy stream of people; "the hurry, the excitement, the feverish, blinding child's play which pretends to be alive, but does not know it——" And again the coughing stopped him. This time she took his hand in her own, pressed it very slightly, then released it. He felt it as the touch of that desert wave upon his soul. "The reception must be in complete and utter resignation. Tainted by lesser things, the disharmony might be——" he began stammeringly.

Again there came interruption, as the rest of the party called impatiently to know if they

were coming up to the hotel. He had not time
to find the completing adjective. Perhaps he
could not find it ever. Perhaps it does not exist
in any modern language. Eternity is not realised to-day; men have no time to know they are
alive for ever; they are too busy. . . .

They all moved in a chattering, merry
group towards the big hotel. Rivers and the
girl were separated.

3

THERE was a dance that evening, but neither
of these took part in it. In the great dining-
room their tables were far apart. He could not
even see her across the sea of intervening heads
and shoulders. The long meal over, he went to
his room, feeling it imperative to be alone. He
did not read, he did not write; but, leaving the
light unlit, he wrapped himself up and leaned
out upon the broad window-sill into the great
Egyptian night. His deep-sunken thoughts,
like to the crowding stars, stood still, yet for
ever took new shapes. He tried to see behind
them, as, when a boy, he had tried to see behind
the constellations—out into space—where there
is nothing.

Below him the lights of Helouan twinkled
like the Pleiades reflected in a pool of water; a
hum of queer soft noises rose to his ears; but

just beyond the houses the desert stood at attention, the vastest thing he had ever known, very stern, yet very comforting, with its peace beyond all comprehension, its delicate, wild terror, and its awful message of immortality. And the attitude of his mind, though he did not know it, was one of prayer. . . . From time to time he went to lie on the bed with paroxysms of coughing. He had overtaxed his strength—his swiftly fading strength. The wave had risen to his lips.

Nearer forty than thirty-five, Paul Rivers had come out to Egypt, plainly understanding that with the greatest care he might last a few weeks longer than if he stayed in England. A few more times to see the sunset and the sunrise, to watch the stars, feel the soft airs of earth upon his cheeks; a few more days of intercourse with his kind, asking and answering questions, wearing the old, familiar clothes he loved, reading his favourite pages, and then—out into the big spaces—where there is nothing.

Yet no one, from his stalwart, energetic figure, would have guessed—no one but the expert mind, not to be deceived, to whom in the first attack of overwhelming despair and desolation he went for final advice. He left that house, as many had left it before, knowing that soon he would need no earthly protection of roof and walls, and that his soul, if it existed, would

be shelterless in the space behind all manifested
life. He had looked forward to fame and position in this world; had, indeed, already achieved
the first step towards his end; and now, with
the vanity of all earthly aims so mercilessly clear
before him, he had turned, in somewhat of a
nervous, concentrated hurry, to make terms
with the Infinite while still the brain was there.
And had, of course, found nothing. For it
takes a lifetime crowded with experiment and
effort to learn even the alphabet of genuine
faith; and what could come of a few weeks'
wild questioning but confusion and bewilder-
ment of mind? It was inevitable. He came out
to Egypt wondering, thinking, questioning, but
chiefly wondering. He had grown, that is, more
childlike, abandoning the futile tool of Reason,
which hitherto had seemed to him the perfect
instrument. Its foolishness stood naked before
him in the pitiless light of the specialist's decision; for "Who can by searching find out
God?"

To be exceedingly careful of over-exertion
was the final warning he brought with him, and,
within a few hours of his arrival, three weeks
ago, he had met this girl and utterly disregarded
it. He took it somewhat thus: "Instead of
lingering I'll enjoy myself and go out—a little
sooner. I'll *live*. The time is very short." His
was not a nature, anyhow, that could heed a

warning. He could not kneel. Upright and unflinching, he went to meet things as they came, reckless, unwise, but certainly not afraid. And this characteristic operated now. He ran to meet Death full tilt in the uncharted spaces that lay behind the stars. With love for a companion, he raced, his speed increasing from day to day, she, as he thought, knowing merely that he sought her, but had not guessed his darker secret that was now his *lesser* secret.

And in the desert, this afternoon of the picnic, the great thing he sped to meet had shown itself with its familiar touch of appalling cold and shadow : familiar, because all minds know of and accept it ; appalling, because, until realised close and with the mental power at the full, it remains but a name the heart refuses to believe in. And he had discovered that its name was—Life.

Rivers had seen the wave that sweeps incessant, tireless, but as a rule invisible, round the great curve of the bulging earth, brushing the nations into the deeps behind. It had followed him home to the streets and houses of Helouan. He saw it now, as he leaned from his window, dim and immense, too huge to break. Its beauty was nameless, undecipherable. His coughing echoed back from the wall of its great sides. . . . And the music floated up at the same time from the ball-room in the opposite wing. The two sounds mingled. Life, which is love, and Death, which is their unchanging partner, held hands beneath the stars.

He leaned out farther to drink in the cool, sweet air. Soon, on this air, his body would be dust, driven, perhaps, against her very cheek, trodden on possibly by her little foot—until, in turn, she joined him too, blown by the same wind loose about the desert. True. Yet at the same time they would always be together, always somewhere side by side, continuing in the vast universe, alive. This new, absolute conviction was in him now. He remembered the curious, sweet perfume in the desert, as of flowers, where yet no flowers are. It was the perfume of life. But in the desert there is no life. Living things that grow and move and utter, are but a protest against death. In the desert they are unnecessary, because death there *is* not. Its overwhelming vitality needs no insolent, visible proof, no protest, no challenge, no little signs of life. The message of the desert is immortality. . . .

He went finally to bed, just before midnight. Hovering magnificently just outside his window, Death watched him while he slept. The wave crept to the level of his eyes. He called her name. . . .

And downstairs, meanwhile, the girl, knowing nothing, wondered where he was, wondered unhappily and restlessly; more—though this she did not understand—wondered motheringly. Until to-day, on the ride home, and from their singular conversation together, she had guessed nothing of his reason for being at Helouan, where so many come in order to find life. She only knew her own. And she was but twenty-five. . . .

Then, in the desert, when that touch of unearthly chill had stolen out of the sand towards sunset, she had realised clearly, astonished she had not seen it long ago, that this man loved her, yet that something prevented his obeying the great impulse. In the life of Paul Rivers, whose presence had profoundly stirred her heart the first time she saw him, there was some obstacle that held him back, a barrier his honour must respect. He could never tell her of his love. It could lead to nothing. Knowing that he was not married, her intuition failed her utterly at first. Then, in their silence on the homeward ride, the truth had somehow pressed up and touched her with its hand of ice. In that disjointed conversation at the end, which reads as it sounded, as though no coherent meaning lay behind the words, and as though both sought to conceal by speech what yet both burned to utter, she had divined his darker secret, and knew that it was the same as her own. She understood then it was Death that had tracked them from the desert, following with its gigantic shadow from the sandy wastes. The cold, the darkness, the silence which cannot answer, the stupendous mystery which is the spell of its inscrutable Presence, had risen about them in the dusk, and kept them company at a little distance, until the lights of Helouan had bade it halt. Life which may not, cannot end, had frightened her.

His time, perhaps, was even shorter than her own. None knew his secret, since he was alone in Egypt and was caring for himself. Similarly, since she bravely kept her terror to herself, her companions had no inkling of her own, aware merely that the disease was in her system and that her orders were to be extremely cautious. This couple, therefore, shared secretly together the two clearest glimpses of eternity life has to offer to the soul. Side by side they looked into the splendid eyes of Love and Death. Life, moreover, with its instinct for simple and terrific drama, had produced this majestic climax, breaking with pathos, at the very moment when it could not be developed—this side of the stars. They stood together upon the stage, a stage emptied of other human players; the audience had gone home and the lights were being lowered; no music sounded; the critics were

a-bed. In this great game of Consequences it
was known where he met her, what he said and
what she answered, possibly what they did and
even what the world thought. But "what the
consequence was" would remain unknown, un-
told. That would happen in the big spaces of
which the desert in its silence, its motionless
serenity, its shelterless, intolerable vastness, is
the perfect symbol. And the desert gives no
answer. It sounds no challenge, for it is complete. Life in the desert makes no sign. It *is*.

4

In the hotel that night there arrived by
chance a famous International dancer, whose
dahabîyeh lay anchored at San Giovanni, in the
Nile below Helouan; and this woman, with her
party, had come to dine and take part in the
festivities. The news spread. After twelve the
lights were lowered, and while the moonlight
flooded the terraces, streaming past pillar and
colonnade, she rendered in the shadowed halls
the music of the Masters, interpreting with an
instinctive genius messages which are eternal
and divine.

Among the crowd of enthralled and delighted guests, the girl sat on the steps and
watched her. The rhythmical interpretation
held a power that seemed, in a sense, inspired;

there lay in it a certain unconscious something
that was pure, unearthly; something that the
stars, wheeling in stately movements over the
sea and desert, know; something the great
winds bring to mountains where they play together; something the forests capture and fix
magically into their gathering of big and little
branches. It was both passionate and spiritual,
wild and tender, intensely human and seduc-
tively non-human. For it was original, taught
of Nature, a revelation of naked, unhampered
life. It comforted, as the desert comforts. It
brought the desert awe into the stuffy corridors
of the hotel, with the moonlight and the whispering of stars, yet behind it ever the silence
of those grey, mysterious, interminable spaces
which utter to themselves the wordless song of
life. For it was the same dim thing, she felt,
that had followed her from the desert several
hours before, halting just outside the streets
and houses as though blocked from further
advance; the thing that had stopped her foolish
painting, skilled though she was, because it
hides behind colour and not in it; the thing that
veiled the meaning in the cryptic sentences she
and he had stammered out together; the thing,
in a word, as near as she could approach it by
any means of interior expression, that the realisation of death for the first time makes comprehensible—Immortality. It was unutterable,

but it *was*. He and she were indissolubly together. Death was no separation. There was no death . . . It was terrible. It was—she had already used the word—awful, full of awe.

"In the desert," thought whispered, as she watched spellbound, "it is impossible even to conceive of death. The idea is meaningless. It simply is not."

The music and the movement filled the air with life which, being there, must continue always, and continuing always can have never had a beginning. Death, therefore, was the great revealer of life. Without it none could realise that they are alive. Others had discovered this before her, but she did not know it. In the desert no one can realise death: it is hope and life that are the only certainty. The entire conception of the Egyptian system was based on this—the conviction, sure and glorious, of life's endless continuation. Their tombs and temples, their pyramids and sphinxes surviving after thousands of years, defy the passage of time and laugh at death; the very bodies of their priests and kings, of their animals even, their fish, their insects, stand to-day as symbols of their stalwart knowledge.

And this girl, as she listened to the music and watched the inspired dancing, remembered it. The message poured into her from many sides, though the desert brought it clearest.

With death peering into her face a few short
weeks ahead, she thought instead of—life. The
desert, as it were, became for her a little fragment of eternity, focused into an intelligible
point for her mind to rest upon with comfort
and comprehension. Her steady, thoughtful
nature stirred towards an objective far beyond
the small enclosure of one narrow lifetime. The
scale of the desert stretched her to the grandeur
of its own imperial meaning, its divine repose,
its unassailable and everlasting majesty. She
looked beyond the wall.

Eternity! That which is endless; without
pause, without beginning, without divisions or
boundaries. The fluttering of her brave yet
frightened spirit ceased, aware with awe of its
own everlastingness. The swiftest motion produces the effect of immobility; excessive light
is darkness; size, run loose into enormity, is the
same as the minutely tiny. Similarly, in the
desert, life, too overwhelming and terrific to
know limit or confinement, lies undetailed and
stupendous, still as deity, a revelation of
nothingness because it is all. Turned golden
beneath its spell that the music and the rhythm
made even more comprehensible, the soul in
her, already lying beneath the shadow of the
great wave, sank into rest and peace, too certain
of itself to fear. And panic fled away. "I am
immortal . . . because I *am*. And what I love

is not apart from me. It is myself. We are together endlessly because we *are*."

Yet in reality, though the big desert brought this, it was Love, which, being of similar parentage, interpreted its vast meaning to her little heart—that sudden love which, without a word of preface or explanation, had come to her a short three weeks before. . . . She went up to her room soon after midnight, abruptly, unexpectedly stricken. Someone, it seemed, had called her name. She passed his door.

The lights had been turned up. The clamour of praise was loud round the figure of the weary dancer as she left in a carriage for her dahabîyeh on the Nile. A low wind whistled round the walls of the great hotel, blowing chill and bitter between the pillars of the colonnades. The girl heard the voices float up to her through the night, and once more, behind the confused sound of the many, she heard her own name called, but more faintly than before, and from very far away. It came through the spaces beyond her open window; it died away again; then—but for the sighing of that bitter wind—silence, the deep silence of the desert.

And these two, Paul Rivers and the girl, between them merely a floor of that stone that built the Pyramids, lay a few moments before the Wave of Sleep engulfed them. And, while they slept, two shadowy forms hovered above the roof of the quiet hotel, melting presently into one, as dreams stole down from the desert and the stars. Immortality whispered to them. On either side rose Life and Death, towering in splendour. Love, joining their spreading wings, fused the gigantic outlines into one. The figures grew smaller, comprehensible. They entered the little windows. Above the beds they paused a moment, watching, waiting, and then, like a wave that is just about to break, they stooped. . . .

And in the brilliant Egyptian sunlight of the morning, as she went downstairs, she passed his door again. She had awakened, but he slept on. He had preceded her. It was next day she learned his room was vacant. . . . Within the month she joined him, and within the year the cool north wind that sweetens Lower Egypt from the sea blew the dust across the desert as before. It is the dust of kings, of queens, of priests, princesses, lovers. It is the dust no earthly power can annihilate. It, too, lasts for ever. There was a little more of it . . . the desert's message slightly added to : Immortality.

L

VII

TRANSITION

JOHN MUDBURY was on his way home from the shops, his arms full of Christmas Presents. It was after six o'clock and the streets were very crowded. He was an ordinary man, lived in an ordinary suburban flat, with an ordinary wife and ordinary children. *He* did not think them ordinary, but everybody else did. He had ordinary presents for each one, a cheap blotter for his wife, a cheap air-gun for the boy, and so forth. He was over fifty, bald, in an office, decent in mind and habits, of uncertain opinions, uncertain politics, and uncertain religion. Yet he considered himself a decided, positive gentleman, quite unaware that the morning newspaper determined his opinions for the day. He just lived—from day to day. Physically, he was fit enough, except for a weak heart (which never troubled him); and his summer holiday was bad golf, while the children bathed and his wife read Garvice on the sands. Like the majority of men, he dreamed idly of the past, muddled away the present, and guessed vaguely—after imaginative reading on occasions—at the future.

"I'd like to survive all right," he said, "provided it's better than this," surveying his wife and children, and thinking of his daily toil. "Otherwise——!" and he shrugged his shoulders as a brave man should.

He went to church regularly. But nothing in church convinced him that he did survive, just as nothing in church enticed him into hoping that he would. On the other hand, nothing in life persuaded him that he didn't, wouldn't, couldn't. "I'm an Evolutionist," he loved to say to thoughtful cronies (over a glass), having never heard that Darwinism had been questioned.

And so he came home gaily, happily, with his bunch of Christmas Presents "for the wife and little ones," stroking himself upon their keen enjoyment and excitement. The night before he had taken "the wife" to see *Magic* at a select London theatre where the Intellectuals went—and had been extraordinarily stirred. He had gone questioningly, yet expecting something out of the common. "It's *not* musical," he warned her, "nor farce, nor comedy, so to speak"; and in answer to her question as to what the critics had said, he had wriggled, sighed, and put his gaudy neck-tie straight four times in quick succession. For no

Man in the Street, with any claim to self-respect, could be expected to understand what the critics had said, even if he understood the Play. And John had answered truthfully: "Oh, they just said things. But the theatre's always full—and that's the only test."

And just now, as he crossed the crowded Circus to catch his 'bus, it chanced that his mind (having glimpsed an advertisement) was full of this particular Play, or, rather, of the effect it had produced upon him at the time. For it had thrilled him—inexplicably: with its marvellous speculative hint, its big audacity, its alert and spiritual beauty. . . . . Thought plunged to find something—plunged after this bizarre suggestion of a bigger universe, after this quasi-jocular suggestion that man is not the only—then dashed full-tilt against a sentence that memory thrust beneath his nose: "Science does *not* exhaust the Universe"—and at the same time dashed full-tilt against destruction of another kind as well. . . .!

How it happened he never exactly knew. He saw a Monster glaring at him with eyes of blazing fire. It was horrible! It rushed upon him. He dodged. . . . Another Monster met him round the corner. Both came at him simultaneously. He dodged again—a leap that might have cleared a hurdle easily, but was too late. Between the pair of them—his heart

literally in his gullet—he was mercilessly caught.
Bones crunched. . . . There was a soft sensation, icy cold and hot as fire. Horns and
voices roared. Battering-rams he saw, and a
carapace of iron. . . . Then dazzling light. . . .
" Always *face* the traffic ! " he remembered
with a frantic yell—and, by some extraordinary
luck, escaped miraculously on to the opposite
pavement.

There was no doubt about it. By the skin
of his teeth he had dodged a rather ugly death.
First . . . he felt for his Presents—all were
safe. And then, instead of congratulating himself and taking breath, he hurried homewards
—on foot, which proved that his mind had lost
control a bit !—thinking only how disappointed
the wife and children would have been if—
well, if anything had happened. Another thing
he realised, oddly enough, was that he no longer
really loved his wife, but had only great affection for her. What made him think of that,
Heaven only knows, but he *did* think of it. He
was an honest man without pretence. This
came as a discovery somehow. He turned a
moment, and saw the crowd gathered about
the entangled taxi-cabs, policemen's helmets
gleaming in the lights of the shop windows
. . . then hurried on again, his thoughts full
of the joy his Presents would give . . . of the
scampering children . . . and of his wife—

bless her silly heart!—eyeing the mysterious parcels. . . .

And, though he never could explain how, he presently stood at the door of the jail-like building that contained his flat, having walked the whole three miles. His thoughts had been so busy and absorbed that he had hardly noticed the length of weary trudge. "Besides," he reflected, thinking of the narrow escape, " I've had a nasty shock. It was a d——d near thing, now I come to think of it. . . ." He still felt a bit shaky and bewildered. Yet, at the same time, he felt extraordinarily jolly and light-hearted.

He counted his Christmas parcels . . . hugged himself in anticipatory joy . . . and let himself in swiftly with his latchkey. " I'm late," he realised, " but when she sees the brown-paper parcels, she'll forget to say a word. God bless the old faithful soul." And he softly used the key a second time and entered his flat on tiptoe. . . . In his mind was the master impulse of that afternoon—the pleasure these Christmas Presents would give his wife and children. . . .

He heard a noise. He hung up hat and coat in the poky vestibule (they never called it " hall ") and moved softly towards the parlour door, holding the packages behind him. Only of them he thought, not of himself—of his

family, that is, not of the packages. Pushing
the door cunningly ajar, he peeped in slyly. To
his amazement the room was full of people. He
withdrew quickly, wondering what it meant.
A party? And without his knowing about
it! Extraordinary! . . . Keen disappointment came over him. But, as he stepped
back, the vestibule, he saw, was full of
people too.

He was uncommonly surprised, yet somehow not surprised at all. People were congratulating him. There was a perfect mob of
them. Moreover, he knew them all—vaguely
remembered them, at least. And they all knew
him.

"Isn't it a game?" laughed someone, patting him on the back. "*They* haven't the least
idea . . . ! "

And the speaker—it was old John Palmer,
the bookkeeper at the office—emphasised the
"they."

"Not the least idea," he answered with a
smile, saying something he didn't understand,
yet knew was right.

His face, apparently, showed the utter be-
wilderment he felt. The shock of the collision
had been greater than he realised evidently. His
mind was wandering. . . . Possibly! Only the
odd thing was—he had never felt so clear-headed
in his life. Ten thousand things grew simple

suddenly. But, how thickly these people pressed about him, and how—familiarly !

"My parcels," he said, joyously pushing his way across the throng. "These are Christmas Presents I've bought for them." He nodded toward the room. "I've saved for weeks—stopped cigars and billiards and—and several other good things—to buy them."

"Good man !" said Palmer with a happy laugh. "It's the heart that counts."

Mudbury looked at him. Palmer had said an amazing truth, only—people would hardly understand and believe him. . . . Would they?

"Eh?" he asked, feeling stuffed and stupid, muddled somewhere between two meanings, one of which was gorgeous and the other stupid beyond belief.

"If you *please*, Mr. Mudbury, step inside. They are expecting you," said a kindly, pompous voice. And, turning sharply, he met the gentle, foolish eyes of Sir James Epiphany, a director of the Bank where he worked.

The effect of the voice was instantaneous from long habit.

"They are," he smiled from his heart, and advanced as from the custom of many years. Oh, how happy and gay he felt ! His affection for his wife was real. Romance, indeed, had gone, but he needed her—and she needed him. And the children—Milly, Bill, and Jean—he deeply loved them. Life was worth living indeed!

In the room was a crowd, but—an astounding silence. John Mudbury looked round him. He advanced towards his wife, who sat in the corner arm-chair with Milly on her knee. A lot of people talked and moved about. Momentarily the crowd increased. He stood in front of them —in front of Milly and his wife. And he spoke —holding out his packages. "It's Christmas Eve," he whispered shyly, " and I've—brought you something — something for everybody. Look!" He held the packages before their eyes.

" Of course, of course," said a voice behind him, " but you may hold them out like that for a century. They'll *never* see them!"

" Of course they won't. But I love to do the old, sweet thing," replied John Mudbury— then wondered with a gasp of stark amazement why he said it.

" *I* think——" whispered Milly, staring round her.

" Well, what do you think?" her mother asked sharply. " You're always thinking something queer."

" I think," the girl continued dreamily, " that Daddy's already here." She paused, then added with a child's impossible conviction, " I'm sure he is. I *feel* him."

There was an extraordinary laugh. Sir James Epiphany laughed. The others—the whole crowd of them—also turned their heads and smiled. But the mother, thrusting the child away from her, rose up suddenly with a violent start. Her face had turned to chalk. She stretched her arms out—into the air before her. She gasped and shivered. There was anguish in her eyes.

"Look!" repeated John, "these are the Presents that I brought."

But his voice apparently was soundless. And, with a spasm of icy pain, he remembered that Palmer and Sir James—some years ago— had died.

"It's magic," he cried, "but—I love you, Jinny—I love you—and—and I have always been true to you—as true as steel. We need each other—oh, can't you see—we go on together—you and I—for ever and ever——"

"*Think*," interrupted an exquisitely tender voice, "don't shout! They can't *hear* you— now." And, turning, John Mudbury met the eyes of Everard Minturn, their President of the year before. Minturn had gone down with the *Titanic*.

He dropped his parcels then. His heart gave an enormous leap of joy.

He saw her face—the face of his wife—look through him.

But the child gazed straight into his eyes. She *saw* him.

The next thing he knew was that he heard something tinkling . . . far, far away. It sounded miles below him—inside him—he was sounding himself—all utterly bewildering—like a bell. It *was* a bell.

Milly stooped down and picked the parcels up. Her face shone with happiness and laughter. . . .

But a man came in soon after, a man with a ridiculous, solemn face, a pencil, and a note-book. He wore a dark blue helmet. Behind him came a string of other men. They carried something . . . something . . . he could not see exactly what it was. But, when he pressed forward through the laughing throng to gaze upon it, he dimly made out two eyes, a nose, a chin, a deep red smear, and a pair of folded hands upon an overcoat. A woman's form fell down upon them then, and he heard soft sounds of children weeping strangely . . . and other sounds . . . as of familiar voices laughing . . . laughing gaily.

"They'll join us presently. It goes like a flash. . . ."

And, turning with great happiness in his heart, he saw that Sir James had said it, holding Palmer by the arm as with some natural yet unexpected love of sympathetic friendship.

"Come on," said Palmer, smiling like a
man who accepts a gift in universal fellowship,
"let's help 'em.   They'll never understand.
. . . Still, we can always try."

The entire throng moved up with laughter
and amusement.   It was a moment of hearty,
genuine life at last.   Delight and Joy and Peace
were everywhere.

Then John Mudbury realised the truth—
that he was dead.

VIII

THE OTHER WING

1

IT used to puzzle him that, after dark, someone *would* look in round the edge of the bedroom door, and withdraw again too rapidly for him to see the face. When the nurse had gone away with the candle this happened: "Good night, Master Tim," she said usually, shading the light with one hand to protect his eyes; "dream of me and I'll dream of you." She went out slowly. The sharp-edged shadow of the door ran across the ceiling like a train. There came a whispered colloquy in the corridor outside, about himself, of course, and—he was alone. He heard her steps going deeper and deeper into the bosom of the old country house; they were audible for a moment on the stone flooring of the hall; and sometimes the dull thump of the baize door into the servants' quarters just reached him, too—then silence. But it was only when the last sound as well as the last sign of her had vanished that the face emerged from its hiding-place and flashed in upon him round the corner. As a rule, too, it came just as he was saying, "Now I'll go to sleep. I won't think any longer. Good night, Master Tim, and happy dreams." He loved to say this to himself; it brought a sense of companionship, as though there were two persons speaking.

The room was on the top of the old house, a big, high-ceilinged room, and his bed against the wall had an iron railing round it; he felt very safe and protected in it. The curtains at the other end of the room were drawn. He lay watching the firelight dancing on the heavy folds, and their pattern, showing a spaniel chasing a long-tailed bird towards a bushy tree, interested and amused him. It was repeated over and over again. He counted the number of dogs, and the number of birds, and the number of trees, but could never make them agree. There was a plan somewhere in that pattern; if only he could discover it, the dogs and birds and trees would "come out right." Hundreds and hundreds of times he had played this game, for the plan in the pattern made it possible to take sides, and the bird and dog were against him. They always won, however; Tim usually fell asleep just when the advantage was on his own side. The curtains hung steadily enough most of the time, but it seemed to him once or twice that they stirred—hiding a dog or bird on purpose to prevent his winning. For instance, he

had eleven birds and eleven trees, and, fixing
them in his mind by saying, "that's eleven
birds and eleven trees, but only ten dogs," his
eyes darted back to find the eleventh dog, when
—the curtain moved and threw all his calculations into confusion again. The eleventh dog
was hidden. He did not quite like the movement; it gave him questionable feelings, rather,
for the curtain did not move of itself. Yet,
usually, he was too intent upon counting the
dogs to feel positive alarm.

Opposite to him was the fireplace, full of
red and yellow coals; and, lying with his head
sideways on the pillow, he could see directly
in between the bars. When the coals settled
with a soft and powdery crash, he turned his
eyes from the curtains to the grate, trying to
discover exactly which bits had fallen. So long
as the glow was there the sound seemed pleasant
enough, but sometimes he awoke later in the
night, the room huge with darkness, the fire
almost out—and the sound was not so pleasant
then. It startled him. The coals did not fall
of themselves. It seemed that someone poked
them cautiously. The shadows were very thick
before the bars. As with the curtains, moreover, the morning aspect of the extinguished
fire, the ice-cold cinders that made a clinking
sound like tin, caused no emotion whatever in
his soul.

And it was usually while he lay waiting for sleep, tired both of the curtain and the coal games, on the point, indeed, of saying, " I'll go to sleep now," that the puzzling thing took place. He would be staring drowsily at the dying fire, perhaps counting the stockings and flannel garments that hung along the high fender-rail when, suddenly, a person looked in with lightning swiftness through the door and vanished again before he could possibly turn his head to see. The appearance and disappearance were accomplished with amazing rapidity always.

It was a head and shoulders that looked in, and the movement combined the speed, the lightness and the silence of a shadow. Only it was not a shadow. A hand held the edge of the door. The face shot round, saw him, and withdrew like lightning. It was utterly beyond him to imagine anything more quick and clever. It darted. He heard no sound. It went. But —it had seen him, looked him all over, examined him, noted what he was doing with that lightning glance. It wanted to know if he were awake still, or asleep. And though it went off, it still watched him from a distance; it waited somewhere; it knew all about him. *Where* it waited no one could ever guess. It came probably, he felt, from beyond the house, possibly from the roof, but most likely from the **garden** or the sky. Yet, though strange, it was not terrible. It was a kindly and protective figure, he felt. And when it happened he never called for help, because the occurrence simply took his voice away.

"It comes from the Nightmare Passage," he decided; "but it's *not* a nightmare." It puzzled him.

Sometimes, moreover, it came more than once in a single night. He was pretty sure— not *quite* positive—that it occupied his room as soon as he was properly asleep. It took possession, sitting perhaps before the dying fire, standing upright behind the heavy curtains, or even lying down in the empty bed his brother used when he was home from school. Perhaps it played the curtain game, perhaps it poked the coals; it knew, at any rate, where the eleventh dog had lain concealed. It certainly came in and out; certainly, too, it did not wish to be seen. For, more than once, on waking suddenly in the midnight blackness, Tim knew it was standing close beside his bed and bending over him. He felt, rather than heard, its presence. It glided quietly away. It moved with marvellous softness, yet he was positive it moved. He felt the difference, so to speak: it had been near him, now it was gone. It came back, too—just as he was falling into sleep again. Its midnight coming and going, how-

M

ever, stood out sharply different from its first shy, tentative approach. For in the firelight it came alone; whereas in the black and silent hours, it had with it—others.

And it was then he made up his mind that its swift and quiet movements were due to the fact that it had wings. It flew. And the others that came with it in the darkness were "its little ones." He also made up his mind that all were friendly, comforting, protective, and that while positively *not* a Nightmare, it yet came somehow along the Nightmare Passage before it reached him. "You see, it's like this," he explained to the nurse: "The big one comes to visit me alone, but it only brings its little ones when I'm *quite* asleep."

"Then the quicker you get to sleep the better, isn't it, Master Tim?"

He replied: "Rather! I always do. Only I wonder where they come *from!*" He spoke, however, as though he had an inkling.

But the nurse was so dull about it that he gave her up and tried his father. "Of course," replied this busy but affectionate parent, "it's either nobody at all, or else it's Sleep coming to carry you away to the land of dreams." He made the statement kindly but somewhat briskly, for he was worried just then about the extra taxes on his land, and the effort to fix his mind on Tim's fanciful world was beyond him at the moment. He lifted the boy on to his knee, kissed and patted him as though he were a favourite dog, and planted him on the rug again with a flying sweep. "Run and ask your mother," he added; "she knows all that kind of thing. Then come back and tell me all about it—another time."

Tim found his mother in an arm-chair before the fire of another room; she was knitting and reading at the same time—a wonderful thing the boy could never understand. She raised her head as he came in, pushed her glasses on to her forehead, and held her arms out. He told her everything, ending up with what his father said.

"You see, it's *not* Jackman, or Thompson, or anyone like that," he exclaimed. "It's someone real."

"But nice," she assured him, "someone who comes to take care of you and see that you're all safe and cosy."

"Oh, yes, I know that. But——"

"I think your father's right," she added quickly. "It's Sleep, I'm sure, who pops in round the door like that. Sleep *has* got wings, I've always heard."

"Then the other thing—the little ones?" he asked. "Are they just sorts of dozes, you think?"

Mother did not answer for a moment. She

turned down the page of her book, closed it slowly, and put it on the table beside her. More slowly still she put her knitting away, arranging the wool and needles with some deliberation.

" Perhaps," she said, drawing the boy closer to her and looking into his big eyes of wonder, " they're dreams ! "

Tim felt a thrill run through him as she said it. He stepped back a foot or so and clapped his hands softly. " Dreams ! " he whispered with enthusiasm and belief; " of course ! I never thought of that."

His mother, having proved her sagacity, then made a mistake. She noted her success, but instead of leaving it there, she elaborated and explained. As Tim expressed it she " went on about it." Therefore he did not listen. He followed his train of thought alone. And presently, he interrupted her long sentences with a conclusion of his own :

" Then I know where She hides," he announced with a touch of awe. " Where She lives, I mean." And without waiting to be asked, he imparted the information : " It's in the Other Wing."

" Ah ! " said his mother, taken by surprise. " How clever of you, Tim ! "—and thus confirmed it.

Thenceforward this was established in his life—that Sleep and her attendant Dreams hid

during the daytime in that unused portion of
the great Elizabethan mansion called the Other
Wing.   This other wing was unoccupied, its
corridors untrodden, its windows shuttered and
its rooms all closed.   At various places green
baize doors led into it, but no one ever opened
them.   For many years this part had been shut
up; and for the children, properly speaking, it
was out of bounds.   They never mentioned it
as a possible place, at any rate; in hide-and-seek
it was not considered, even; there was a hint of
the inaccessible about the Other Wing.
Shadows, dust, and silence had it to themselves.

But Tim, having ideas of his own about
everything, possessed special information about
the Other Wing.   He believed it *was* inhabited.
Who occupied the immense series of empty
rooms, who trod the spacious corridors, who
passed to and fro behind the shuttered windows,
he had not known exactly.   He had called these
occupants "they," and the most important
among them was "The Ruler."   The Ruler of
the Other Wing was a kind of deity, powerful,
far away, ever present yet never seen.

And about this Ruler he had a wonderful
conception for a little boy; he connected her,
somehow, with deep thoughts of his own, the
deepest of all.   When he made up adventures to
the moon, to the stars, or to the bottom of the
sea, adventures that he lived inside himself, as

it were—to reach them he must invariably pass through the chambers of the Other Wing. Those corridors and halls, the Nightmare Passage among them, lay along the route; they were the first stage of the journey. Once the green baize doors swung to behind him and the long dim passage stretched ahead, he was well on his way into the adventure of the moment; the Nightmare Passage once passed, he was safe from capture; but once the shutters of a window had been flung open, he was free of the gigantic world that lay beyond. For then light poured in and he could see his way.

The conception, for a child, was curious. It established a correspondence between the mysterious chambers of the Other Wing and the occupied, but unguessed chambers of his Inner Being. Through these chambers, through these darkened corridors, along a passage, sometimes dangerous, or at least of questionable repute, he must pass to find all adventures that were *real*. The light—when he pierced far enough to take the shutters down—was discovery. Tim did not actually think, much less say, all this. He was aware of it, however. He felt it. The Other Wing was inside himself as well as through the green baize doors. His inner map of wonder included both of them.

But now, for the first time in his life, he knew who lived there and who the Ruler was.

A shutter had fallen of its own accord; light poured in; he made a guess, and Mother had confirmed it. Sleep and her Little Ones, the host of dreams, were the daylight occupants. They stole out when the darkness fell. All adventures in life began and ended by a dream —discoverable by first passing through the Other Wing.

2

AND, having settled this, his one desire now was to travel over the map upon journeys of exploration and discovery. The map inside himself he knew already, but the map of the Other Wing he had not seen. His imagination knew it, he had a clear mental picture of rooms and halls and passages, but his feet had never trod the silent floors where dust and shadows hid the flock of dreams by day. The mighty chambers where Sleep ruled he longed to stand in, to see the Ruler face to face. He made up his mind to get into the Other Wing.

To accomplish this was difficult; but Tim was a determined youngster, and he meant to try; he meant, also, to succeed. He deliberated. At night he could not possibly manage it; in any case, the Ruler and her host all left it after dark to fly about the world; the Wing would be empty, and the emptiness would frighten him. Therefore he must make a day-

light visit; and it was a daylight visit he decided
on. He deliberated more. There were rules
and risks involved: it meant going out of
bounds, the danger of being seen, the certainty
of being questioned by some idle and inquisitive
grown-up : " Where in the world have you been
all this time? "—and so forth. These things he
thought out carefully, and though he arrived at
no solution, he felt satisfied that it would be all
right. That is, he recognised the risks. To be
thus prepared was half the battle, for nothing
then could take him by surprise.

The notion that he might slip in from the
garden was soon abandoned; the red bricks
showed no openings; there was no door; from
the courtyard, also, entrance was impracticable;
even on tiptoe he could barely reach the broad
window-sills of stone. When playing alone, or
walking with the French governess, he examined
every outside possibility. None offered. The
shutters, supposing he could reach them, were
thick and solid.

Meanwhile, when opportunity offered, he
stood against the outside walls and listened, his
ear pressed against the tight red bricks; the
towers and gables of the Wing rose overhead;
he heard the wind go whispering along the
eaves; he imagined tiptoe movements and a
sound of wings inside. Sleep and her Little
Ones were busily preparing for their journeys

after dark; they hid, but they did not sleep; in
this unused Wing, vaster alone than any other
country house he had ever seen, Sleep taught
and trained her flock of feathered Dreams. It
was very wonderful. They probably supplied
the entire County. But more wonderful still
was the thought that the Ruler herself should
take the trouble to come to his particular room
and personally watch over him all night long.
That was amazing. And it flashed across his
imaginative, inquiring mind: "Perhaps they
take me with them! The moment I'm asleep!
That's why she comes to see me!"

Yet his chief preoccupation was, how Sleep
got out. Through the green baize doors, of
course! By a process of elimination he arrived
at a conclusion: he, too, must enter through a
green baize door and risk detection.

Of late, the lightning visits had ceased. The
silent, darting figure had not peeped in and
vanished as it used to do. He fell asleep too
quickly now, almost before Jackman reached
the hall, and long before the fire began to die.
Also, the dogs and birds upon the curtains
always matched the trees exactly, and he won
the curtain game quite easily; there was never
a dog or bird too many; the curtain never
stirred. It had been thus ever since his talk
with Mother and Father. And so he came to
make a second discovery: His parents did not

really believe in his Figure. She kept away on that account. They doubted her; she hid. Here was still another incentive to go and find her out. He ached for her, she was so kind, she gave herself so much trouble—just for his little self in the big and lonely bedroom. Yet his parents spoke of her as though she were of no account. He longed to see her, face to face, and tell her that *he* believed in her and loved her. For he was positive she would like to hear it. She cared. Though he had fallen asleep of late too quickly for him to see her flash in at the door, he had known nicer dreams than ever in his life before—travelling dreams. And it was she who sent them. More—he was sure she took him out with her.

One evening, in the dusk of a March day, his opportunity came; and only just in time, for his brother, Jack, was expected home from school on the morrow, and with Jack in the other bed, no Figure would ever care to show itself. Also it was Easter, and after Easter, though Tim was not aware of it at the time, he was to say good-bye finally to governesses and become a day-boarder at a preparatory school for Wellington. The opportunity offered itself so naturally, moreover, that Tim took it without hesitation. It never occurred to him to question, much less to refuse it. The thing was obviously meant to be. For he found himself unexpectedly in front of a green baize door; and the green baize door was—swinging! Somebody, therefore, had just passed through it.

It had come about in this wise. Father, away in Scotland, at Inglemuir, the shooting place, was expected back next morning; Mother had driven over to the church upon some Easter business or other; and the governess had been allowed her holiday at home in France. Tim, therefore, had the run of the house, and in the hour between tea and bed-time he made good use of it. Fully able to defy such second-rate obstacles as nurses and butlers, he explored all manner of forbidden places with ardent thoroughness, arriving finally in the sacred precincts of his father's study. This wonderful room was the very heart and centre of the whole big house; he had been birched here long ago; here, too, his father had told him with a grave yet smiling face: "You've got a new companion, Tim, a little sister; you must be very kind to her." Also, it was the place where all the money was kept. What he called "father's jolly smell" was strong in it—papers, tobacco, books, flavoured by hunting crops and gunpowder.

At first he felt awed, standing motionless just inside the door; but presently, recovering equilibrium, he moved cautiously on tiptoe towards the gigantic desk where important papers were piled in untidy patches. These he did not touch; but beside them his quick eye noted the jagged piece of iron shell his father brought home from his Crimean campaign and now used as a letter-weight. It was difficult to lift, however. He climbed into the comfortable chair and swung round and round. It was a swivel-chair, and he sank down among the cushions in it, staring at the strange things on the great desk before him, as if fascinated. Next he turned away and saw the stick-rack in the corner—this, he knew, he was allowed to touch. He had played with these sticks before. There were twenty, perhaps, all told, with curious carved handles, brought from every corner of the world; many of them cut by his father's own hand in queer and distant places. And, among them, Tim fixed his eye upon a cane with an ivory handle, a slender, polished cane that he had always coveted tremendously. It was the kind he meant to use when he became a man. It bent, it quivered, and when he swished it through the air it trembled like a riding-whip, and made a whistling noise. Yet it was very strong in spite of its elastic qualities. A family treasure, it was also an old-fashioned relic; it had been his great-grandfather's walking stick. Something of another century clung visibly about it still. It had dignity and grace and leisure in its very aspect. And it suddenly

occurred to him : " How great-grandpapa must
miss it ! Wouldn't he just love to have it back
again ! "

How it happened exactly, Tim did not know,
but a few minutes later he found himself walking
about the deserted halls and passages of the
house with the air of an elderly gentleman of a
hundred years ago, proud as a courtier, flourish-
ing the stick like an Eighteenth Century dandy
in the Mall. That the cane reached to his
shoulder made no difference; he held it accord-
ingly, swaggering on his way. He was off upon
an adventure. He dived down through the by-
ways of the Other Wing inside himself, as
though the stick transported him to the days of
the old gentleman who had used it in another
century.

It may seem strange to those who dwell in
smaller houses, but in this rambling Elizabethan
mansion there were whole sections that, even to
Tim, were strange and unfamiliar. In his mind
the map of the Other Wing was clearer by far
than the geography of the part he travelled
daily. He came to passages and dim-lit halls,
long corridors of stone beyond the Picture Gallery; narrow, wainscoted connecting-channels
with four steps down and a little later two steps
up; deserted chambers with arches guarding
them—all hung with the soft March twilight
and all bewilderingly unrecognised. With a

sense of adventure born of naughtiness he went
carelessly along, farther and farther into the
heart of this unfamiliar country, swinging the
cane, one thumb stuck into the arm-pit of his
blue serge suit, whistling softly to himself, excited yet keenly on the alert—and suddenly
found himself opposite a door that checked all
further advance. It was a green baize door.
And it was swinging.

He stopped abruptly, facing it. He stared,
he gripped his cane more tightly, he held his
breath. "The Other Wing!" he gasped in a
swallowed whisper.

It was an entrance, but an entrance he had
never seen before. He thought he knew every
door by heart; but this one was new. He stood
motionless for several minutes, watching it; the
door had two halves, but one half only was
swinging, each swing shorter than the one
before; he heard the little puffs of air it made;
it settled finally, the last movements very short
and rapid; it stopped. And the boy's heart,
after similar rapid strokes, stopped also—for a
moment.

"Someone's just gone through," he gulped.
And even as he said it he knew who the someone was. The conviction just dropped into him.
"It's great-grandpapa; he knows I've got his
stick. He wants it!" On the heels of this
flashed instantly another amazing certainty.

" He sleeps in there. He's having dreams. That's what being dead means."

His first impulse, then, took the form of, " I must let Father know; it'll make him burst for joy ! " but his second was for himself—to finish his adventure. And it was this, naturally enough, that gained the day. He could tell his father later. His first duty was plainly to go through the door into the Other Wing. He must give the stick back to its owner. He must *hand* it back.

The test of will and character came now. Tim had imagination, and so knew the meaning of fear; but there was nothing craven in him. He could howl and scream and stamp like any other person of his age when the occasion called for such behaviour, but such occasions were due to temper roused by a thwarted will, and the histrionics were half " pretended " to produce a calculated effect. There was no one to thwart his will at present. He also knew how to be afraid of Nothing, to be afraid without ostensible cause that is—which was merely " nerves." He could have " the shudders " with the best of them.

But, when a real thing faced him, Tim's character emerged to meet it. He would clench his hands, brace his muscles, set his teeth—and wish to heaven he was bigger. But he would not flinch. Being imaginative, he lived the worst

a dozen times before it happened, yet in the final
crash he stood up like a man. He had that
highest pluck—the courage of a sensitive temperament. And at this particular juncture,
somewhat ticklish for a boy of eight or nine, it
did not fail him. He lifted the cane and pushed
the swinging door wide open. Then he walked
through it—into the Other Wing.

8

THE green baize door swung to behind him;
he was even sufficiently master of himself to
turn and close it with a steady hand, because he
did not care to hear the series of muffled thuds
its lessening swings would cause. But he realised clearly his position, knew he was doing a
tremendous thing.

Holding the cane between fingers very
tightly clenched, he advanced bravely along the
corridor that stretched before him. And all fear
left him from that moment, replaced, it seemed,
by a mild and exquisite surprise. His footsteps
made no sound, he walked on air; instead of
darkness, or the twilight he expected, a diffused
and gentle light that seemed like the silver on
the lawn when a half-moon sails a cloudless sky,
lay everywhere. He knew his way, moreover,
knew exactly where he was and whither he was
going. The corridor was as familiar to him as

the floor of his own bedroom; he recognised the
shape and length of it; it agreed exactly with
the map he had constructed long ago. Though
he had never, to the best of his knowledge,
entered it before, he knew with intimacy its
every detail.

And thus the surprise he felt was mild and
far from disconcerting. "I'm here again!"
was the kind of thought he had. It was *how* he
got here that caused the faint surprise, apparently. He no longer swaggered, however, but
walked carefully, and half on tiptoe, holding the
ivory handle of the cane with a kind of affectionate respect. And as he advanced, the light
closed softly up behind him, obliterating the
way by which he had come. But this he did
not know, because he did not look behind him.
He only looked in front, where the corridor
stretched its silvery length towards the great
chamber where he knew the cane must be sur-
rendered. The person who had preceded him
down this ancient corridor, passing through the
green baize door just before he reached it, this
person, his father's grandfather, now stood in
that great chamber, waiting to receive his own.
Tim knew it as surely as he knew he breathed.
At the far end he even made out the larger
patch of silvery light which marked its gaping
doorway.

There was another thing he knew as well—

N

that this corridor he moved along between rooms
with fast-closed doors, was the Nightmare Corridor; often and often he had traversed it; each
room was occupied. "This is the Nightmare
Passage," he whispered to himself, "but I
know the Ruler—it doesn't matter. None of
the Nightmares can get out or do anything."
He heard them, none the less, inside, as he
passed by; he heard them scratching to get out.
The feeling of security made him reckless; he
took unnecessary risks; he brushed the panels
as he passed. And the love of keen sensation
for its own sake, the desire to feel "an awful
thrill," tempted him once so sharply that he
suddenly raised his stick and poked a fast-shut
door with it!

He was not prepared for the result, but he
gained the sensation and the thrill. For the
door opened with instant swiftness half an inch,
a hand emerged, caught the stick and tried to
draw it in. Tim sprang back as if he had been
struck. He pulled at the ivory handle with all
his strength, but his strength was less than
nothing. He tried to shout, but his voice had
gone. A terror of the moon came over him, for
he was unable to loosen his hold of the handle;
his fingers had become a part of it. An appalling
weakness turned him helpless. He was dragged
inch by inch towards the fearful door. The end
of the stick was already through the narrow

crack. He could not see the hand that pulled, but he knew it was gigantic. He understood now why the world was strange, why horses galloped furiously, and why trains whistled as they raced through stations. All the comedy and terror of nightmare gripped his heart with pincers made of ice. The disproportion was abominable. The final collapse rushed over him when, without a sign of warning, the door slammed silently, and between the jamb and the wall the cane was crushed as flat as if it were a bulrush. So irresistible was the force behind the door that the solid stick just went flat as the stalk of a bulrush.

He looked at it. It *was* a bulrush.

He did not laugh; the absurdity was so distressingly unnatural. The horror of finding a bulrush where he had expected a polished cane —this hideous and appalling detail held the nameless horror of the nightmare. It betrayed him utterly. Why had he not always known really that the stick was not a stick, but a thin and hollow reed . . .?

Then the cane was safely in his hand, unbroken. He stood looking at it. The Nightmare was in full swing. He heard another door opening behind his back, a door he had not touched. There was just time to see a hand thrusting and waving dreadfully, horribly, at him through the narrow crack—just time to realise that this was another Nightmare acting in atrocious concert with the first, when he saw closely beside him, towering to the ceiling, the protective, kindly Figure that visited his bedroom. In the turning movement he made to meet the attack, he became aware of her. And his terror passed. It was a nightmare terror merely. The infinite horror vanished. Only the comedy remained. He smiled.

He saw her dimly only, she was so vast, but he saw her, the Ruler of the Other Wing at last, and knew that he was safe again. He gazed with a tremendous love and wonder, trying to see her clearly; but the face was hidden far aloft and seemed to melt into the sky beyond the roof. He discerned that she was larger than the Night, only far, far softer, with wings that folded above him more tenderly even than his mother's arms; that there were points of light like stars among the feathers, and that she was vast enough to cover millions and millions of people all at once. Moreover, she did not fade or go, so far as he could see, but spread herself in such a way that he lost sight of her. She spread over the entire Wing . . .

And Tim remembered that this was all quite natural really. He had often and often been down this corridor before; the Nightmare Corridor was no new experience; it had to be faced as usual. Once knowing what hid inside the rooms, he was bound to tempt them out. They drew, enticed, attracted him; this was their power. It was their special strength that they could suck him helplessly towards them, and that he was obliged to go. He understood exactly why he was tempted to tap with the cane upon their awful doors, but, having done so, he had accepted the challenge and could now continue his journey quietly and safely. The Ruler of the Other Wing had taken him in charge.

A delicious sense of carelessness came on him. There was softness as of water in the solid things about him, nothing that could hurt or bruise. Holding the cane firmly by its ivory handle, he went forward along the corridor, walking as on air.

The end was quickly reached: He stood upon the threshold of the mighty chamber where he knew the owner of the cane was waiting; the long corridor lay behind him, in front he saw the spacious dimensions of a lofty hall that gave him the feeling of being in the Crystal Palace, Euston Station, or St. Paul's. High, narrow windows, cut deeply into the wall, stood in a row upon the other side; an enormous open fireplace of burning logs was on his right; thick tapestries hung from the ceiling to the floor of stone; and in the centre of the chamber was a massive table of dark, shining wood, great chairs with carved stiff backs set here and there beside it. And in the biggest of these throne-like chairs there sat a figure looking at him gravely—the figure of an old, old man.

Yet there was no surprise in the boy's fast-beating heart; there was a thrill of pleasure and excitement only, a feeling of satisfaction. He had known quite well the figure would be there, known also it would look like this exactly. He stepped forward on to the floor of stone without a trace of fear or trembling, holding the precious cane in two hands now before him, as though to present it to its owner. He felt proud and pleased. He had run risks for this.

And the figure rose quietly to meet him, advancing in a stately manner over the hard stone floor. The eyes looked gravely, sweetly down at him, the aquiline nose stood out. Tim knew him perfectly : the knee-breeches of shining satin, the gleaming buckles on the shoes, the neat dark stockings, the lace and ruffles about neck and wrists, the coloured waistcoat opening so widely—all the details of the picture over father's mantelpiece, where it hung between two Crimean bayonets, were reproduced in life before his eyes at last. Only the polished cane with the ivory handle was not there.

Tim went three steps nearer to the advancing figure and held out both his hands with the cane laid crosswise on them.

" I've brought it, great-grandpapa," he

said, in a faint but clear and steady tone; "here
it is."

And the other stooped a little, put out three
fingers half concealed by falling lace, and took
it by the ivory handle. He made a courtly bow
to Tim. He smiled, but though there was
pleasure, it was a grave, sad smile. He spoke
then : the voice was slow and very deep. There
was a delicate softness in it, the suave politeness
of an older day.

"Thank you," he said; "I value it. It was
given to me by my grandfather. I forgot it
when I——" His voice grew indistinct a
little.

"Yes?" said Tim.

"When I—left," the old gentleman repeated.

"Oh," said Tim, thinking how beautiful
and kind the gracious figure was.

The old man ran his slender fingers carefully
along the cane, feeling the polished surface with
satisfaction. He lingered specially over the
smoothness of the ivory handle. He was evidently very pleased.

"I was not quite myself—er—at the
moment," he went on gently; "my memory
failed me somewhat." He sighed, as though
an immense relief was in him.

"*I* forget things, too—sometimes," Tim
mentioned sympathetically. He simply loved

his great-grandfather. He hoped—for a
moment—he would be lifted up and kissed.
" I'm *awfully* glad I brought it," he added—
" that you've got it again."

The other turned his kind grey eyes upon
him; the smile on his face was full of gratitude
as he looked down.

" Thank you, my boy. I am truly and
deeply indebted to you. You courted danger
for my sake. Others have tried before, but the
Nightmare Passage—er——" He broke off.
He tapped the stick firmly on the stone flooring,
as though to test it. Bending a trifle, he put
his weight upon it. " Ah ! " he exclaimed with
a short sigh of relief, " I can now——"

His voice again grew indistinct; Tim did not
catch the words.

" Yes? " he asked again, aware for the first
time that a touch of awe was in his heart.

" —get about again," the other continued
very low. " Without my cane," he added, the
voice failing with each word the old lips uttered,
" I could not . . . possibly . . . allow myself
. . . to be seen. It was indeed . . . deplorable
. . . unpardonable of me . . . to forget in such
a way. Zounds, sir . . . ! I—I . . ."

His voice sank away suddenly into a sound
of wind. He straightened up, tapping the iron
ferrule of his cane on the stones in a series of
loud knocks. Tim felt a strange sensation creep

into his legs. The queer words frightened him a little.

The old man took a step towards him. He still smiled, but there was a new meaning in the smile. A sudden earnestness had replaced the courtly, leisurely manner. The next words seemed to blow down upon the boy from above, as though a cold wind brought them from the sky outside.

Yet the words, he knew, were kindly meant, and very sensible. It was only the abrupt change that startled him. Great-grandpapa, after all, was but a man! This distant sound recalled something in him to that outside world from which the cold wind blew.

"My eternal thanks to you," he heard, while the voice and face and figure seemed to withdraw deeper and deeper into the heart of the mighty chamber. "I shall not forget your kindness and your courage. It is a debt I can, fortunately, one day repay. . . . But now you had best return, and with dispatch. For your head and arm lie heavily on the table, the documents are scattered, there is a cushion fallen . . . and my son's son is in the house. . . . Farewell! You had best leave me quickly. See! *She* stands behind you, waiting. Go with her! Go now . . . !"

The entire scene had vanished even before the final words were uttered. Tim felt empty

space about him. A vast, shadowy Figure bore
him through it as with mighty wings. He flew,
he rushed, he remembered nothing more—until
he heard another voice and felt a heavy hand
upon his shoulder.

"Tim, you rascal! What are you doing in
my study? And in the dark, like this!"

He looked up into his father's face without
a word. He felt dazed. The next minute his
father had caught him up and kissed him.

"Ragamuffin! How did you guess I was
coming back to-night?" He shook him play-
fully and kissed his tumbling hair. "And
you've been asleep, too, into the bargain. Well
—how's everything at home—eh? Jack's coming back from school to-morrow, you know,
and . . ."

4

JACK came home, indeed, the following day,
and when the Easter holidays were over, the
governess stayed abroad and Tim went off to
adventures of another kind in the preparatory
school for Wellington. Life slipped rapidly
along with him; he grew into a man; his mother
and his father died; Jack followed them within
a little space; Tim inherited, married, settled
down into his great possessions—and opened up
the Other Wing. The dreams of imaginative
boyhood all had faded; perhaps he had merely

put them away, or perhaps he had forgotten them.   At any rate, he never spoke of such things now, and when his Irish wife mentioned her belief that the old country house possessed a family ghost, even declaring that she had met an Eighteenth Century figure of a man in the corridors, " an old, old man who bends down upon a stick "—Tim only laughed and said :

" That's as it ought to be !   And if these awful land taxes force us to sell some day, a respectable ghost will increase the market value."

But one night he woke and heard a tapping on the floor.   He sat up in bed and listened. There was a chilly feeling down his back.   Belief had long since gone out of him ; he felt uncannily afraid.   The sound came nearer and nearer ; there were light footsteps with it.   The door opened—it opened a little wider, that is, for it already stood ajar—and there upon the threshold stood a figure that it seemed he knew. He saw the face as with all the vivid sharpness of reality.   There was a smile upon it, but a smile of warning and alarm.   The arm was raised.   Tim saw the slender hand, lace falling down upon the long, thin fingers, and in them, tightly gripped, a polished cane.   Shaking the cane twice to and fro in the air, the face thrust forward, spoke certain words, and—vanished. But the words were inaudible ; for, though the lips distinctly moved, no sound, apparently, came from them.

And Tim sprang out of bed. The room was full of darkness. He turned the light on. The door, he saw, was shut as usual. He had, of course, been dreaming. But he noticed a curious odour in the air. He sniffed it once or twice—then grasped the truth. It was a smell of burning!

Fortunately, he awoke just in time. . . .

He was acclaimed a hero for his promptitude. After many days, when the damage was repaired, and nerves had settled down once more into the calm routine of country life, he told the story to his wife—the entire story. He told the adventure of his imaginative boyhood with it. She asked to see the old family cane. And it was this request of hers that brought back to memory a detail Tim had entirely forgotten all these years. He remembered it suddenly again —the loss of the cane, the hubbub his father kicked up about it, the endless, futile search. For the stick had never been found, and Tim, who was questioned very closely concerning it, swore with all his might that he had not the smallest notion where it was. Which was, of course, the truth.

IX

THE OCCUPANT OF THE ROOM

He arrived late at night by the yellow diligence, stiff and cramped after the toilsome ascent of three slow hours. The village, a single mass of shadow, was already asleep. Only in front of the little hotel was there noise and light and bustle—for a moment. The horses, with tired, slouching gait, crossed the road and disappeared into the stable of their own accord, their harness trailing in the dust; and the lumbering diligence stood for the night where they had dragged it —the body of a great yellow-sided beetle with broken legs.

In spite of his physical weariness the schoolmaster, revelling in the first hours of his ten-guinea holiday, felt exhilarated. For the high Alpine valley was marvellously still; stars twinkled over the torn ridges of the Dent du Midi where spectral snows gleamed against rocks that looked like ebony; and the keen air smelt of pine forests, dew-soaked pastures, and freshly sawn wood. He took it all in with a kind of bewildered delight for a few minutes, while the

other three passengers gave directions about
their luggage and went to their rooms. Then
he turned and walked over the coarse matting
into the glare of the hall, only just able to resist
stopping to examine the big mountain map that
hung upon the wall by the door.

And, with a sudden disagreeable shock, he
came down from the ideal to the actual. For
at the inn—the only inn—there was no vacant
room. Even the available sofas were occupied. . . .

How stupid he had been not to write! Yet
it had been impossible, he remembered, for he
had come to the decision suddenly that morning
in Geneva, enticed by the brilliance of the
weather after a week of rain.

They talked endlessly, this gold-braided
porter and the hard-faced old woman—her face
was hard, he noticed—gesticulating all the time,
and pointing all about the village with sugges-
tions that he ill understood, for his French was
limited and their *patois* was fearful.

"*There!*"—he might find a room, "or
there! But we are, *hélas*, full—more full than
we care about. To-morrow, perhaps—if So-
and-So give up their rooms——!" And then,
with much shrugging of shoulders, the hard-
faced old woman stared at the gold-braided
porter, and the porter stared sleepily at the
schoolmaster.

At length, however, by some process of hope he did not himself understand, and following directions given by the old woman that were utterly unintelligible, he went out into the street and walked towards a dark group of houses she had pointed out to him. He only knew that he meant to thunder at a door and ask for a room. He was too weary to think out details. The porter half made to go with him, but turned back at the last moment to speak with the old woman. The houses sketched themselves dimly in the general blackness. The air was cold. The whole valley was filled with the rush and thunder of falling water. He was thinking vaguely that the dawn could not be very far away, and that he might even spend the night wandering in the woods, when there was a sharp noise behind him and he turned to see a figure hurrying after him. It was the porter—running.

And in the little hall of the inn there began again a confused three-cornered conversation, with frequent muttered colloquy and whispered asides in *patois* between the woman and the porter—the net result of which was that, "If Monsieur did not object—there *was* a room, after all, on the first floor—only it was in a sense 'engaged.' That is to say——"

But the schoolmaster took the room without inquiring too closely into the puzzle that had somehow provided it so suddenly. The ethics of hotel-keeping had nothing to do with him. If the woman offered him quarters it was not for him to argue with her whether the said quarters were legitimately hers to offer.

But the porter, evidently a little thrilled, accompanied the guest up to the room and supplied in a mixture of French and English details omitted by the landlady—and Minturn, the schoolmaster, soon shared the thrill with him, and found himself in the atmosphere of a possible tragedy.

All who know the peculiar excitement that belongs to lofty mountain valleys where dangerous climbing is a chief feature of the attractions, will understand a certain faint element of high alarm that goes with the picture. One looks up at the desolate, soaring ridges and thinks involuntarily of the men who find their pleasure for days and nights together scaling perilous summits among the clouds, and conquering inch by inch the icy peaks that for ever shake their dark terror in the sky. The atmosphere of adventure, spiced with the possible horror of a very grim order of tragedy, is inseparable from any imaginative contemplation of the scene; and the idea Minturn gleaned from the half-frightened porter lost nothing by his ignorance of the language. This English-woman, the real occupant of the room, had insisted on going without a guide. She had left

just before daybreak two days before—the
porter had seen her start—and . . . she had
not returned! The route was difficult and
dangerous, yet not impossible for a skilled
climber, even a solitary one. And the Englishwoman was an experienced mountaineer. Also,
she was self-willed, careless of advice, bored by
warnings, self-confident to a degree. Queer,
moreover; for she kept entirely to herself, and
sometimes remained in her room with locked
doors, admitting no one, for days together: a
" crank," evidently, of the first water.

This much Minturn gathered clearly enough
from the porter's talk while his luggage was
brought in and the room set to rights; further,
too, that the search party had gone out and
might, of course, return at any moment. In
which case—— Thus the room was empty, yet
still hers. " If Monsieur did not object—if the
risk he ran of having to turn out suddenly in the
night——" It was the loquacious porter who
furnished the details that made the transaction
questionable; and Minturn dismissed the loquacious porter as soon as possible, and prepared to
get into the hastily arranged bed and snatch all
the hours of sleep he could before he was turned
out.

At first, it must be admitted, he felt uncomfortable—distinctly uncomfortable. He was in
someone else's room. He had really no right to

o

be there. It was in the nature of an unwarrantable intrusion; and while he unpacked he kept looking over his shoulder as though someone were watching him from the corners. Any moment, it seemed, he would hear a step in the passage, a knock would come at the door, the door would open, and there he would see this vigorous Englishwoman looking him up and down with anger. Worse still—he would hear her voice asking him what he was doing in her room—her bedroom. Of course, he had an adequate explanation, but still——!

Then, reflecting that he was already half undressed, the humour of it flashed for a second across his mind, and he laughed—*quietly*. And at once, after that laughter, under his breath, came the sudden sense of tragedy he had felt before. Perhaps, even while he smiled, her body lay broken and cold upon those awful heights, the wind of snow playing over her hair, her glazed eyes staring sightless up to the stars. . . . It made him shudder. The sense of this woman whom he had never seen, whose name even he did not know, became extraordinarily real. Almost he could imagine that she was somewhere in the room with him, hidden, observing all he did.

He opened the door softly to put his boots outside, and when he closed it again he turned the key. Then he finished unpacking **and** distributed his few things about the room. It was soon done; for, in the first place, he had only a small Gladstone and a knapsack, and secondly, the only place where he could spread his clothes was the sofa. There was no chest of drawers, and the cupboard, an unusually large and solid one, was locked. The Englishwoman's things had evidently been hastily put away in it. The only sign of her recent presence was a bunch of faded *Alpenrosen* standing in a glass jar upon the washhand stand. This, and a certain faint perfume, were all that remained. In spite, however, of these very slight evidences, the whole room was pervaded with a curious sense of occupancy that he found exceedingly distasteful. One moment the atmosphere seemed subtly charged with a " just left " feeling; the next it was a queer awareness of " still here " that made him turn and look hurriedly behind him.

Altogether, the room inspired him with a singular aversion, and the strength of this aversion seemed the only excuse for his tossing the faded flowers out of the window, and then hanging his mackintosh upon the cupboard door in such a way as to screen it as much as possible from view. For the sight of that big, ugly cupboard, filled with the clothing of a woman who might then be beyond any further need of covering—thus his imagination insisted on picturing it—touched in him a startled sense of the

incongruous that did not stop there, but crept
through his mind gradually till it merged somehow into a sense of a rather grotesque horror.
At any rate, the sight of that cupboard was
offensive, and he covered it almost instinctively.
Then, turning out the electric light, he got into
bed.

But the instant the room was dark he realised that it was more than he could stand; for,
with the blackness, there came a sudden rush of
cold that he found it hard to explain. And the
odd thing was that, when he lit the candle beside his bed, he noticed that his hand trembled.

This, of course, was too much. His imagination was taking liberties and must be called to
heel. Yet the way he called it to order was significant, and its very deliberateness betrayed a
mind that has already admitted fear. And fear,
once in, is difficult to dislodge. He lay there
upon his elbow in bed and carefully took note
of all the objects in the room—with the intention, as it were, of taking an inventory of everything his senses perceived, then drawing a line,
adding them up finally, and saying with decision,
" That's all the room contains! I've counted
every single thing. There is nothing more.
Now—I may sleep in peace! "

And it was during this absurd process of
enumerating the furniture of the room that the
dreadful sense of distressing lassitude came over

him that made it difficult even to finish counting. It came swiftly, yet with an amazing kind of violence that overwhelmed him softly and easily with a sensation of enervating weariness hard to describe. And its first effect was to banish fear. He no longer possessed enough energy to feel really afraid or nervous. The cold remained, but the alarm vanished. And into every corner of his usually vigorous personality crept the insidious poison of a *muscular* fatigue —at first—that in a few seconds, it seemed, translated itself into *spiritual* inertia. A sudden consciousness of the foolishness, the crass futility, of life, of effort, of fighting—of all that makes life worth living, shot into every fibre of his being, and left him utterly weak. A spirit of black pessimism that was not even vigorous enough to assert itself, invaded the secret chambers of his heart. . . .

Every picture that presented itself to his mind came dressed in grey shadows : those bored and sweating horses toiling up the ascent to— nothing ! that hard-faced landlady taking so much trouble to let her desire for gain conquer her sense of morality—for a few francs ! That gold-braided porter, so talkative, fussy, energetic, and so anxious to tell all he knew ! What was the use of them all ? And for himself, what in the world was the good of all the labour and drudgery he went through in that preparatory school where he was junior master? What could it lead to? Wherein lay the value of so much uncertain toil, when the ultimate secrets of life were hidden and no one knew the final goal? How foolish was effort, discipline, work! How vain was pleasure! How trivial the noblest life! . . .

With a fearful jump that nearly upset the candle Minturn pulled himself together. Such vicious thoughts were usually so remote from his normal character that the sudden vile invasion produced a swift reaction. Yet, only for a moment. Instantly, again, the black depression descended upon him like a wave. His work—it could lead to nothing but the dreary labour of a small headmastership after all—seemed as vain and foolish as his holiday in the Alps. What an idiot he had been, to be sure, to come out with a knapsack merely to work himself into a state of exhaustion climbing over toilsome mountains that led to nowhere—resulted in nothing. A dreariness of the grave possessed him. Life was a ghastly fraud! Religion a childish humbug! Everything was merely a trap—a trap of death; a coloured toy that Nature used as a decoy! But a decoy for what? For nothing! There was no meaning in anything. The only *real* thing was—DEATH. And the happiest people were those who found it soonest.

Then why wait for it to come?

He sprang out of bed, thoroughly frightened. This was horrible. Surely mere physical fatigue could not produce a world so black, an outlook so dismal, a cowardice that struck with such sudden hopelessness at the very roots of life? For, normally, he was cheerful and strong, full of the tides of healthy living; and this appalling lassitude swept the very basis of his personality into Nothingness and the desire for death. It was like the development of a Secondary Personality. He had read, of course, how certain persons who suffered shocks developed thereafter entirely different characteristics, memory, tastes, and so forth. It had all rather frightened him. Though scientific men vouched for it, it was hardly to be believed. Yet here was a similar thing taking place in his own consciousness. He was, beyond question, experiencing all the mental variations of—*someone else!* It was un-moral. It was awful. It was —well, after all, at the same time, it was uncommonly interesting.

And this interest he began to feel was the first sign of his returning normal Self. For to feel interest is to live, and to love life.

He sprang into the middle of the room— then switched on the electric light. And the first thing that struck his eye was—the big cupboard.

"Hallo! There's that — beastly cupboard ! " he exclaimed to himself, involuntarily, yet aloud. It held all the clothes, the swinging skirts and coats and summer blouses of the dead woman. For he knew now—somehow or other —that she *was* dead. . . .

At that moment, through the open windows, rushed the sound of falling water, bringing with it a vivid realisation of the desolate, snow-swept heights. He saw her—positively *saw* her !— lying where she had fallen, the frost upon her cheeks, the snow-dust eddying about her hair and eyes, her broken limbs pushing against the lumps of ice. For a moment the sense of spiritual lassitude—of the emptiness of life— vanished before this picture of broken effort—of a small human force battling pluckily, yet in vain, against the impersonal and pitiless Potencies of Inanimate Nature—and he found himself again, his normal self. Then, instantly, returned again that terrible sense of cold, nothingness, emptiness. . . .

And he found himself standing opposite the big cupboard where her clothes were. He suddenly wanted to see those clothes—things she had used and worn. Quite close he stood, almost touching it. The next second he had touched it. His knuckles struck upon the wood.

Why he knocked is hard to say. It was an instinctive movement probably. Something in his deepest self dictated it—ordered it. He knocked at the door. And the dull sound upon the wood into the stillness of that room brought —horror. Why it should have done so he found it as hard to explain to himself as why he should have felt impelled to knock. The fact remains that when he heard the faint reverberation inside the cupboard, it brought with it so vivid a realisation of the woman's presence that he stood there shivering upon the floor with a dreadful sense of anticipation : he almost expected to hear an answering knock from within—the rustling of the hanging skirts perhaps—or, worse still, to see the locked door slowly open towards him.

And from that moment, he declares that in some way or other he must have partially lost control of himself, or at least of his better judgment; for he became possessed by such an overmastering desire to tear open that cupboard door and see the clothes within, that he tried every key in the room in the vain effort to unlock it, and then, finally, before he quite realised what he was doing—rang the bell !

But, having rung the bell for no obvious or intelligent reason at two o'clock in the morning, he then stood waiting in the middle of the floor for the servant to come, conscious for the first time that something outside his ordinary self had pushed him towards the act. It was almost like an internal voice that directed him . . . and thus, when at last steps came down the passage and he faced the cross and sleepy chambermaid, amazed at being summoned at such an hour, he found no difficulty in the matter of what he should say. For the same power that insisted he should open the cupboard door also impelled him to utter words over which he apparently had no control.

" It's not *you* I rang for ! " he said with decision and impatience " I want a man. Wake the porter and send him up to me at once— hurry ! I tell you, hurry——! "

And when the girl had gone, frightened at his earnestness, Minturn realised that the words surprised himself as much as they surprised her. Until they were out of his mouth he had not known what exactly he was saying. But now he understood that some force foreign to his own personality was using his mind and organs. The black depression that had possessed him a few moments before was also part of it. The powerful mood of this vanished woman had somehow momentarily taken possession of him —communicated, possibly, by the atmosphere of things in the room still belonging to her. But even now, when the porter, without coat or collar, stood beside him in the room, he did not understand why he insisted, with a positive fury admitting no denial, that the key of that cupboard must be found and the door instantly opened.

The scene was a curious one. After some perplexed whispering with the chambermaid at the end of the passage, the porter managed to find and produce the key in question. Neither he nor the girl knew clearly what this excited Englishman was up to, or why he was so passionately intent upon opening the cupboard at two o'clock in the morning. They watched him with an air of wondering what was going to happen next. But something of his curious earnestness, even of his late fear, communicated itself to them, and the sound of the key grating in the lock made them both jump.

They held their breath as the creaking door swung slowly open. All heard the clatter of that other key as it fell against the wooden floor —within. The cupboard had been locked *from the inside*. But it was the scared housemaid, from her position in the corridor, who first saw —and with a wild scream fell crashing against the bannisters.

The porter made no attempt to save her. The schoolmaster and himself made a simultaneous rush towards the door, now wide open. They, too, had seen.

There were no clothes, skirts or blouses on the pegs, but they saw the body of the Englishwoman suspended in mid-air, the head bent for-

wards. Jarred by the movement of unlocking,
the body swung slowly round to face them. . . .
Pinned upon the inside of the door was a hotel
envelope with the following words pencilled in
straggling writing :

    " Tired — unhappy — hopelessly depressed.
. . . I cannot face life any longer. . . . All is
black. I must put an end to it. . . . I meant
to do it on the mountains, but was afraid. I
slipped back to my room unobserved. This way
is easiest and best. . . ."

X

CAIN'S ATONEMENT

So many thousands to-day have deliberately put Self aside, and are ready to yield their lives for an ideal, that it is not surprising a few of them should have registered experiences of a novel order. For to step aside from Self is to enter a larger world, to be open to new impressions. If Powers of Good exist in the universe at all, they can hardly be inactive at the present time. . . .

The case of two men, who may be called Jones and Smith, occurs to the mind in this connection. Whether a veil actually was lifted for a moment, or whether the tension of long and terrible months resulted in an exaltation of emotion, the experience claims significance. Smith, to whom the experience came, holds the firm belief that it was real. Jones, though it involved him too, remained unaware.

It is a somewhat personal story, their peculiar relationship dating from early youth : a kind of unwilling antipathy was born between them, yet an antipathy that had no touch of hate or even of dislike. It was rather in the nature

of an instinctive rivalry. Some tie operated that
flung them ever into the same arena with strange
persistence, and ever as opponents. An inevitable fate delighted to throw them together in
a sense that made them rivals; small as well as
large affairs betrayed this malicious tendency of
the gods. It showed itself in earliest days, at
school, at Cambridge, in travel, even in house-
parties and the lighter social intercourse.
Though distant cousins, their families were not
intimate, and there was no obvious reason why
their paths should fall so persistently together.
Yet their paths did so, crossing and recrossing
in the way described. Sooner or later, in all his
undertakings, Smith would note the shadow of
Jones darkening the ground in front of him; and
later, when called to the Bar in his chosen pro-
fession, he found most frequently that the
learned counsel in opposition to him was the
owner of this shadow, Jones. In another matter,
too, they became rivals, for the same girl, oddly
enough, attracted both, and though she accepted
neither offer of marriage (during Smith's lifetime!), the attitude between them was that of
unwilling rivals. For they were friends as well.

Jones, it appears, was hardly aware that any
rivalry existed; he did not think of Smith as an
opponent, and as an adversary, never. He did
notice, however, the constantly recurring meet-
ings, for more than once he commented on them

with good-humoured amusement. Smith, on the other hand, was conscious of a depth and strength in the tie that certainly intrigued him; being of a thoughtful, introspective nature, he was keenly sensible of the strange competition in their lives, and sought in various ways for its explanation, though without success. The desire to find out was very strong in him. And this was natural enough, owing to the singular fact that in all their battles he was the one to lose. Invariably Jones got the best of every conflict. Smith always paid; sometimes he paid with interest.

Occasionally, too, he seemed forced to injure himself while contributing to his cousin's success. It was very curious. He reflected much upon it; he wondered what the origin of their tie and rivalry might be, but especially why it was that he invariably lost, and why he was so often obliged to help his rival to the point even of his own detriment. Tempted to bitterness sometimes, he did not yield to it, however; the relationship remained frank and pleasant; if anything, it deepened.

He remembered once, for instance, giving his cousin a chance introduction which yet led, a little later, to the third party offering certain evidence which lost him an important case— Jones, of course, winning it. The third party, too, angry at being dragged into the case, turned hostile to him, thwarting various subsequent projects. In no other way could Jones have procured this particular evidence; he did not know of its existence even. That chance introduction did it all. There was nothing the least dishonourable on the part of Jones—it was just the chance of the dice. The dice were always loaded against Smith—and there were other instances of similar kind.

About this time, moreover, a singular feeling that had lain vaguely in his mind for some years past, took more definite form. It suddenly assumed the character of a conviction, that yet had no evidence to support it. A voice, long whispering in the depths of him, became much louder, grew into a statement that he accepted without further ado : "I'm paying off a debt," he phrased it, "an old, old debt is being discharged. I owe him this—my help and so forth." He accepted it, that is, as just; and this certainty of justice kept sweet his heart and mind, shutting the door on bitterness or envy. The thought, however, though it recurred persistently with each encounter, brought no explanation.

When the war broke out both offered their services; as members of the O.T.C., they got commissions quickly; but it was a chance remark of Smith's that made his friend join the very regiment he himself was in. They trained

together, were in the same retreats and the same
advances together. Their friendship deepened.
Under the stress of circumstances the tie did
not dissolve, but strengthened. It was indubit-
ably real, therefore. Then, oddly enough, they
were both wounded in the same engagement.

And it was here the remarkable fate that
jointly haunted them betrayed itself more clearly
than in any previous incident of their long relationship—Smith was wounded in the act of
protecting his cousin. How it happened is con-
fusing to a layman, but each apparently was
leading a bombing-party, and the two parties
came together. They found themselves shoulder
to shoulder, both brimmed with that pluck
which is complete indifference to Self; they exchanged a word of excited greeting; and the
same second one of those rare opportunities
of advantage presented itself which only the
highest courage could make use of. Neither,
certainly, was thinking of personal reward; it
was merely that each saw the chance by which
instant heroism might gain a surprise advantage
for their side. The risk was heavy, but there
was a chance; and success would mean a decisive
result, to say nothing of high distinction for the
man who obtained it—if he survived. Smith,
being a few yards ahead of his cousin, had the
moment in his grasp. He was in the act of dashing forward when something made him pause.

P

A bomb in mid-air, flung from the opposing trench, was falling; it seemed immediately above him; he saw that it would just miss himself, but land full upon his cousin—whose head was turned the other way. By stretching out his hand, Smith knew he could field it like a cricket ball. There was an interval of a second and a half, he judged. He hesitated—perhaps a quarter of a second—then he acted. He caught it. It was the obvious thing to do. He flung it back into the opposing trench.

The rapidity of thought is hard to realise. In that second and a half Smith was aware of many things: He saved his cousin's life unquestionably; unquestionably also Jones seized the opportunity that otherwise was his cousin's. But it was neither of these reflections that filled Smith's mind. The dominant impression was another. It flashed into actual words inside his excited brain: "I must risk it. I owe it to him —and more besides!" He was, further, aware of another impulse than the obvious one. In the first fraction of a second it was overwhelmingly established. And it was this: that the entire episode was familiar to him. A subtle familiarity was present. All this had happened before. He had already—elsewhere—seen death descending upon his cousin from the air. Yet with a difference. The "difference" escaped him; the familiarity was vivid. That he missed the deadly detonators in making the catch, or that the fuse delayed, he called good luck. He only remembers that he flung the gruesome weapon back whence it had come, and that its explosion in the opposite trench materially helped his cousin to find glory in the place of death. The slight delay, however, resulted in his receiving a bullet through the chest—a bullet he would not otherwise have received, presumably.

It was some days later, gravely wounded, that he discovered his cousin in another bed across the darkened floor. They exchanged remarks. Jones was already "decorated," it seemed, having snatched success from his cousin's hands, while little aware whose help had made it possible. . . . And once again there stole across the inmost mind of Smith that strange, insistent whisper: "I owed it to him . . . but, by God, I owe more than that . . . I mean to pay it too . . . !"

There was not a trace of bitterness or envy now; only this profound conviction, of obscurest origin, that it was right and absolutely just—full, honest repayment of a debt incurred. Some ancient balance of account was being settled; there was no "chance"; injustice, caprice played no rôle at all. . . . And a deeper understanding of life's ironies crept into him; for if everything was just, there was no room for whimpering.

And the voice persisted above the sound of busy footsteps in the ward : " I owe it . . . I'll pay it gladly . . .! "

Through the pain and weakness the whisper died away. He was exhausted. There were periods of unconsciousness, but there were periods of half-consciousness as well; then flashes of another kind of consciousness altogether, when, bathed in high, soft light, he was aware of things he could not quite account for. He *saw*. It was absolutely real. Only, the critical faculty was gone. He did not question what he saw, as he stared across at his cousin's bed. He knew. Perhaps the beaten, worn-out body let something through at last. The nerves, overstrained to numbness, lay very still. The physical system, battered and depleted, made no cry. The clamour of the flesh was hushed. He was aware, however, of an undeniable exaltation of the spirit in him, as he lay and gazed towards his cousin's bed. . . .

Across the night of time, it seemed to him, the picture stole before his inner eye with a certainty that left no room for doubt. It was not the cells of memory in his brain of To-day that gave up their dead, it was the eternal Self in him that remembered and understood—the soul. . . .

With that satisfaction which is born of full comprehension, he watched the light glow and

spread about the little bed. Thick matting
deadened the footsteps of nurses, orderlies, doctors. New cases were brought in, " old " cases
were carried out; he ignored them; he saw only
the light above his cousin's bed grow stronger.
He lay still and stared. It came neither from
the ceiling nor the floor; it unfolded like a cloud
of shining smoke. And the little lamp, the
sheets, the figure framed between them—all
these slid cleverly away and vanished utterly.
He stood in another place that had lain behind
all these appearances—a landscape with wooded
hills, a foaming river, the sun just sinking below
the forest, and dusk creeping from a gorge along
the lonely banks. In the warm air there was a
perfume of great flowers and heavy-scented
trees; there were fire-flies, and the taste of spray
from the tumbling river was on his lips. Across
the water a large bird flapped its heavy wings,
as it moved down-stream to find another fishing
place. For he and his companion had disturbed
it as they broke out of the thick foliage and
reached the river-bank. The companion, moreover, was his brother; they ever hunted together; there was a passionate link between
them born of blood and of affection—they were
twins. . . .

It all was as clear as though of Yesterday.
In his heart was the lust of the hunt; in his
blood was the lust of woman; and thick behind

these lurked the jealousy and fierce desire of a primitive day. But, though clear as of Yesterday, he knew that it was of long, long ago. . . . And his brother came up close beside him, resting his bloody spear with a clattering sound against the boulders on the shore. He saw the gleaming of the metal in the sunset, he saw the shining glitter of the spray upon the boulders, he saw his brother's eyes look straight into his own. And in them shone a light that was neither the reflection of the sunset, nor the excitement of the hunt just over.

"It escaped us," said his brother. "Yet I know my first spear struck."

"It followed the fawn that crossed," was the reply. "Besides, we came down wind, thus giving it warning. Our flocks, at any rate, are safer——"

The other laughed significantly.

"It is not the safety of our flocks that troubles me just now, brother," he interrupted eagerly, while the light burned more deeply in his eyes. "It is, rather, that *she* waits for me by the fire across the river, and that I would get to her. With your help added to my love," he went on in a trusting voice, "the gods have shown me the favour of true happiness!" He pointed with his spear to a camp-fire on the farther bank, turning his head as he strode forward to plunge into the stream and swim across.

For a moment, then, the other felt his natural love turn into bitter hate. His own fierce passion, unconfessed, concealed, burst into instant flame. That the girl should become his brother's wife sent the blood surging through his veins in fury. He felt his life and all that he desired go down in ashes. . . . He watched his brother stride towards the water, the deerskin cast across one naked shoulder—when another object caught his practised eye. In mid-air it passed suddenly, like a shining gleam; it seemed to hang a second; then it swept swiftly forward past his head—and downward. It had leaped with a blazing fury from the overhanging bank behind; he saw the blood still streaming from its wounded flank. It must land—he saw it with a secret, awful pleasure—full upon the striding figure whose head was turned away.

The swiftness of that leap, however, was not so swift but that he could easily have used his spear. Indeed, he gripped it strongly. His skill, his strength, his aim—he knew them well enough. But hate and love, fastening upon his heart, held all his muscles still. He hesitated. He was no murderer, yet he paused. He heard the roar, the ugly thud, the crash, the cry for help—too late . . . and when, an instant afterwards, his steel plunged into the great beast's heart, the human heart and life he might have saved lay still for ever. . . . He heard the water rushing past, an icy wind came down the gorge against his naked back, he saw the fire shine upon the farther bank . . . and the figure of a girl in skins was wading across, seeking out the shallow places in the dusk, and calling loudly as she came. . . . Then darkness hid the entire landscape, yet a darkness that was deeper, bluer than the velvet of the night alone. . . .

And he shrieked aloud in his remorseful anguish : " May the gods forgive me, for I did not mean it ! Oh, that I might undo . . . that I might repay . . . ! "

That his cries disturbed the weary occupants in more than one bed is certain, but he remembers chiefly that a nurse was quickly by his side, and that something she gave him soothed his violent pain and helped him into deeper sleep again. There was, he noticed, anyhow, no longer the soft, clear, blazing light about his cousin's bed. He saw only the faint glitter of the oil-lamps down the length of the great room. . . .

And some weeks later he went back to fight. The picture, however, never left his memory. It stayed with him as an actual reality that was neither delusion nor hallucination. He believed that he understood at last the meaning of the tie that had fettered him and puzzled him so long. The memory of those far-off days of shepherding beneath the stars of long ago remained vividly beside him. He kept his secret, however. In many a talk with his cousin beneath the nearer stars of Flanders no word of it ever passed his lips.

The friendship between them, meanwhile, experienced a curious deepening, though unacknowledged in any spoken words. Smith, at any rate, on his side, put into it an affection that was a brave man's love. He watched over his cousin. In the fighting especially, when possible, he sought to protect and shield him, regardless of his own personal safety. He delighted secretly in the honours his cousin had already won. He himself was not yet even mentioned in dispatches, and no public distinction of any kind had come his way.

His V.C. eventually—well, he was no longer occupying his body when it was bestowed. He had already " left." . . . He was now conscious, possibly, of other experiences besides that one of ancient, primitive days when he and his brother were shepherding beneath other stars. But the reckless heroism which saved his cousin under fire may later enshrine another memory which, at some far future time, shall reawaken as an " hallucination " from a Past that to-day is called the Present. . . . The notion, at any rate, flashed across his mind before he " left."

XI

AN EGYPTIAN HORNET

THE very word has an angry, malignant sound that brings the idea of attack vividly into the mind. There is a vicious sting about it somewhere—even a foreigner, ignorant of the meaning must feel it. A hornet is wicked; it darts and stabs; it pierces, aiming without provocation for the face and eyes. The name suggests a metallic droning of evil wings, fierce flight, and poisonous assault. Though black and yellow, it sounds scarlet. There is blood in it. A striped tiger of the air in concentrated form! There is no escape—if it attacks.

In Egypt an ordinary bee is the size of an English hornet, but the Egyptian hornet is enormous. It is truly monstrous—an ominous, flying terror. It shares that universal quality of the land of the Sphinx and Pyramids—great size. It is a formidable insect, worse than scorpion or tarantula. The Rev. James Milligan, meeting one for the first time, realised the meaning of another word as well, a word he used prolifically in his eloquent sermons—devil.

An Egyptian Hornet

One morning in February, when the heat
began to bring the insects out, he rose as usual
betimes and went across the wide stone corridor
to his bath. The desert already glared in through
the open windows. The heat would be afflicting
later in the day, but at this early hour the cool
north wind blew pleasantly down the hotel passages. It was Sunday, and at half-past eight
o'clock he would appear to conduct the morning
service for the English visitors. The floor of the
passageway was cold beneath his feet in their
thin native slippers of bright yellow. He was
neither young nor old; his salary was comfortable; he had a competency of his own, without
wife or children to absorb it; the dry climate
had been recommended to him; and—the big
hotel took him in for next to nothing. And he
was thoroughly pleased with himself, for he was
a sleek, vain, pompous, well-advertised personality, but mean as a rat. No worries of any kind
were on his mind as, carrying sponge and towel,
scented soap and a bottle of Scrubb's ammonia,
he travelled amiably across the deserted, shining
corridor to the bathroom. And nothing went
wrong with the Rev. James Milligan until he
opened the door, and his eye fell upon a gleaming, suspicious-looking object clinging to the
window-pane in front of him.

And even then, at first, he felt no anxiety
or alarm, but merely a natural curiosity to know

exactly what it was—this little clot of an odd-shaped, elongated thing that stuck there on the wooden framework six feet before his aquiline nose. He went straight up to it to see—then stopped dead. His heart gave a distinct, un-clerical leap. His lips formed themselves into unregenerate shape. He gasped : " Good God ! What is it? " For something unholy, something wicked as a secret sin, stuck there before his eyes in the patch of blazing sunshine. He caught his breath.

For a moment he was unable to move, as though the sight half fascinated him. Then, cautiously and very slowly—stealthily, in fact—he withdrew towards the door he had just entered. Fearful of making the smallest sound, he retraced his steps on tiptoe. His yellow slip-pers shuffled. His dry sponge fell, and bounded till it settled, rolling close beneath the horribly attractive object facing him. From the safety of the open door, with ample space for retreat behind him, he paused and stared. His entire being focused itself in his eyes. It was a hornet that he saw. It hung there, motionless and threatening, between him and the bathroom door. And at first he merely exclaimed—below his breath—" Good God ! It's an Egyptian hornet ! "

Being a man with a reputation for decided action, however, he soon recovered himself. He was well schooled in self-control. When people left his church at the beginning of the sermon, no muscle of his face betrayed the wounded vanity and annoyance that burned deep in his heart. But a hornet sitting directly in his path was a very different matter. He realised in a flash that he was poorly clothed—in a word, that he was practically half naked.

From a distance he examined this intrusion of the devil. It was calm and very still. It was wonderfully made, both before and behind. Its wings were folded upon its terrible body. Long, sinuous things, pointed like temptation, barbed as well, stuck out of it. There was poison, and yet grace, in its exquisite presentment. Its shiny black was beautiful, and the yellow stripes upon its sleek, curved abdomen were like the gleaming ornaments upon some feminine body of the seductive world he preached against. Almost, he saw an abandoned dancer on the stage. And then, swiftly in his impressionable soul, the simile changed, and he saw instead more blunt and aggressive forms of destruction. The well-filled body, tapering to a horrid point, reminded him of those perfect engines of death that reduce hundreds to annihilation unawares —torpedoes, shells, projectiles, crammed with secret, desolating powers. Its wings, its awful, quiet head, its delicate, slim waist, its stripes of brilliant saffron—all these seemed the concentrated prototype of abominations made cleverly by the brain of man, and beautifully painted to disguise their invisible freight of cruel death.

" Bah! " he exclaimed, ashamed of his prolific imagination. "It's only a hornet after all —an insect! " And he contrived a hurried, careful plan. He aimed a towel at it, rolled up into a ball—but did not throw it. He might miss. He remembered that his ankles were unprotected. Instead, he paused again, examining the black and yellow object in safe retirement near the door, as one day he hoped to watch the world in leisurely retirement in the country. It did not move. It was fixed and terrible. It made no sound. Its wings were folded. Not even the black antennæ, blunt at the tips like clubs, showed the least stir or tremble. It breathed, however. He watched the rise and fall of the evil body; it breathed air in and out as he himself did. The creature, he realised, had lungs and heart and organs. It had a brain! Its mind was active all this time. It knew it was being watched. It merely waited. Any second, with a whiz of fury, and with perfect accuracy of aim, it might dart at him and strike. If he threw the towel and missed—it certainly would.

There were other occupants of the corridor, however, and a sound of steps approaching gave

him the decision to act. He would lose his bath
if he hesitated much longer. He felt ashamed
of his timidity, though " pusillanimity " was the
word thought selected owing to the pulpit
vocabulary it was his habit to prefer. He went
with extreme caution towards the inner bathroom door, passing the point of danger so close
that his skin turned hot and cold. With one
foot gingerly extended he recovered his sponge.
The hornet did not move a muscle. But—it had
seen him pass. It merely waited. All dangerous
insects had that trick. It knew quite well he
was inside ; it knew quite well he must come out
a few minutes later ; it also knew quite well that
he was—naked.

Once inside the little room, he closed the
door with exceeding gentleness, lest the vibration might stir the fearful insect to attack. The
bath was already filled, and he plunged to his
neck with a feeling of comparative security. A
window into the outside passage he also closed,
so that nothing could possibly come in. And
steam soon charged the air and left its blurred
deposit on the glass. For ten minutes he could
enjoy himself and pretend that he was safe. For
ten minutes he did so. He behaved carelessly,
as though nothing mattered, and as though all
the courage in the world were his. He splashed
and soaped and sponged, making a lot of reckless noise. He got out and dried himself.

Slowly the steam subsided, the air grew clearer, he put on dressing-gown and slippers. It was time to go out.

Unable to devise any further reason for delay, he opened the door softly half an inch—peeped out—and instantly closed it again with a resounding bang. He had heard a drone of wings. The insect had left its perch and now buzzed upon the floor directly in his path. The air seemed full of stings; he felt stabs all over him; his unprotected portions winced with the expectancy of pain. The beast knew he was coming out, and was waiting for him. In that brief instant he had felt its sting all over him, on his unprotected ankles, on his back, his neck, his cheeks, in his eyes, and on the bald clearing that adorned his Anglican head. Through the closed door he heard the ominous, dull murmur of his striped adversary as it beat its angry wings. Its oiled and wicked sting shot in and out with fury. Its deft legs worked. He saw its tiny waist already writhing with the lust of battle. Ugh! That tiny waist! A moment's steady nerve and he could have severed that cunning body from the directing brain with one swift, well-directed thrust. But his nerve had utterly deserted him.

Human motives, even in the professedly holy, are an involved affair at any time. Just now, in the Rev. James Milligan, they were

quite inextricably mixed. He claims this explanation, at any rate, in excuse of his abominable subsequent behaviour. For, exactly at this
moment, when he had decided to admit
cowardice by ringing for the Arab servant, a
step was audible in the corridor outside, and
courage came with it into his disreputable heart.
It was the step of the man he cordially "dis-
approved of," using the pulpit version of
"hated and despised." He had overstayed his
time, and the bath was in demand by Mr.
Mullins. Mr. Mullins invariably followed him
at seven-thirty; it was now a quarter to eight.
And Mr. Mullins was a wretched drinking man
—"a sot."

In a flash the plan was conceived and put
into execution. The temptation, of course, was
of the devil. Mr. Milligan hid the motive from
himself, pretending he hardly recognised it.
The plan was what men call a dirty trick; it was
also irresistibly seductive. He opened the door,
stepped boldly, nose in the air, right over the
hideous insect on the floor, and fairly pranced
into the outer passage. The brief transit
brought a hundred horrible sensations—that the
hornet would rise and sting his leg, that it would
cling to his dressing-gown and stab his spine,
that he would step upon it and die, like Achilles,
of a heel exposed. But with these, and conquering them, was one other stronger emotion

Q

that robbed the lesser terrors of their potency—
that Mr. Mullins would run precisely the same
risks five seconds later, unprepared. He heard
the gloating insect buzz and scratch the oilcloth.
But it was behind him. *He* was safe!

" Good morning to you, Mr. Mullins," he
observed with a gracious smile. " I trust I have
not kept you waiting."

" Mornin'! " grunted Mullins sourly in
reply, as he passed him with a distinctly hostile
and contemptuous air. For Mullins, though
depraved, perhaps, was an honest man, abhor-
ring parsons and making no secret of his opinions
—whence the bitter feeling.

All men, except those very big ones who are
super-men, have something astonishingly despicable in them. The despicable thing in Milligan came uppermost now. He fairly chuckled.
He met the snub with a calm, forgiving smile,
and continued his shambling gait with what
dignity he could towards his bedroom opposite.
Then he turned his head to see. His enemy
would meet an infuriated hornet—an Egyptian
hornet!—and might not notice it. He might
step on it. He might not. But he was bound
to disturb it, and rouse it to attack. The
chances were enormously on the clerical side.
And its sting meant death.

" May God forgive me! " ran subconsciously
through his mind. And side by side with the

repentant prayer ran also a recognition of the
tempter's eternal skill : " I hope the devil it will
sting him ! "

It happened very quickly. The Rev. James
Milligan lingered a moment by his door to
watch. He saw Mullins, the disgusting Mullins,
step blithely into the bathroom passage; he saw
him pause, shrink back, and raise his arm to
protect his face. He heard him swear out
aloud : " What's the d——d thing doing here?
Have I really got 'em again——? " And then
he heard him laugh—a hearty, guffawing laugh
of genuine relief—— " It's *real!* "

The moment of revulsion was overwhelming.
It filled the churchly heart with anguish and
bitter disappointment. For a space he hated the
whole race of men.

For the instant Mr. Mullins realised that the
insect was not a fiery illusion of his disordered
nerves; he went forward without the smallest
hesitation. With his towel he knocked down
the flying terror. Then he stooped. He
gathered up the venomous thing his well-aimed
blow had stricken so easily to the floor. He
advanced with it, held at arm's length, to the
window. He tossed it out carelessly. The
Egyptian hornet flew away uninjured, and Mr.
Mullins—the Mr. Mullins who drank, gave
nothing to the church, attended no services,
hated parsons, and proclaimed the fact with

enthusiasm—this same detestable Mr. Mullins
went to his unearned bath without a scratch.
But first he saw his enemy standing in the doorway across the passage, watching him—and understood. That was the awful part of it.
Mullins would make a story of it, and the story
would go the round of the hotel.

The Rev. James Milligan, however, proved
that his reputation for self-control was not un-
deserved. He conducted morning service half
an hour later with an expression of peace upon
his handsome face. He conquered all outward
sign of inward spiritual vexation; the wicked,
he consoled himself, ever flourish like green bay
trees. It was notorious that the righteous never
have any luck at all! That was bad enough. But
what was worse—and the Rev. James Milligan
remembered for very long—was the superior
ease with which Mullins had relegated both himself and hornet to the same level of comparative
insignificance. Mullins ignored them both—
which proved that he felt himself superior. Infinitely worse than the sting of any hornet in the
world : he really was superior.

XII

BY WATER

THE night before young Larsen left to take up
his new appointment in Egypt he went to the
clairvoyante. He neither believed nor disbe-
lieved. He felt no interest, for he already knew
his past and did not wish to know his future.
"Just to please me, Jim," the girl pleaded.
"The woman is wonderful. Before I had been
five minutes with her she told me your initials,
so there *must* be something in it." "She read
your thought," he smiled indulgently. "Even
I can do that!" But the girl was in earnest.
He yielded; and that night at his farewell
dinner he came to give his report of the interview.

The result was meagre and unconvincing:
money was coming to him, he was soon to make
a voyage, and—he would never marry. "So
you see how silly it all is," he laughed, for they
were to be married when his first promotion
came. He gave the details, however, making a
little story of it in the way he knew she loved.

"But was that all, Jim?" The girl asked

it, looking rather hard into his face. "Aren't you hiding something from me?" He hesitated a moment, then burst out laughing at her clever discernment. "There *was* a little more," he confessed, "but you take it all so seriously; I——"

He had to tell it then, of course. The woman had told him a lot of gibberish about friendly and unfriendly elements. "She said water was unfriendly to me; I was to be careful of water, or else I should come to harm by it. Fresh water only," he hastened to add, seeing that the idea of shipwreck was in her mind.

"Drowning?" came the question quickly.

"Yes," he admitted with reluctance, but still laughing; "she did say drowning, though drowning in no ordinary way."

The girl's face showed uneasiness a moment. "What does that mean—drowning in no ordinary way?" There was a catch in her breath.

But that he could not tell her, because he did not know himself. He gave, therefore, the woman's exact words: "You will drown, but will not know you drown."

It was unwise of him. He wished afterwards he had invented a happier report, or had kept this detail back. "I'm safe in Egypt, anyhow," he laughed. "I shall be a clever man if I can find enough water in the desert to do me harm!" And all the way from Trieste to

Alexandria he remembered the promise she had extracted—that he would never once go on the Nile unless duty made it imperative for him to do so. He kept that promise like the literal, faithful soul he was. His love was equal to the somewhat quixotic sacrifice it occasionally involved. Fresh water in Egypt there was practically none other, and in any case the natron works where his duty lay had their headquarters some distance out into the desert. The river, with its banks of welcome, refreshing verdure, was not even visible.

Months passed quickly, and the time for leave came within measurable distance. In the long interval luck had played the cards kindly for him, vacancies had occurred, early promotion seemed likely, and his letters were full of plans to bring her out to share a little house of their own. His health, however, had not improved; the dryness did not suit him; even in this short period his blood had thinned, his nervous system deteriorated, and, contrary to the doctor's prophecy, the waterless air had told upon his sleep. A damp climate liked him best. And once the sun had touched him with its fiery finger.

His letters made no mention of this. He described the life to her, the work, the sport, the pleasant people, and his chances of increased pay and early marriage. And a week

before he sailed he rode out upon a final act of
duty to inspect the latest diggings his Company
were making. His course lay some twenty
miles into the desert behind El-Chobak towards
the limestone hills of Guebel Haidi, and he
went alone, carrying lunch and tea, for it was
the weekly holiday òf Friday, and the men were
not at work.

The accident was ordinary enough. On his
way back in the heat of early afternoon his
pony stumbled against a boulder on the
treacherous desert film, threw him heavily,
broke the girth, bolted before he could seize
the reins again, and left him stranded some ten
or twelve miles from home. There was a pain
in his knee that made walking difficult, a buzz-
ing in his head that troubled sight and made
the landscape swim, while, worse than either,
his provisions, fastened to the saddle, had vanished with the frightened pony into those blazing leagues of sand. He was alone in the
Desert, beneath the pitiless afternoon sun,
twelve miles of utterly exhausting country between him and safety.

Under normal conditions he could have
covered the distance in four hours, reaching
home by dark; but his knee pained him so that
a mile an hour proved the best he could possibly
do. He reflected a few minutes. The wisest
course was to sit down and wait till the pony

told its obvious story to the stable, and help should come. And this was what he did, for the scorching heat and glare were dangerous; they were terrible; he was shaken and bewildered by his fall, hungry and weak into the bargain; and an hour's painful scrambling over the baked and burning little gorges must have speedily caused complete prostration. He sat down and rubbed his aching knee. It was quite a little adventure. Yet, though he knew the Desert might not be lightly trifled with, he felt at the moment nothing more than this— and the amusing description of it he would give in his letter, or—intoxicating thought—by word of mouth. In the heat of the sun he began to feel drowsy. He was exhausted. A soft torpor crept over him. He dozed. He fell asleep.

It was a long, a dreamless sleep . . . for when he woke at length the sun had just gone down, the dusk lay awfully upon the enormous desert, and the air was chilly. The cold had waked him. Quickly, as though on purpose, the red glow faded from the sky; the first stars shone; it was dark; the heavens were deep violet. He looked round and realised that his sense of direction had gone entirely. Great hunger was in him. The cold already was bitter as the wind rose, but the pain in his knee having eased, he got up and walked a little—and

in a moment lost sight of the spot where
he had been lying. The shadowy desert swallowed it. "Ah," he realised, "this is not an
English field or moor. I'm in the Desert!"
The safe thing to do was to remain exactly
where he was; only thus could the rescuers find
him; once he wandered he was done for. It
was strange the search-party had not yet arrived.
To keep warm, however, he was compelled to
move, so he made a little pile of stones to mark
the place, and walked round and round it in a
circle of some dozen yards' diameter. He
limped badly, and the hunger gnawed dreadfully; but, after all, the adventure was not so
terrible. The amusing side of it kept uppermost still. Though fragile in body, his spirit
was not unduly timid or imaginative; he *could*
last out the night, or, if the worst came to the
worst, the next day as well. But when he
watched the little group of stones, he saw that
there were dozens of them, scores, hundreds,
thousands of these little groups of stones. The
desert's face, of course, is thickly strewn with
them. The original one was lost in the first
five minutes. So he sat down again. But the
biting cold, and the wind that licked his very
skin beneath the light clothing, soon forced him
up again. It was ominous; and the night huge
and shelterless. The shaft of green zodiacal
light that hung so strangely in the western sky

for hours had faded away; the stars were out in
their bright thousands; no guide was anywhere;
the wind moaned and puffed among the sandy
mounds; the vast sheet of desert stretched
mockingly upon the world; he heard the jackals
cry. . . .

And with the jackals' cry came suddenly the
unwelcome realisation that no play was in this
adventure any more, but that a bleak reality
stared at him through the surrounding darkness.
He faced it—at bay. He was genuinely lost.
Thought blocked in him. "I must be calm and
think," he said aloud. His voice woke no echo;
it was small and dead; something gigantic ate
it instantly. He got up and walked again.
Why did no one come? Hours had passed.
The pony had long ago found its stable, or—
had it run madly in another direction altogether?
He worked out possibilities, tightening his belt.
The cold was searching; he never had been,
never could be warm again; the hot sunshine of
a few hours ago seemed the merest dream. Unfamiliar with hardship, he knew not what to do,
but he took his coat and shirt off, vigorously
rubbed his skin where the dried perspiration of
the afternoon still caused clammy shivers, swung
his arms furiously like a London cabman, and
quickly dressed again. Though the wind upon
his bare back was biting, he felt warmer a little.
He lay down exhausted, sheltered by an over-

hanging limestone crag, and took snatches of fitful dog's-sleep, while the wind drove overhead and the dry sand pricked his skin. One face continually was near him; one pair of tender eyes; two dear hands smoothed him; he smelt the perfume of light brown hair. It was all natural enough. His whole thought, in his misery, ran to her in England—England where there was soft fresh grass, big sheltering trees, hemlock and honeysuckle in the hedges—while the hard black Desert guarded him, and consciousness dipped away at little intervals under this dry and pitiless Egyptian sky. . . .

It was perhaps five in the morning when a voice spoke and he started up with a sudden jerk —the voice of that clairvoyante woman. The sentence fled away into the darkness, but one word remained : *Water!* At first he wondered, but at once explanation came. Cause and effect were obvious. The clue was physical. His body needed water, and so the thought came up into his mind. He was thirsty.

This was the moment when fear first really touched him. Hunger was manageable, more or less—for a day or two, certainly. But thirst! Thirst and the Desert were an evil pair that, by cumulative suggestion gathering since childhood days, brought terror in. Once in the mind it could not be dislodged. In spite of his best efforts, the ghastly thing grew passionately—because his thirst grew too. He had smoked much; had eaten spiced things at lunch; had breathed in alkali with the dry, scorched air. He searched for a cool flint pebble to put into his burning mouth, but found only angular scraps of dusty limestone. There were no pebbles here. The cold helped a little to counteract, but already he knew in himself subconsciously the dread of something that was coming. What was it? He tried to hide the thought and bury it out of sight. The utter futility of his tiny strength against the power of the universe appalled him. And then he knew. It was the sun. The merciless sun was on the way, already rising. Its return was like the presage of execution. . . .

It came. With true horror he watched the marvellous swift dawn break across the sandy sea. The eastern sky glowed hurriedly as from crimson fires. Ridges, not noticeable in the starlight, turned black in endless series, like flat-topped billows of a frozen ocean. Wide streaks of blue and yellow followed, as the sky dropped sheets of mauve light upon the wind-eaten cliffs and showed their under sides. They did not advance; they waited till the sun was up—and then they moved; they rose and sank; they shifted as the sunshine lifted them and the shadows crept away. But in an hour there would be no shadows any more. There would be no shade.

The little groups of stones began to dance. It was horrible. The unbroken, huge expanse lay round him, warming up, twelve hours of blazing hell to come. Already the monstrous Desert glared, each bit familiar, since each bit was a repetition of the bit before, behind, on either side. It laughed at guidance and direction. He rose and walked; for miles he walked, though how many, north, south, or west, he knew not. The frantic thing was in him now, the fury of the Desert; he took its pace, its endless, tireless stride, the stride of the burning, murderous Desert that is waterless. He felt it alive—a blindly heaving desire in it to reduce him to its conditionless, awful dryness. He felt —yet knowing this was feverish and *not* to be believed—that his own small life lay on its mighty surface, a mere dot in space, a mere heap of little stones. His emotions, his fears, his hopes, his ambition, his love—mere bundled group of little unimportant stones that danced with apparent activity for a moment, then were merged in the undifferentiated surface underneath. He was included in a purpose greater than his own.

The will made a plucky effort then. "A night and a day," he laughed, while his lips cracked smartingly with the stretching of the skin, "what is it? Many a chap has lasted days and days . . .!" Yes, only he was not of that rare company. He was ordinary, unaccustomed to privation, weak, untrained of spirit, unacquainted with stern resistance. He knew not how to spare himself. The Desert struck him where it pleased—all over. It played with him. His tongue was swollen; the parched throat could not swallow. He sank. . . . An hour he lay there, just wit enough in him to choose the top of a mound where he could be most easily seen. He lay two hours, three, four hours. . . . The heat blazed down upon him like a furnace. . . . The sky, when he opened his eyes once, was empty . . . then a speck became visible in the blue expanse; and presently another speck. They came from nowhere. They hovered very high, almost out of sight. They appeared, they disappeared, they—re-appeared. Nearer and nearer they swung down, in sweeping stealthy circles . . . little dancing groups of them, miles away but ever drawing closer—the vultures. . . .

He had strained his ears so long for sounds of feet and voices that it seemed he could no longer hear at all. Hearing had ceased within him. Then came the water-dreams, with their agonising torture. He heard *that* . . . heard it running in silvery streams and rivulets across green English meadows. It rippled with silvery music. He heard it splash. He dipped hands and feet and head in it—in deep, clear pools of

generous depth. He drank; with his skin
he drank, not with mouth and throat alone.
Delicious! Ice clinked in effervescent, sparkling water against a glass. He swam and
plunged. Water gushed freely over back and
shoulders, gallons and gallons of it, bathfuls and
to spare, a flood of gushing, crystal, cool, life-
giving liquid. . . . And then he stood in a
beech wood and felt the streaming deluge of
delicious summer rain upon his face; heard it
drip luxuriantly upon a million thirsty leaves.
The wet trunks shone, the damp moss spread
its perfume, ferns waved heavily in the moist
atmosphere. He was soaked to the skin in it.
A mountain torrent, fresh from fields of snow,
dashed foaming past, and the spray fell in a
shower upon his cheeks and hair. He dived
—head foremost. . . . Ah, he was up to the
neck . . . and *she* was with him; they were
under water together; he saw her eyes gleaming
into his own beneath the copious flood.

The voice, however, was not hers. . . . " You
will drown, yet you will not know you drown.
. . .!" His swollen tongue called out a name.
But no sound was audible. He closed his eyes.
There came sweet unconsciousness. . . .

A sound in that instant *was* audible, though.
It was a voice—voices—and the thud of animal
hoofs upon the sand. The specks had vanished
from the sky as mysteriously as they came.

And, as though in answer to the sound, he made
a movement—but an automatic, an unconscious
movement. He did not know he moved. And
the body, uncontrolled, lost its precarious
balance. He rolled; but he did not know he
rolled. Slowly, over the edge of the sloping
mound of sand, he turned sideways. Like a log
of wood he slid gradually, turning over and over,
nothing to stop him—to the bottom. A few
feet only, and not even steep; just steep enough
to keep rolling slowly. There was a—splash.
But he did not know there was a splash.

They found him in a pool of water—one of
these rare pools the Desert Bedouin mark pre-
ciously for their own. He had lain within three
yards of it for hours. He was drowned . . .
but he did not know he drowned. . . .

R

XIII

H. S. H.

In the mountain Club Hut, to which he had escaped after weeks of gaiety in the capital, Delane, young travelling Englishman, sat alone, and listened to the wind that beat the pines with violence. The firelight danced over the bare stone floor and raftered ceiling, giving the room an air of movement, and though the solid walls held steady against the wild spring hurricane, the cannonading of the wind seemed to threaten the foundations. For the mountain shook, the forest roared, and the shadows had a way of running everywhere as though the little building trembled. Delane watched and listened. He piled the logs on. From time to time he glanced nervously over his shoulder, restless, half uneasy, as a burst of spray from the branches dashed against the window, or a gust of unusual vehemence shook the door. Over-wearied with his long day's climb among impossible conditions, he now realised, in this mountain refuge, his utter loneliness; for his mind gave birth to that unwelcome symptom of true loneliness—

that he was not, after all, alone. Continually
he heard steps and voices in the storm. Another
wanderer, another climber out of season like
himself, would presently arrive, and sleep was
out of the question until first he heard that
knocking on the door. Almost—he expected
someone.

He went for the tenth time to the little
window. He peered forth into the thick darkness of the dropping night, shading his eyes
against the streaming pane to screen the firelight
in an attempt to see if another climber—perhaps
a climber in distress—were visible. The surroundings were desolate and savage, well named
the Devil's Saddle. Black-faced precipices,
streaked with melting snow, rose towering to
the north, where the heights were hidden in
seas of vapour; waterfalls poured into abysses
on two sides; a wall of impenetrable forest
pressed up from the south; and the dangerous
ridge he had climbed all day slid off wickedly
into a sky of surging cloud. But no human
figure was, of course, distinguishable, for both
the lateness of the hour and the elemental fury
of the night rendered it most unlikely. He
turned away with a start, as the tempest delivered a blow with massive impact against his
very face. Then, clearing the remnants of his
frugal supper from the table, he hung his soaking clothes at a new angle before the fire, made

sure the door was fastened on the inside, climbed into the bunk where white pillows and thick Austrian blankets looked so inviting, and prepared finally for sleep.

"I must be over-tired," he sighed, after half an hour's weary tossing, and went back to make up the sinking fire. Wood is plentiful in these climbers' huts; he heaped it on. But this time he lit the little oil lamp as well, realising—though unwilling to acknowledge it—that it was not over-fatigue that banished sleep, but this unwelcome sense of expecting someone, of being not quite alone. For the feeling persisted and increased. He drew the wooden bench close up to the fire, turned the lamp as high as it would go, and wished unaccountably for the morning. Light was a very pleasant thing; and darkness now, for the first time since childhood, troubled him. It was outside; but it might so easily come in and swamp, obliterate, extinguish. The darkness seemed a positive thing. Already, somehow, it was established in his mind—this sense of enormous, aggressive darkness that veiled an undesirable hint of personality. Some shadow from the peaks or from the forest, immense and threatening, pervaded all his thought. "This can't be entirely nerves," he whispered to himself. "I'm not so tired as all that!" And he made the fire roar. He shivered and drew closer to the blaze. "I'm

out of condition; that's part of it," he realised,
and remembered with loathing the weeks of
luxurious indulgence just behind him.

For Delane had rather wasted his year of
educational travel. Straight front Oxford, and
well supplied with money, he had first saturated
his mind in the latest Continental thought—the
science of France, the metaphysics and philo-
sophy of Germany—and had then been caught
aside by the gaiety of capitals where the lights
are not turned out at midnight by a Sunday
School police. He had been surfeited, physically, emotionally, and intellectually, till his mind
and body longed hungrily for simple living again
and simple teaching—above all, the latter. The
Road of Excess leads to the Palace of Wisdom
—for certain temperaments (as Blake forgot to
add), of which Delane was one. For there was
stuff in the youth, and the reaction had set in
with violent abruptness. His system rebelled.
He cut loose energetically from all soft delights,
and craved for severity, pure air, solitude and
hardship. Clean and simple conditions he must
have without delay, and the tonic of physical
battling. It was too early in the year to climb
seriously, for the snow was still dangerous and
the weather wild, but he had chosen this most
isolated of all the mountain huts in order to
make sure of solitude, and had come, without
guide or companion, for a week's strenuous life

in wild surroundings, and to take stock of himself with a view to full recovery.

And all day long as he climbed the desolate, unsafe ridge, his mind—good, wholesome, natural symptom—had reverted to his childhood days, to the solid worldly wisdom of his church-going father, and to the early teaching (oh, how sweet and refreshing in its literal spirit!) at his mother's knee. Now, as he watched the blazing logs, it came back to him again with redoubled force; the simple, precious, old-world stories of heaven and hell, of a paternal Deity, and of a daring, subtle, personal devil——

The interruption to his thoughts came with startling suddenness, as the roaring night descended against the windows with a thundering violence that shook the walls and sucked the flame half-way up the wide stone chimney. The oil lamp flickered and went out. Darkness invaded the room for a second, and Delane sprang from his bench, thinking the wet snow had loosened far above and was about to sweep the hut into the depths. And he was still standing, trembling and uncertain, in the middle of the room, when a deep and sighing hush followed sharp upon the elemental outburst, and in the hush, like a whisper after thunder, he heard a curious steady sound that, at first, he thought must be a footstep by the door. It was then instantly repeated. But it was not a

step. It was someone knocking on the heavy
oaken panels—a firm, authoritative sound, as
though the new arrival had the right to enter
and was already impatient at the delay.

The Englishman recovered himself instantly,
realising with keen relief the new arrival—at
last.

"Another climber like myself, of course,"
he said, "or perhaps the man who comes to
prepare the hut for others. The season has
begun." And he went over quickly, without a
further qualm, to unbolt the door.

"Forgive!" he exclaimed in German, as he
threw it wide, "I was half asleep before the fire.
It is a terrible night. Come in to food and
shelter, for both are here, and you shall share
such supper as I possess."

And a tall, cloaked figure passed him swiftly
with a gust of angry wind from the impenetrable blackness of the world beyond. On the
threshold, for a second, his outline stood full in
the blaze of firelight with the sheet of darkness behind it, stately, erect, commanding, his
cloak torn fiercely by the wind, but the face
hidden by a low-brimmed hat; and an instant
later the door shut with resounding clamour
upon the hurricane, and the two men turned to
confront one another in the little room.

Delane then realised two things sharply, both
of them fleeting impressions, but acutely vivid:

First, that the outside darkness seemed to have
entered and established itself between him and
the new arrival; and, secondly, that the
stranger's face was difficult to focus for clear
sight, although the covering hat was now re-
moved. There was a blur upon it somewhere.
And this the Englishman ascribed partly to the
flickering effect of firelight, and partly to the
lightning glare of the man's masterful and
terrific eyes, which made his own sight waver
in some curious fashion as he gazed upon him.
These impressions, however, were but moment-
ary and passing, due doubtless to the condition
of his nerves and to the semi-shock of the
dramatic, even theatrical entrance. Delane's
senses, in this wild setting, were guilty of ex-
aggeration. For now, while helping the man
remove his cloak, speaking naturally of shelter,
food, and the savage weather, he lost this first
distortion and his mind recovered sane propor-
tion. The stranger, after all, though striking,
was not of appearance so uncommon as to cause
alarm; the light and the low doorway had
touched his stature with illusion. He dwindled.
And the great eyes, upon calmer subsequent
inspection, lost their original fierce lightning.
The entering darkness, moreover, was but an
effect of the upheaving night behind him as he
strode across the threshold. The closed door
proved it.

And yet, as Delane continued his quieter examination, there remained, he saw, the startling quality which had caused that first magnifying in his mind. His senses, while reporting accurately, insisted upon this arresting and uncommon touch : there was, about this late wanderer of the night, some evasive, lofty strangeness that set him utterly apart from ordinary men.

The Englishman, while he relit the lamp, examined him searchingly, surreptitiously, but with a touch of passionate curiosity he could not in the least account for nor explain. There were contradictions of perplexing character about him. For the first presentment had been of splendid youth, while on the face, though vigorous and gloriously handsome, he now discerned the stamp of tremendous age. It was worn and tired. While radiant with strength and health and power, it wore as well this certain signature of deep exhaustion that great experience rather than physical weariness brings. Moreover, he discovered in it, in some way he could not hope to describe, man, woman, and child. There was a dark, sad earnestness about it, yet a touch of humour too; patience, tenderness, and sweetness held the mouth; and behind the high pale forehead intellect sat enthroned and watchful. In it were both love and hatred, longing and despair;

an expression of being ever on the defensive, yet hugely mutinous; an air both hunted and beseeching; great knowledge and great woe.

Delane gave up the search, aware that something unalterably splendid stood before him. Solemnity and beauty swept him too. His was never the grotesque assumption that man must be the highest being in the universe, nor that a thing is a miracle merely because it has never happened before. He groped, while explanation and analysis both halted. "A great teacher," thought fluttered through him, "or a mighty rebel! A distinguished personality beyond all question! Who can he be?" There was something regal that put respect upon his imagination instantly. And he remembered the legend of the countryside that Ludwig of Bavaria was said to be about when nights were very wild. He wondered. Into his speech and manner crept unawares an attitude of deference that was almost reverence, and with it— whence came the other quality?—a searching pity.

"You must be wearied out," he said respectfully, busying himself about the room, "as well as cold and wet. This fire will dry you, sir, and meanwhile I will prepare quickly such food as there is, if you will eat." For the other carried no knapsack, nor was he clothed for the severity of mountain travel.

"I have already eaten," said the stranger courteously, "and, with my thanks to you, I am neither wet nor tired. The afflictions that I bear are of another kind, though ones that you shall more easily, I am sure, relieve."

He spoke as a man whose words set troops in action, and Delane glanced at him, deeply moved by the surprising phrase, yet hardly marvelling that it should be so. He found no ready answer. But there was evidently question in his look, for the other continued, and this time with a smile that betrayed sheer winning beauty as of a tender woman:

"I saw the light and came to it. It is unusual—at this time."

His voice was resonant, yet not rough. There was a ringing quality about it that the bare room emphasised. It charmed the young Englishman inexplicably. Also, it woke in him a sense of infinite pathos.

"You are a climber, sir, like myself," Delane resumed, lifting his eyes a moment uneasily from the coffee he brewed over a corner of the fire. "You know this neighbourhood, perhaps? Better, at any rate, than I can know it?" His German halted rather. He chose his words with difficulty. There was uncommon trouble in his mind.

"I know all wild and desolate places," replied the other, half wistfully yet with a wintry

mournfulness in his voice and eyes, "for I
feel at home in them, and their stern companionship my nature craves as solace. But,
unlike yourself, I am no climber."

"The heights have no attraction for you?"
asked Delane, as he mingled steaming milk and
coffee in the wooden bowl, marvelling what
brought him then so high above the valleys.
"It is their difficulty and danger that fascinate
me always. I find the loneliness of the summits
intoxicating in a sense."

And, regardless of refusal, he set the bread
and meat before him, the apple and the tiny
packet of salt, then turned away to place the
coffee pot beside the fire again. But, as he did
so, a singular gesture of the other caught his eyes.
Before touching bowl or plate, the stranger
took the fruit and brushed his lips with it. He
kissed it, then set it on the ground and crushed
it into pulp beneath his heel. And, seeing this,
the young Englishman knew something dreadfully arrested in his mind, for, as he looked away,
pretending the act was unobserved, a thing of
ice and darkness moved past him through the
room, so that the pot trembled in his hand,
rattling sharply against the hearthstone where
he stooped. He could only interpret it as an
act of madness, and the myth of the sad,
drowned monarch wandering through this enchanted region, pressed into him again unsought

and urgent. It was a full minute before he had
control of his heart and hand again.

The bowl was half emptied, and the man was
smiling—this time the smile of a child who im-
plores the comfort of enveloping and understanding arms.

"I am a wanderer rather than a climber,"
he was saying, as though there had been no
interval, "for, though the lonely summits suit
me well, I now find in them only—terror. My
feet lose their sureness, and my head its steady
balance. I prefer the hidden gorges of these
mountains, and the shadows of the covering
forests. My days"—his voice drew the loneliness of uttermost space into its piteous accents
—"are passed in darkness. I can never climb
again."

He spoke this time, indeed, as a man whose
nerve was gone for ever. It was pitiable almost
to tears. And Delane, unable to explain the
amazing contradictions, felt recklessly, furiously
drawn to this trapped wanderer with the mien
of a king yet the air and speech sometimes of
a woman and sometimes of an outcast child.

"Ah, then you have known accidents,"
Delane replied with outer calmness, as he lit his
pipe, trying in vain to keep his hand as steady
as his voice. "You have been in one perhaps.
The effect, I have been told, is——"

The power and sweetness in that resonant

voice took his breath away as he heard it break
in upon his own uncertain accents :

"I fell," the stranger replied impressively,
as the rain and wind wailed past the building
mournfully, "yet it was no part of any accident. For it was no common fall," he added
with a magnificent gesture of disdain, "while
yet it broke my heart in two." He stooped
a little as he uttered the next words with a
crying pathos that an outcast woman might
have used. "I am," he said, "engulfed in intolerable loneliness. I can never climb again."

With a shiver impossible to control, half of
terror, half of pity, Delane moved a step nearer
to the marvellous stranger. The spirit of Ludwig, exiled and distraught, had gripped his soul
with a weakening terror; but now sheer beauty
lifted him above all personal shrinking. There
seemed some echo of lost divinity, worn, wild
yet grandiose, through which this significant
language strained towards a personal message
—for himself.

"In loneliness?" he faltered, sympathy
rising in a flood.

"For my Kingdom that is lost to me for
ever," met him in deep, throbbing tones that
set the air on fire. "For my imperial ancient
heights that jealousy took from me——"

The stranger paused, with an indescribable
air of broken dignity and pain.

Outside the tempest paused a moment before
the awful elemental crash that followed. A bel-
lowing of many winds descended like artillery
upon the world. A burst of smoke rushed from
the fireplace about them both, shrouding the
stranger momentarily in a flying veil. And
Delane stood up, uncomfortable in his very
bones. "What can it be?" he asked himself
sharply. "Who is this being that he should
use such language?" He watched alarm chase
pity, aware that the conversation held something beyond experience. But the pity returned
in greater and ever greater flood. And love
surged through him too. It was significant, he
remembered afterwards, that he felt it incum-
bent upon himself to stand. Curious, too, how
the thought of that mad, drowned monarch
haunted memory with such persistence. Some
vast emotion that he could not name drove out
his subsequent words. The smoke had cleared,
and a strange, high stillness held the world. The
rain streamed down in torrents, isolating these
two somehow from the haunts of men. And the
Englishman stared then into a countenance
grown mighty with woe and loneliness. There
stood darkly in it this incommunicable magnifi-
cence of pain that mingled awe with the pity
he had felt. The kingly eyes looked clear into
his own, completing his subjugation out of time.
"I would follow you," ran his thought upon

its knees, "follow you with obedience for ever
and ever, even into a last damnation. For you
are sublime. You shall come again into your
Kingdom, if my own small worship——"

Then blackness sponged the reckless thought
away. He spoke aloud in its place a more
guarded, careful thing:

"I am aware," he faltered, yet conscious
that he bowed, "of standing before a Great One
of some world unknown to me. Who he may
be I have but the privilege of wondering. He
has spoken darkly of a Kingdom that is lost.
Yet he is still, I see, a Monarch." And he
lowered his head and shoulders involuntarily.

For an instant, then, as he said it, the eyes
before him flashed their original terrific lightnings. The darkness of the common world
faded before the entrance of an Outer Darkness.
From gulfs of terror at his feet rose shadows
out of the night of time, and a passionate
anguish as of sudden madness seized his heart
and shook it.

He listened breathlessly for the words that
followed. It seemed some wind of unutterable
despair passed in the breath from those non-
human lips:

"I am still a Monarch, yes; but my Kingdom is taken from me, for I have no single
subject. Lost in a loneliness that lies out of
space and time, I am become a throneless Ruler,

and my hopelessness is more than I can bear."
The beseeching pathos of the voice tore him in
two. The Deity himself, it seemed, stood there
accused of jealousy, of sin and cruelty. The
stranger rose. The power about him brought
the picture of a planet, throned in mid-heaven
and poised beyond assault. "Not otherwise,"
boomed the startling words as though an
avalanche found syllables, "could I now show
myself to—you."

Delane was trembling horribly. He felt the
next words slip off his tongue unconsciously.
The shattering truth had dawned upon his soul
at last.

"Then the light you saw, and came to
——?" he whispered.

"Was the light in your heart that guided
me," came the answer, sweet, beguiling as the
music in a woman's tones; "the light of your
instant, brief desire that held love in it." He
made an opening movement with his arms as he
continued, smiling like stars in summer. "For
you summoned me; summoned me by your dear
and precious belief: how dear, how precious,
none can know but I who stand before you."

His figure drew up with an imperial air of
proud dominion. His feet were set among the
constellations. The opening movement of his
arms continued slowly. And the music in his
tones seemed merged in distant thunder.

s

"For your single, brief belief," he smiled with the grandeur of a condescending Emperor, "shall give my vanished Kingdom back to me."

And with an air of native majesty he held his hand out—to be kissed.

The black hurricane of night, the terror of frozen peaks, the yawning horror of the great abyss outside—all three crowded into the Englishman's mind with a crushing impact that blocked delivery of any word or action. It was not that he refused, it was not that he withdrew, but that Life stood paralysed and rigid. The flow stopped dead for the first time since he had left his mother's womb. The God in him was turned to stone and rendered ineffective. For an appalling instant God was *not*.

He realised the stupendous moment. Before him, drinking his little soul out merely by his Presence, stood one whose habit of mind, not alone his external accidents, were imperial with black prerogative before the first man drew the breath of life. August procedure was native to his inner process of existence. The stars and confines of the universe owned his sway before he fell, to trifle away the dreary little centuries by haunting the minds of feeble men and women, by hiding himself in nursery cupboards, and by grinning with stained gargoyles from the roofs of city churches. . . .

And the lad's life stammered, flickered,

threatened to go out before the enveloping terror of the revelation.

"I called to you . . . but called to you in play," thought whispered somewhere deep below the level of any speech, yet not so low that the audacious sound of it did not crash above the elements outside; "for . . . till now . . . you have been to me but a coated bogy . . . that my brain disowned with laughter . . . and my heart thought picturesque. If you are here . . . *alive!* May God forgive me for my . . ."

It seemed as though tears—the tears of love and profound commiseration—drowned the very seed of thought itself.

A sound stopped him that was like a collapse in heaven. Some ruin, as of a falling world, passed through his little timid heart. He did not yield, but he understood—with an understanding which seemed the delicate first sign of yielding—the seductiveness of evil, the sweet delight of surrendering the Will with utter recklessness to those swelling forces which disintegrate the heroic soul in man. He remembered. It was true. In the reaction from excess he *had* definitely called upon his childhood's teaching with a passing moment of genuine belief. And now that yearning of a fraction of a second bore its awful fruit. The luscious Capitals where he had rioted passed in a coloured stream before his eyes; the Wine, the Woman,

and the Song stood there before him, clothed
in that Power which lies insinuatingly disguised
behind their little passing show of innocence.
Their glamour donned this domino of regal and
virile grandeur. He felt entangled beyond recovery. The idea of God seemed sterile and
without reality. The one real thing, the one
desirable thing, the one possible, strong and
beautiful thing—was to bend his head and kiss
those imperial fingers. ˙ He moved noiselessly
towards the Hand. He put out his own to take
it and raise it towards his mouth——

When there rose in his mind with startling
vividness a small, soft picture of a child's nursery, a picture of a little boy, kneeling in scanty
night-gown with pink upturned soles, and asking ridiculous, audacious things of a shining
Figure seated on a summer cloud above the
kitchen-garden walnut tree.

The tiny symbol flashed and went its way,
yet not before it had lit the entire world with
glory. For there came an absolutely routing
power with it. In that half-forgotten instant's
craving for the simple teaching of his childhood
days, Belief had conjured with two immense
traditions. This was the second of them. The
appearance of the one had inevitably produced
the passage of its opposite. . . .

And the Hand that floated in the air before
him to be kissed sank slowly down below the

possible level of his lips. He shrank away.
Though laughter tempted something in his
brain, there still clung about his heart the first
aching, pitying terror. But size retreated,
dwindling somehow as it went. The wind and
rain obliterated every other sound; yet in that
bare, unfurnished room of a climber's mountain
hut, there was a silence, above the roar, that
drank in everything and broke the back of
speech. In opposition to this masquerading
splendour Delane had set up a personal, paternal
Deity.

"I thought of you, perhaps," cried the voice
of self-defence, "but I did not call to you with
real belief. And, by the name of God, I did
not summon you. For your sweetness, as your
power, sicken me; and your hand is black with
the curses of all the mothers in the world, whose
prayers and tears——"

He stopped dead, overwhelmed by the
cruelty of his reckless utterance.

And the Other moved towards him slowly.
It was like the summit of some peaked and
terrible height that moved. He spoke. He
changed appallingly.

"But _I_ claim," he roared, "your heart. I
claim you by that instant of belief you felt.
For by that alone you shall restore to me my
vanished Kingdom. You shall worship me."

In the countenance was a sudden power;

but, behind the stupefying roar, there was weakness in the voice as of an imploring and beseeching child. Again, deep love and searching pity seared the Englishman's heart as he replied in the gentlest accents he could find to master :

"And I claim *you*," he said, "by my understanding sympathy, and by my sorrow for your God-forsaken loneliness, and by my love. For no Kingdom built on hate can stand against the love you would deny——"

Words failed him then, as he saw the majesty fade slowly from the face, grown small and shadowy. One last expression of desperate energy in the eyes struck lightnings from the smoky air, as with an abandoned movement of the entire figure, he drew back, it seemed, towards the door behind him.

Delane moved slowly after him, opening his arms. Tenderness and big compassion flung wide the gates of love within him. He found strange language, too, although actual, spoken words did not produce them further than his entrails where they had their birth :

"Toys in the world are plentiful, Sire, and you may have them for your masterpiece of play. But you must seek them where they still survive; in the churches, and in isolated lands where thought lies unawakened. For they are the children's blocks of make-believe whose palaces, like your once tremendous kingdom, have no true existence for the thinking mind.''

And he stretched his hands towards him with the gesture of one who sought to help and save, then paused as he realised that his arms enclosed sheer blackness, with the emptiness of wind and driving rain.

For the door of the hut stood open, and Delane, upon the threshold, faced the sheet of night above the abyss. He heard the waterfalls in the valley far below. The forest flapped and tossed its myriad branches. Cold draughts swept down from spectral fields of melting snow above; and the blackness turned momentarily into the semblance of towers and bastions of thick beaten gloom. Above one soaring turret, then, a space of sky appeared, swept naked by a violent, lost wind—an opening of purple into limitless distance. For one second, amid the vapours, it was visible, empty and untenanted. The next, there sailed across its small diameter, a falling Star. With an air of slow and endless leisure, yet at the same time with terrific speed, it dived behind the ragged curtain of the clouds, and the space closed up again. Blackness returned upon the heavens.

And through this blackness, plunging into that abyss of woe whence he had momentarily risen, the figure of the marvellous stranger melted utterly away. Delane, for a fleeting second, was aware of the earnestness in the sad, imploring countenance; of its sweetness and its power so strangely mingled; of its mysterious grandeur; and of its pathetic childishness. But, already, it was sunk into interminable distance. A star that would be baleful, yet was merely glorious, passed on its endless wandering among the teeming systems of the universe. Behind the fixed and steady stars, secure in their appointed places, it set. It vanished into the pit of unknown emptiness. It was gone.

" God help you ! " sighed across the sea of wailing branches, echoing down the dark abyss below. " God give you rest at last ! "

For he saw a princely, nay, an imperial Being, homeless for ever, and for ever wandering, hunted as by keen remorseless winds about a universe that held no corner for his feet, his majesty unworshipped, his reign a mockery, his Court unfurnished, and his courtiers mere shadows of deep space. . . .

And a thin, grey dawn, stealing up behind clearing summits in the east, crept then against the windows of the mountain hut. It brought with it a treacherous, sharp air that made the sleeper draw another blanket near to shelter him from the sudden cold. For the fire had died out, and an icy draught sucked steadily beneath the doorway.

XIV

THE TRADITION

THE noises outside the little flat at first were very disconcerting after living in the country. They made sleep difficult. At the cottage in Sussex where the family had lived, night brought deep, comfortable silence, unless the wind was high, when the pine trees round the duck-pond made a sound like surf, or, if the gale was from the south-west, the orchard roared a bit unpleasantly.

But in London it was very different; sleep was easier in the daytime than at night. For, after nightfall, the rumble of the traffic became spasmodic instead of continuous; the motor-horns startled like warnings of alarm; after comparative silence the furious rushing of a taxi-cab touched the nerves. From dinner till eleven o'clock the streets subsided gradually; then came the army from theatres, parties, and late dinners, hurrying home to bed. The motor-horns during this hour were lively and incessant, like bugles of a regiment moving into battle. The parents rarely retired until this attack was

over. If quick about it, sleep was possible then
before the flying of the night-birds—an uncertain squadron—screamed half the street awake
again. But, these finally disposed of, a delightful hush settled down upon the neighbourhood,
profounder far than any peace of the countryside. The deep rumble of the produce wagons,
coming in to the big London markets from the
farms—generally about three A.M.—held no
disturbing quality.

But sometimes in the stillness of very early
morning, when streets were empty and pavements all deserted, there was a sound of another
kind that was startling and unwelcome. For it
was ominous. It came with a clattering violence
that made nerves quiver and forced the heart to
pause and listen. A strange resonance was in
it, a volume of sound, moreover, that was hardly
justified by its cause. For it was hoofs. A
horse swept hurrying up the deserted street, and
was close upon the building in a moment. It
was audible suddenly, no gradual approach from
a distance, but as though it turned a corner from
soft ground that muffled the hoofs, on to the
echoing, hard paving that emphasised the dreadful clatter. Nor did it die away again when
once the house was reached. It ceased as
abruptly as it came. The hoofs did not go
away.

It was the mother who heard them first, and

drew her husband's attention to their disagreeable quality.

"It is the mail-vans, dear," he answered. "They go at four A.M. to catch the early trains into the country."

She looked up sharply, as though something in his tone surprised her.

"But there's no sound of wheels," she said. And then, as he did not reply, she added gravely, "You have heard it too, John. I can tell."

"I have," he said. "I have heard it—twice."

And they looked at one another searchingly, each trying to read the other's mind. She did not question him; he did not propose writing to complain in a newspaper; both understood something that neither of them quite believed.

"I heard it first," she then said softly, "the night before Jack got the fever. And, as I listened, I heard him crying. But when I went in to see he was asleep. The noise stopped just outside the building." There was a shadow in her eyes as she said this, and a hush crept in between her words. "I did not hear it *go*." She said this almost beneath her breath.

He looked a moment at the ground; then, coming towards her, he took her in his arms and kissed her. And she clung very tightly to him.

"Sometimes," he said in a quiet voice, " a

mounted policeman passes down the street, I
think."

"It is a horse," she answered. But whether
it was a question or mere corroboration he did
not ask, for at that moment the doctor arrived,
and the question of little Jack's health became
the paramount matter of immediate interest.
The great man's verdict was uncommonly dis-
quieting.

All that night they sat up in the sick room.
It was strangely still, as though by one accord the
traffic avoided the house where a little boy hung
between life and death. The motor-horns even
had a muffled sound, and heavy drays and wagons
used the side streets; there were fewer taxi-
cabs about, or else they flew by noiselessly. Yet
no straw was down; the expense prohibited that.
And towards morning, very early, the mother
decided to watch alone. She had been a trained
nurse before her marriage, accustomed when she
was younger to long vigils. "You go down,
dear, and get a little sleep," she urged in a
whisper. "He's quiet now. At five o'clock
I'll come for you to take my place."

"You'll fetch me at once," he whispered,
"if——" then hesitated as though breath
failed him. A moment he stood there staring
from her face to the bed. "If you hear anything," he finished. She nodded, and he went
downstairs to his study, not to his bedroom.

He left the door ajar. He sat in darkness, listening. Mother, he knew, was listening, too, beside the bed. His heart was very full, for he did not believe the boy could live till morning. The picture of the room was all the time before his eyes—the shaded lamp, the table with the medicines, the little wasted figure beneath the blankets, and mother close beside it, listening. He sat alert, ready to fly upstairs at the smallest cry.

But no sound broke the stillness; the entire neighbourhood was silent; all London slept. He heard the clock strike three in the dining-room at the end of the corridor. It was still enough for that. There was not even the heavy rumble of a single produce wagon, though usually they passed about this time on their way to Smithfield and Covent Garden markets. He waited, far too anxious to close his eyes. . . . At four o'clock he would go up and relieve her vigil. Four, he knew, was the time when life sinks to its lowest ebb. . . . Then, in the middle of his reflections, thought stopped dead, and it seemed his heart stopped too.

Far away, but coming nearer with extraordinary rapidity, a sharp, clear sound broke out of the surrounding stillness—a horse's hoofs. At first it was so distant that it might have been almost on the high roads of the country, but the amazing speed with which it came closer, and the sudden increase of the beating sound was such, that by the time he turned his head it seemed to have entered the street outside. It was within a hundred yards of the building. The next second it was before the very door. And something in him blenched. He knew a moment's complete paralysis. The abrupt cessation of the heavy clatter was strangest of all. It came like lightning, it struck, it paused. It did not go away again. Yet the sound of it was still beating in his ears as he dashed up-stairs three steps at a time. It seemed in the house as well, on the stairs behind him, in the little passage-way, *inside the very bedroom.* It was an appalling sound. Yet he entered a room that was quiet, orderly, and calm. It was silent. Beside the bed his wife sat, holding Jack's hand and stroking it. She was soothing him; her face was very peaceful. No sound but her gentle whisper was audible.

He controlled himself by a tremendous effort, but his face betrayed his consternation and distress. "Hush," she said beneath her breath, "he's sleeping much more calmly now. The crisis, bless God, is over, I do believe. I dared not leave him."

He saw in a moment that she was right, and an untellable relief passed over him. He sat down beside her, very cold, yet perspiring with heat.

" You heard——? " he asked after a pause.

" Nothing," she replied quickly, " except his pitiful, wild words when the delirium was on him. It's passed. It lasted but a moment, or I'd have called you."

He stared closely into her tired eyes. " And his words? " he asked in a whisper. Whereupon she told him quietly that the little chap had sat up with wide-opened eyes and talked excitedly about a " great, great horse " he heard, but that was not " coming for him." " He laughed and said he would not go with it because he 'was not ready yet.' Some scrap of talk he had overheard from us," she added, " when we discussed the traffic once. . . ."

" But *you* heard nothing? " he repeated almost impatiently.

No, she had heard nothing. After all, then, he *had* dozed a moment in his chair. . . .

Four weeks later Jack, entirely convalescent, was playing a restricted game of hide-and-seek with his sister in the flat. It was really a forbidden joy, owing to noise and risk of breakages, but he had unusual privileges after his grave illness. It was dusk. The lamps in the street were being lit. " Quietly, remember; your mother's resting in her room," were the father's orders. She had just returned from a week by the sea, recuperating from the strain of nursing for so many nights. The traffic rolled and boomed along the streets below.

"Jack! Do come on and hide. It's your turn. I hid last."

But the boy was standing spellbound by the window, staring hard at something on the pavement. Sybil called and tugged in vain. Tears threatened. Jack would not budge. He declared he saw something.

"Oh, you're always seeing something. I wish you'd go and hide. It's only because you can't think of a good place, really."

"Look!" he cried in a voice of wonder. And as he said it his father rose quickly from his chair before the fire.

"Look!" the child repeated with delight and excitement. "It's a great, great horse. And it's perfectly white all over." His sister joined him at the window. "Where? Where? I can't see it. Oh, *do* show me!"

Their father was standing close behind them now. "I heard it," he was whispering, but so low the children did not notice him. His face was very pale.

"Straight in front of our door, stupid! Can't you see it? Oh, I do wish it had come for me. It's *such* a beauty!" And he clapped his hands with pleasure and excitement. "Quick, quick! I can hear it. It's going away again!"

But, while the children stood half squabbling by the window, their father leaned over a sofa in the adjoining room above a figure whose heart in sleep had quietly stopped its beating. The great, great horse had come. But this time he had not only heard its wonderful arrival. He had also heard it go. It seemed he heard the awful hoofs beat down the sky, far, far away, and very swiftly, dying into silence, finally up among the stars.

T

XV

A VICTIM OF HIGHER SPACE

"THERE'S a hextraordinary gentleman to see you, sir," said the new man.

"Why 'extraordinary'?" asked **Dr.** Silence, drawing the tips of his thin fingers through his brown beard. His eyes twinkled pleasantly. "Why 'extraordinary,' Barker?" he repeated encouragingly, noticing the perplexed expression in the man's eyes.

"He's so—so thin, sir. I could hardly see 'im at all—at first. He was inside the house before I could ask the name," he added, remembering strict orders.

"And who brought him here?"

"He come alone, sir, in a closed cab. He pushed by me before I could say a word—making no noise not what I could hear. He seemed to move very soft——"

The man stopped short with obvious embarrassment, as though he had already said enough to jeopardise his new situation, but trying hard to show that he remembered the instructions and warnings he had received with regard to the admission of strangers not properly accredited.

" And where is the gentleman now? " asked Dr. Silence, turning away to conceal his amusement.

"I really couldn't exactly say, sir. I left him standing in the 'all——"

The doctor looked up sharply. " But why in the hall, Barker? Why not in the waiting-room? " He fixed his piercing though kindly eyes on the man's face. " Did he frighten you? " he asked quickly.

"I think he did, sir, if I may say so. I seemed to lose sight of him, as it were——" The man stammered, evidently convinced by now that he had earned his dismissal. " He come in so funny, just like a cold wind," he added boldly, setting his heels at attention and looking his master full in the face.

The doctor made an internal note of the man's halting description; he was pleased that the slight evidence of intuition which had induced him to engage Barker had not entirely failed at the first trial. Dr. Silence sought for this qualification in all his assistants, from secretary to serving-man, and if it surrounded him with a somewhat singular crew, the drawbacks were more than compensated for on the whole by their occasional flashes of insight.

"So the gentleman made you feel queer, did he?"

"That was it, I think, sir," repeated the man stolidly.

"And he brings no kind of introduction to me—no letter or anything?" asked the doctor, with feigned surprise, as though he knew what was coming.

The man fumbled, both in mind and pockets, and finally produced an envelope.

"I beg pardon, sir," he said, greatly flustered; "the gentleman handed me this for you."

It was a note from a discerning friend, who had never yet sent him a case that was not vitally interesting from one point or another.

"Please see the bearer of this note," the brief message ran, "though I doubt if even you can do much to help him."

John Silence paused a moment, so as to gather from the mind of the writer all that lay behind the brief words of the letter. Then he looked up at his servant with a graver expression than he had yet worn.

"Go back and find this gentleman," he said, "and show him into the green study. Do not reply to his question, or speak more than actually necessary; but think kind, helpful, sympathetic thoughts as strongly as you can, Barker. You remember what I told you about the importance of thinking, when I engaged you. Put curiosity out of your mind, and think gently, sympathetically, affectionately, if you can."

He smiled, and Barker, who had recovered his composure in the doctor's presence, bowed silently and went out.

There were two different reception rooms in Dr. Silence's house. One, intended for persons who imagined they needed spiritual assistance when really they were only candidates for the asylum, had padded walls, and was well supplied with various concealed contrivances by means of which sudden violence could be instantly met and overcome. It was, however, rarely used. The other, intended for the reception of genuine cases of spiritual distress and out-of-the-way afflictions of a psychic nature, was entirely draped and furnished in a soothing deep green, calculated to induce calmness and repose of mind. And this room was the one in which Dr. Silence interviewed the majority of his " queer " cases, and the one into which he had directed Barker to show his present caller.

To begin with, the arm-chair in which the patient was always directed to sit, was nailed to the floor, since its immovability tended to impart this same excellent characteristic to the occupant. Patients invariably grew excited when talking about themselves, and their excitement tended to confuse their thoughts and to exag-

gerate their language. The immobility of the
chair helped to counteract this. After repeated
endeavours to drag it forward, or push it back,
they ended by resigning themselves to sitting
quietly. And with the futility of fidgeting there
followed a calmer state of mind.

Upon the floor, and at intervals in the wall
immediately behind, were certain tiny green
buttons, practically unnoticeable, which on being
pressed permitted a soothing and persuasive
narcotic to rise invisibly about the occupant of
the chair. The effect upon the excitable patient
was rapid, admirable, and harmless. The green
study was further provided with a secret spy-
hole; for John Silence liked when possible to
observe his patient's face before it had assumed
that mask the features of the human countenance invariably wear in the presence of another
person. A man sitting alone wears a psychic
expression; and this expression is the man himself. It disappears the moment another person
joins him. And Dr. Silence often learned more
from a few moments' secret observation of a face
than from hours of conversation with its owner
afterwards.

A very light, almost a dancing step followed
Barker's heavy tread towards the green room,
and a moment afterwards the man came in and
announced that the gentleman was waiting. He
was still pale and his manner nervous.

"Never mind, Barker," the doctor said kindly; "if you were not intuitive the man would have had no effect upon you at all. You only need training and development. And when you have learned to interpret these feelings and sensations better, you will feel no fear, but only a great sympathy."

"Yes, sir; thank you, sir!" And Barker bowed and made his escape, while Dr. Silence, an amused smile lurking about the corners of his mouth, made his way noiselessly down the passage and put his eye to the spy-hole in the door of the green study.

This spy-hole was so placed that it commanded a view of almost the entire room, and, looking through it, the doctor saw a hat, gloves, and umbrella lying on a chair by the table, but searched at first in vain for their owner.

The windows were both closed and a brisk fire burned in the grate. There were various signs —signs intelligible at least to a keenly intuitive soul—that the room was occupied, yet so far as human beings were concerned, it seemed undeniably empty. No one sat in the chairs; no one stood on the mat before the fire; there was no sign even that a patient was anywhere close against the wall, examining the Böcklin reproductions—as patients so often did when they thought they were alone—and therefore rather difficult to see from the spy-hole. Ordinarily speaking, there was no one in the room. It was unoccupied.

Yet **Dr.** Silence was quite well aware that a human being *was* in the room. His sensitive system never failed to let him know the proximity of an incarnate or discarnate being. Even in the dark he could tell that. And he now knew positively that his patient—the patient who had alarmed Barker, and had then tripped down the corridor with that dancing footstep— was somewhere concealed within the four walls commanded by his spy-hole. He also realised —and this was most unusual—that this individual whom he desired to watch knew that he was being watched. And, further, that the stranger himself was also watching in his turn. In fact, that it was he, the doctor, who was being observed—and by an observer as keen and trained as himself.

An inkling of the true state of the case began to dawn upon him, and he was on the verge of entering—indeed, his hand already touched the door-knob—when his eye, still glued to the spy-hole, detected a slight movement. Directly opposite, between him and the fireplace, something stirred. He watched very attentively and made certain that he was not mistaken. An object on the mantelpiece—it was a blue vase— disappeared from view. It passed out of sight together with the portion of the marble mantelpiece on which it rested. Next, that part of the fire and grate and brass fender immediately below it vanished entirely, as though a slice had been taken clean out of them.

Dr. Silence then understood that something between him and these objects was slowly coming into being, something that concealed them and obstructed his vision by inserting itself in the line of sight between them and himself.

He quietly awaited further results before going in.

First he saw a thin perpendicular line tracing itself from just above the height of the clock and continuing downwards till it reached the woolly fire-mat. This line grew wider, broadened, grew solid. It was no shadow; it was something substantial. It defined itself more and more. Then suddenly, at the top of the line, and about on a level with the face of the clock, he saw a small luminous disc gazing steadily at him. It was a human eye, looking straight into his own, pressed there against the spy-hole. And it was bright with intelligence. Dr. Silence held his breath for a moment—and stared back at it.

Then, like someone moving out of deep shadow into light, he saw the figure of a man come sliding sideways into view, a whitish face following the eye, and the perpendicular line he had first observed broadening out and developing into the complete figure of a human being.

It was the patient. He had apparently been standing there in front of the fire all the time. A second eye had followed the first, and both of them stared steadily at the spy-hole, sharply concentrated, yet with a sly twinkle of humour and amusement that made it impossible for the doctor to maintain his position any longer.

He opened the door and went in quickly. As he did so he noticed for the first time the sound of a German band coming in noisily through the open ventilators. In some intuitive, unaccountable fashion the music connected itself with the patient he was about to interview. This sort of prevision was not unfamiliar to him. It always explained itself later.

The man, he saw, was of middle age and of very ordinary appearance; so ordinary, in fact, that he was difficult to describe—his only peculiarity being his extreme thinness. Pleasant— that is, good—vibrations issued from his atmosphere and met Dr. Silence as he advanced to greet him, yet vibrations alive with currents and discharges betraying the perturbed and dis- ordered condition of his mind and brain. There was evidently something wholly out of the usual in the state of his thoughts. Yet, though strange, it was not altogether distressing; it was not the impression that the broken and violent atmosphere of the insane produces upon the mind. Dr. Silence realised in a flash that here was a case of absorbing interest that might require all his powers to handle properly.

"I was watching you through my little peep-hole—as you saw," he began, with a pleasant smile, advancing to shake hands. "I find it of the greatest assistance sometimes——"

But the patient interrupted him at once. His voice was hurried and had odd, shrill changes in it, breaking from high to low in unexpected fashion. One moment it thundered, the next it almost squeaked.

"I understand without explanation," he broke in rapidly. "You get the true note of a man in that way—when he thinks himself unobserved. I quite agree. Only, in my case, I fear, you saw very little. My case, as you of course grasp, Dr. Silence, is extremely peculiar, uncomfortably peculiar. Indeed, unless Sir William had positively assured me——"

"My friend has sent you to me," the doctor interrupted gravely, with a gentle note of authority, "and that is quite sufficient. Pray, be seated, Mr.——"

"Mudge—Racine Mudge," returned the other.

"Take this comfortable one, Mr. Mudge," leading him to the fixed chair, "and tell me your condition in your own way and at your own pace. My whole day is at your service if you require it."

Mr. Mudge moved towards the chair in question and then hesitated.

"You will promise me not to use the narcotic buttons," he said, before sitting down. "I do not need them. Also I ought to mention that anything you think of vividly will reach my mind. That is apparently part of my peculiar case." He sat down with a sigh and arranged his thin legs and body into a position of comfort. Evidently he was very sensitive to the thoughts of others, for the picture of the green buttons had only entered the doctor's mind for a second, yet the other had instantly snapped it up. Dr. Silence noticed, too, that Mr. Mudge held on tightly with both hands to the arms of the chair.

"I'm rather glad the chair is nailed to the floor," he remarked, as he settled himself more comfortably. "It suits me admirably. The fact is—and this is my case in a nutshell—which is all that a doctor of your marvellous development requires—the fact is, Dr. Silence, I am a victim of Higher Space. That's what's the matter with me—Higher Space!"

The two looked at each other for a space in silence, the little patient holding tightly to the arms of the chair which "suited him admirably," and looking up with staring eyes, his atmosphere positively trembling with the waves of some unknown activity; while the doctor smiled kindly and sympathetically, and put his whole person as far as possible into the mental condition of the other.

"Higher Space," repeated Mr. Mudge, "that's what it is. Now, do you think you can help me with *that* ? "

There was a pause during which the men's eyes steadily searched down below the surface of their respective personalities. Then Dr. Silence spoke.

"I am quite sure I can help," he answered quietly; "sympathy must always help, and suffering always claims my sympathy. I see you have suffered cruelly. You must tell me all about your case, and when I hear the gradual steps by which you reached this strange condition, I have no doubt I can be of assistance to you."

He drew a chair up beside his interlocutor and laid a hand on his shoulder for a moment. His whole being radiated kindness, intelligence, desire to help.

"For instance," he went on, "I feel sure it was the result of no mere chance that you became familiar with the terrors of what you term Higher Space; for higher space is no mere external measurement. It is, of course, a spiritual state, a spiritual condition, an inner development, and one that we must recognise as abnormal, since it is beyond the reach of the

senses at the present stage of evolution. Higher
Space is a mystical state."

"Oh!" cried the other, rubbing his bird-
like hands with pleasure, "the relief it is to me
to talk to someone who can understand! Of
course what you say is the utter truth. And
you are right that no mere chance led me to
my present condition, but, on the other hand,
prolonged and deliberate study. Yet chance in
a sense now governs it. I mean, my entering
the condition of higher space seems to depend
upon the chance of this and that circumstance."
He sighed and paused a moment. "For instance," he continued, starting, "the mere
sound of that German band sent me off. Not
that all music will do so, but certain sounds,
certain vibrations, at once key me up to the
requisite pitch, and off I go. Wagner's music
always does it, and that band must have been
playing a stray bit of Wagner. But I'll come
to all that later. Only, first"—he smiled
deprecatingly—"I must ask you to send away
your man from the spy-hole."

John Silence looked up with a start, for Mr.
Mudge's back was to the door, and there was
no mirror. He saw the brown eye of Barker
glued to the little circle of glass, and he crossed
the room without a word and snapped down the
black shutter provided for the purpose, and then
heard Barker shuffle away along the passage.

"Now," continued the little man in the chair, "I can go on. You have managed to put me completely at my ease, and I feel I may tell you my whole case without shame or reserve. You will understand. But you must be patient with me if I go into details that are already familiar to you—details of higher space, I mean—and if I seem stupid when I have to describe things that transcend the power of language and are really therefore indescribable."

"My dear friend," put in the other calmly, "that goes without saying. To know higher space is an experience that defies description, and one is obliged to make use of more or less intelligible symbols. But, pray, proceed. Your vivid thoughts will tell me more than your halting words."

An immense sigh of relief proceeded from the little figure half lost in the depths of the chair. Such intelligent sympathy meeting him half-way was a new experience, and it touched his heart at once. He leaned back, relaxing his tight hold of the arms, and began in his thin, scale-like voice.

"My mother was a Frenchwoman, and my father an Essex bargeman," he said abruptly. "Hence my name—Racine and Mudge. My father died before I ever saw him. My mother inherited money from her Bordeaux relations, and when she died soon after, I was left alone

with wealth and a strange freedom. I had no
guardian, trustees, sisters, brothers, or any connection in the world to look after me. I grew
up, therefore, utterly without education. This
much was to my advantage; I learned none of
that deceitful rubbish taught in schools, and so
had nothing to unlearn when I awakened to my
true love—mathematics, higher mathematics
and higher geometry. These, however, I
seemed to know instinctively. It was like the
memory of what I had deeply studied before;
the principles were in my blood, and I simply
raced through the ordinary stages, and beyond,
and then did the same with geometry. Afterwards, when I read the books on these subjects,
I understood how swift and undeviating the
knowledge had come back to me. It was simply
memory. It was simply re-collecting the
memories of what I had known before in a previous existence and required no books to teach
me."

In his growing excitement, Mr. Mudge
attempted to drag the chair forward a little nearer
to his listener, and then smiled faintly as he re-
signed himself instantly again to its immobility,
and plunged anew into the recital of his singular
"disease."

"The audacious speculations of Bolyai, the
amazing theories of Gauss—that through a point
more than *one* line could be drawn parallel to a

given line; the possibility that the angles of a triangle are together *greater* than two right angles, if drawn upon immense curvatures— the breathless intuitions of Beltrami and Lobatchewsky—all these I hurried through, and emerged, panting but unsatisfied, upon the verge of my—my new world, my higher space possibilities—in a word, my disease!

"How I got there," he resumed after a brief pause, during which he appeared to be listening nervously for an approaching sound, "is more than I can put intelligibly into words. I can only hope to leave your mind with an intuitive comprehension of the possibility of what I say.

"Here, however, came a change. At this point I was no longer absorbing the fruits of studies I had made before; it was the beginning of new efforts to learn for the first time, and I had to go slowly and laboriously through terrible work. Here I sought for the theories and speculations of others. But books were few and far between, and with the exception of one man—a 'dreamer,' the world called him—whose audacity and piercing intuition amazed and delighted me beyond description, I found no one to guide or help.

"You, of course, Dr. Silence, understand something of what I am driving at with these stammering words, though you cannot perhaps

U

yet guess what depths of pain my new knowledge brought me to, nor why an acquaintance with a new dimension of space should prove a source of misery and terror."

Mr. Racine Mudge, remembering that the chair would not move, did the next best thing he could in his desire to draw nearer to the attentive man facing him, and sat forward upon the very edge of the cushions, crossing his legs and gesticulating with both hands as though he saw into this region of new space he was attempting to describe, and might any moment tumble into it bodily from the edge of the chair and disappear from view. John Silence, separated from him by three paces, sat with his eyes fixed upon the thin white face opposite, noting every word and every gesture with deep attention.

" This room we now sit in, Dr. Silence, has one side open to space—to higher space. A closed box only *seems* closed. There is a way in and out of a soap bubble without breaking the skin."

" You tell me no new thing," the doctor interposed gently.

" Hence, if higher space exists and our world borders upon it and lies partially in it, it follows necessarily that we see only portions of all objects. We never see their true and complete shape. We see their three measurements, but not their fourth. The new direction is concealed from us, and when I hold this book and move my hand all round it I have not really made a complete circuit. We only perceive those portions of any object which exist in our three dimensions, the rest escapes us. But, once learn to see in higher space, and objects will appear as they actually are. Only they will thus be hardly recognisable!

"Now you may begin to grasp something of what I am coming to."

"I am beginning to understand something of what you must have suffered," observed the doctor soothingly, "for I have made similar experiments myself, and only stopped just in time——"

"You are the one man in all the world who can understand, *and* sympathise," exclaimed Mr. Mudge, grasping his hand and holding it tightly while he spoke. The nailed chair prevented further excitability.

"Well," he resumed, after a moment's pause, "I procured the implements and the coloured blocks for practical experiment, and I followed the instructions carefully till I had arrived at an imaginative conception of four-dimensional space. The tessaract, the figure whose boundaries are cubes, I knew by heart. That is to say, I knew it and saw it mentally, for my eye, of course, could never take in a

new measurement, nor my hands and feet
handle it.

" So, at least, I thought," he added, making
a wry face. " I had reached the stage, you see,
when I could *imagine* in a new dimension. I
was able to conceive the shape of that new figure
which is intrinsically different to all we know
—the shape of the tessaract. I could perceive
in four dimensions. When, therefore, I looked
at a cube I could see all its sides at once. Its
top was not foreshortened, nor its farther side
and base invisible. I saw the whole thing out
flat, so to speak. Moreover, I also saw its
content—its in-sides."

" You were not yourself able to enter this
new world? " interrupted Dr. Silence.

" Not then. I was only able to conceive
intuitively what it was like and how exactly it
must look. Later, when I slipped in there and
saw objects in their entirety, unlimited by the
paucity of our poor three measurements, I very
nearly lost my life. For, you see, space does
not stop at a single new dimension, a fourth.
It extends in all possible new ones, and we must
conceive it as containing any number of new
dimensions. In other words, there is no space
at all, but only a condition. But, meanwhile,
I had come to grasp the strange fact that the
objects in our normal world appear to us only
partially."

Mr. Mudge moved farther forward till he was balanced dangerously on the very edge of the chair. "From this starting point," he resumed, "I began my studies and experiments, and continued them for years. I had money, and I was without friends. I lived in solitude and experimented. My intellect, of course, had little part in the work, for intellectually it was all unthinkable. Never was the limitation of mere reason more plainly demonstrated. It was mystically, intuitively, spiritually that I began to advance. And what I learnt, and knew, and did is all impossible to put into language, since it describes experiences transcending the experiences of men. It is only some óf the results —what you would call the symptoms of my disease—that I can give you, and even these must often appear absurd contradictions and impossible paradoxes.

"I can only tell you, Dr. Silence"—his manner became grave suddenly—"that I reached sometimes a point of view whence all the great puzzle of the world became plain to me, and I understood what they call in the Yoga books 'The Great Heresy of Separateness'; why all great teachers have urged the necessity of man loving his neighbour as himself; how men are all really *one;* and why the utter loss of self is necessary to salvation and the discovery of the true life of the soul."

He paused a moment and drew breath.

"Your speculations have been my own long ago," the doctor said quietly. "I fully realise the force of your words. Men are doubtless not separate at all—in the sense they imagine."

"All this about the very much higher space I only dimly, very dimly conceived, of course," the other went on, raising his voice again by jerks; "but what did happen to me was the humbler accident of—the simpler disaster—oh dear, how shall I put it——?"

He stammered and showed visible signs of distress.

"It was simply this," he resumed with a sudden rush of words, "that, accidentally, as the result of my years of experiment, I one day slipped bodily into the next world, the world of four dimensions, yet without knowing precisely how I got there, or how I could get back again. I discovered, that is, that my ordinary three-dimensional body was but an expression—a partial projection—of my higher four-dimensional body!

"Now you understand what I meant much earlier in our talk when I spoke of chance. I cannot control my entrance or exit. Certain people, certain human atmospheres, certain wandering forces, thoughts, desires even—the radiations of certain combinations of colour, and above all, the vibrations of certain kinds of music, will suddenly throw me into a state of what I can only describe as an intense and terrific inner vibration—and behold I am off! Off in the direction at right angles to all our known directions! Off in the direction the cube takes when it begins to trace the outlines of the new figure, the tessaract! Off into my breathless and semi-divine higher space! Off, *inside myself*, into the world of four dimensions! "

He gasped and dropped back into the depths of the immovable chair.

" And there," he whispered, his voice issuing from among the cushions, " there I have to stay until these vibrations subside, or until they do something which I cannot find words to describe properly or intelligibly to you—and then, behold, I am back again. First, that is, I disappear. Then I reappear. Only "—he sighed —" I cannot control my entrance nor my exit."

" Just so," exclaimed Dr. Silence, " and that is why a few——"

" Why a few moments ago," interrupted Mr. Mudge, taking the words out of his mouth, " you found me gone, and then saw me return. The music of that wretched German band sent me off. Your intense thinking about me brought me back—when the band had stopped its Wagner. I saw you approach the peep-hole and I saw Barker's intention of doing so later. For me no interiors are hidden. I see inside.

When in that state the content of your mind, as of your body, is open to me as the day. Oh dear, oh dear, oh dear ! "

Mr. Mudge stopped and mopped his brow. A light trembling ran over the surface of his small body like wind over grass. He still held tightly to the arms of the chair.

"At first," he presently resumed, "my new experiences were so vividly interesting that I felt no alarm. There was no room for it. The alarm came a little later."

"Then you actually penetrated far enough into that state to experience yourself as a normal portion of it?" asked the doctor, leaning forward, deeply interested.

Mr. Mudge nodded a perspiring face in reply.

"I did," he whispered, "undoubtedly I did. I am coming to all that. It began first at night, when I realised that sleep brought no loss of consciousness——"

"The spirit, of course, can never sleep. Only the body becomes unconscious," interposed John Silence.

"Yes, we know that—theoretically. At night, of course, the spirit is active elsewhere, and we have no memory of where and how, simply because the brain stays behind and receives no record. But I found that, while remaining conscious, I also retained memory.

I had attained to the state of continuous consciousness, for at night regularly, with the first approaches of drowsiness, I entered *nolens volens* the four dimensional world.

"For a time this happened frequently, and I could not control it; though later I found a way to regulate it better. Apparently sleep is unnecessary in the higher—the four dimensional —body. Yes, perhaps. But I should infinitely have preferred dull sleep to the knowledge. For, unable to control my movements, I wandered to and fro, attracted owing to my partial development and premature arrival, to parts of this new world that alarmed me more and more. It was the awful waste and drift of a monstrous world, so utterly different to all we know and see that I cannot even hint at the nature of the sights and objects and beings in it. More than that, I cannot even remember them. I cannot now picture them to myself even, but can recall only the *memory of the impression* they made upon me, the horror and devastating terror of it all. To be in several places at once, for instance——"

"Perfectly," interrupted John Silence, noticing the increase of the other's excitement, "I understand exactly. But now, please, tell me a little more of this alarm you experienced, and how it affected you."

"It's not the disappearing and reappearing

U*

per se that I mind," continued Mr. Mudge,
"so much as certain other things. It's seeing
people and objects in their weird entirety, in
their true and complete shapes, that is so distressing. It introduced me to a world of mon-
sters. Horses, dogs, cats, all of which I loved;
people, trees, children; all that I have considered beautiful in life—everything, from a
human face to a cathedral—appear to me in a
different shape and aspect to all I have known
before. Instead of seeing their partial expression in three dimensions, I saw them complete—
in four. I cannot perhaps convince you why
this should be terrible, but I assure you that it
is so. To hear the human voice proceeding
from this novel appearance which I scarcely
recognise as a human body is ghastly, simply
ghastly. To see inside everything and everybody is a form of insight peculiarly distressing.
To be so confused in geography as to find myself one moment at the North Pole, and the next
at Clapham Junction—or possibly at both places
simultaneously—is absurdly terrifying. Your
imagination will readily furnish other details
without my multiplying my experiences now.
But you have no idea what it all means, and
how I suffer."

Mr. Mudge paused in his panting account
and lay back in his chair. He still held tightly
to the arms as though they could keep him in

the world of sanity and three measurements, and only now and again released his left hand in order to mop his face. He looked very thin and white and oddly unsubstantial, and he stared about him as though he saw into this other space he had been talking about.

John Silence, too, felt warm. He had listened to every word and had made many notes. The presence of this man had an exhilarating effect upon him. It seemed as if Mr. Racine Mudge still carried about with him something of that breathless higher-space condition he had been describing. At any rate, Dr. Silence had himself advanced sufficiently far himself to realise that the visions of this extraordinary little person had a basis of truth for their origin.

After a pause that prolonged itself into minutes, he crossed the room and unlocked a drawer in a bookcase, taking out a small book with a red cover. It had a lock to it, and he produced a key out of his pocket and proceeded to open the covers. The bright eyes of Mr. Mudge never left him for a single second.

"It almost seems a pity," he said at length, "to cure you, Mr. Mudge. You are on the way to discovery of great things. Though you may lose your life in the process—that is, your life here in the world of three dimensions—you would lose thereby nothing of great value —you will pardon my apparent rudeness, I know—and you might gain what is infinitely greater. Your suffering, of course, lies in the fact that you alternate between the two worlds and are never wholly in one or the other. Also, I rather imagine, though I cannot be certain of this from any personal experiments, that you have here and there penetrated even into space of more than four dimensions, and have hence experienced the terror you speak of."

The perspiring son of the Essex bargeman and the woman of Normandy bent his head several times in assent, but uttered no word in reply.

"Some strange psychic predisposition, dating no doubt from one of your former lives, has favoured the development of your 'disease'; and the fact that you had no normal training at school or college, no leading by the poor intellect into the culs-de-sac falsely called knowledge, has further caused your exceedingly rapid movement along the lines of direct inner experience. None of the knowledge you have foreshadowed has come to you through the senses, of course."

Mr. Mudge, sitting in his immovable chair, began to tremble slightly. A wind again seemed to pass over his surface and again to set it curiously in motion like a field of grass.

"You are merely talking to gain time," he said hurriedly, in a shaking voice. "This thinking aloud delays us. I see ahead what you are coming to, only please be quick, for something is going to happen. A band is again coming down the street, and if it plays—if it plays Wagner—I shall be off in a twinkling."

"Precisely. I will be quick. I was leading up to the point of how to effect your cure. The way is this : You must simply learn to block the entrances—prevent the *centres* acting."

"True, true, utterly true!" exclaimed the little man, dodging about nervously in the depths of the chair. "But how, in the name of space, can that be done?"

"By concentration. They are all within you, these centres, although outer causes such as colour, music, and other things lead you towards them. These external things you cannot hope to destroy, but once the entrances are blocked, they will lead you only to bricked walls and closed channels. You will no longer be able to find the way."

"Quick, quick!" cried the bobbing figure in the chair. "How is this concentration to be effected?"

"This little book," continued Dr. Silence calmly, "will explain to you the way." He tapped the cover. "Let me now read out to you certain simple instructions, composed, as I see you divine, entirely from my own personal experiences in the same direction. Follow these instructions and you will no longer enter the state of higher space.   The entrances will be blocked effectively.''

Mr. Mudge sat bolt upright in his chair to listen, and John Silence cleared his throat and began to read slowly in a very distinct voice.

But before he had uttered a dozen words, something happened.   A sound of street music entered the room through the open ventilators, for a band had begun to play in the stable mews at the back of the house—the March from *Tannhäuser*.   Odd as it may seem that a German band should twice within the space of an hour enter the same mews and play Wagner, it was nevertheless the fact.

Mr. Racine Mudge heard it.   He uttered a sharp, squeaking cry and twisted his arms with nervous energy round the chair.   A piteous look that was not far from tears spread over his white face.   Grey shadows followed it— the grey of fear.   He began to struggle convulsively.

"Hold me fast!   Catch me!   For God's sake, keep me here!   I'm on the rush already.   Oh, it's frightful!" he cried in tones of anguish, his voice as thin as a reed.

Dr. Silence made a plunge forward to seize him, but in a flash, before he could cover the space between them, Mr. Racine Mudge, screaming and struggling, seemed to shoot past

him into invisibility. He disappeared like an
arrow from a bow propelled at infinite speed,
and his voice no longer sounded in the external
air, but seemed in some curious way to make
itself heard somewhere within the depths of the
doctor's own being. It was almost like a faint
singing cry in his head, like a voice of dream,
a voice of vision and unreality.

"Alcohol, alcohol!" it cried faintly, with
distance in it, "give me alcohol! It's the
quickest way. Alcohol, before I'm out of
reach!"

The doctor, accustomed to rapid decisions
and even more rapid action, remembered that a
brandy flask stood upon the mantelpiece, and in
less than a second he had seized it and was holding it out towards the space above the chair
recently occupied by the visible Mudge. But,
before his very eyes, and long ere he could
unscrew the metal stopper, he saw the contents
of the closed glass phial sink and lessen as
though someone were drinking violently and
greedily of the liquor within.

"Thanks! Enough! It deadens the vibrations!" cried the faint voice in his interior,
as he withdrew the flask and set it back upon
the mantelpiece. He understood that in
Mudge's present condition one side of the flask
was open to space and he could drink without
removing the stopper. He could hardly have

had a more interesting proof of what he had
been hearing described at such length.

But the next moment—the very same
moment it almost seemed—the German band
stopped midway in its tune—and there was Mr.
Mudge back in his chair again, gasping and
panting!

"Quick!" he shrieked, "stop that band!
Send it away! Catch hold of me! Block the
entrances! Block the entrances! Give me the
red book! Oh, oh, oh-h-h-h!!!"

The music had begun again. It was merely
a temporary interruption. The *Tannhäuser*
March started again, this time at a tremendous
pace that made it sound like a rapid two-
step, as though the instruments played against
time.

But the brief interruption gave Dr. Silence
a moment in which to collect his scattering
thoughts, and before the band had got through
half a bar, he had flung forward upon the chair
and held Mr. Racine Mudge, the struggling
little victim of Higher Space, in a grip of iron.
His arms went all round his diminutive person,
taking in a good part of the chair at the same
time. He was not a big man, yet he seemed
to smother Mudge completely.

Yet, even as he did so, and felt the wriggling
form underneath him, it began to melt and slip
away like air or water. The wood of the arm-

chair somehow disentangled itself from between his own arms and those of Mudge. The phenomenon known as the passage of matter through matter took place. The little man seemed actually to be interfused with the other's being. Dr. Silence could just see his face beneath him. It puckered and grew dark as though from some great internal effort. He heard the thin, reedy voice cry in his ear to " Block the entrances, block the entrances! " and then—but how in the world describe what is indescribable?

John Silence half rose up to watch. Racine Mudge, his face distorted beyond all recognition, was making a marvellous inward movement, as though doubling back upon himself. He turned funnel-wise like water in a whirling vortex, and then appeared to break up somewhat as a reflection breaks up and divides in a distorting convex mirror. He went neither forward nor backwards, neither to the right nor the left, neither up nor down. But he went. He went utterly. He simply flashed away out of sight like a vanishing projectile.

All but one leg! Dr. Silence just had the time and the presence of mind to seize upon the left ankle and boot as it disappeared, and to this he held on for several seconds like grim death. Yet all the time he knew it was a foolish and useless thing to do.

The foot was in his grasp one moment, and the next it seemed—this was the only way he could describe it—inside his own skin and bones, and at the same time outside his hand and all round it. It seemed mingled in some amazing way with his own flesh and blood. Then it was gone, and he was tightly grasping a mere draught of heated air.

"Gone! gone! gone!" cried a faint, whispering voice somewhere deep within his own consciousness. "Lost! lost! lost!" it repeated, growing fainter and fainter till at length it vanished into nothing and the last signs of Mr. Racine Mudge vanished with it.

John Silence locked his red book and replaced it in the cabinet, which he fastened with a click, and when Barker answered the bell he inquired if Mr. Mudge had left a card upon the table. It appeared that he had, and when the servant returned with it, Dr. Silence read the address and made a note of it. It was in North London.

"Mr. Mudge has gone," he said quietly to Barker, noticing his expression of alarm.

"He's not taken his 'at with him, sir."

"Mr. Mudge requires no hat where he is now," continued the doctor, stooping to poke the fire. "But he may return for it——"

"And the humbrella, sir."

"And the umbrella."

"He didn't go out *my* way, sir, if you please," stuttered the amazed servant, his curiosity overcoming his nervousness.

"Mr. Mudge has his own way of coming and going, and prefers it. If he returns by the door at any time remember to bring him instantly to me, and be kind and gentle with him and ask no questions. Also, remember, Barker, to think pleasantly, sympathetically, affectionately of him while he is away. Mr. Mudge is a very suffering gentleman."

Barker bowed and went out of the room backwards, gasping and feeling round the inside of his collar with three very hot fingers of one hand.

It was two days later when he brought in a telegram to the study. Dr. Silence opened it, and read as follows:

"Bombay. Just slipped out again. All safe. Have blocked entrances. Thousand thanks. Address Cooks, London.—MUDGE."

Dr. Silence looked up and saw Barker staring at him bewilderingly. It occurred to him that somehow he knew the contents of the telegram.

"Make a parcel of Mr. Mudge's things," he said briefly, "and address them Thomas Cook & Sons, Ludgate Circus. And send them there exactly a month from to-day, marked ' To be called for.' "

" Yes, sir," said Barker, leaving the room with a deep sigh and a hurried glance at the waste-paper basket where his master had dropped the pink paper.

PRINTED BY CASSELL & COMPANY, LIMITED, LA BELLE SAUVAGE, LONDON, E.C.
F.30,117

www.ingramcontent.com/pod-product-compliance
Lightning Source LLC
Chambersburg PA
CBHW032237010726
47494CB00002B/525